Demon Blade

This book is a work of fiction, except for the parts that are true.

Dedication

Dedicated to Katrina and Harper

Contents

Chapter 1

LONDON - 1888

Thick fog clung to the district like manure on a blanket, making it harder to peer through the gloom of Whitechapel's dark and grungy streets. A pitiful group of urchins, their bony frames covered in sodden rags, ran past him. One, a boy who looked due for his annual bath, bumped into him.

By instinct, Khan caught the boy's wrist and squeezed as the lad's nimble fingers swept across his jacket pockets. A pained yelp of surprise escaped the mouth of the urchin. He would have cried louder and longer if not for Khan's cold stare that subdued the boy.

"Sorry, sir." The boy yelped and struggled to free his fist from Khan's iron grip. "It was an accident, sir."

Khan prised the youth's fingers apart to check they held nothing. For a moment, he studied the boy's ruddy face, a hodgepodge of muck and bruises.

"You're one of Taylor's urchins?"

Mention of the name stopped the boy's struggling. "I dunno him, sir." As soon as the words left his lips, he resumed struggling against Khan's steel grip.

Earlier, Khan had spotted the pickpocket amongst Bob Taylor's army of children, so he recognised the boy's lie. Taylor enlisted young orphans as pickpockets and thieves; he cultivated such fierce loyalty, not one child betrayed him to authorities if caught. Khan hated lies, but he allowed a smile to flick across the corner of his mouth still. If the boy showed intense allegiance to Taylor, then Khan's association with Taylor was safe. Khan leaned forward to study him closer, allowing a pale finger of distant gaslight to cross his long gaunt face. The lad gasped in fright at Khan's obsidian eyes staring at him from deep eye sockets.

"Mr Khan!" The boy's astonishment was clear. "I didn't recognise you, sir. I'm sorry."

Khan remained silent, regarding him for another second. The other kids had stopped running to watch things from an adjoining street corner; Khan could feel their shifty gazes. He glanced across at them, and they withdrew back into the shades of evening. Khan released the child who lingered, unable to decide whether he should run away or keep staring at the giant he only recognised by name and mysterious reputation.

He dropped his head to the lad's level. "Boo!" In a flash, the boy scampered away, stumbling with frightened feet after his friends. Khan smiled to himself. He was fond of children, but he didn't want them hovering around him either.

Khan often kept to himself, and evidently, the youngsters saw him earlier with their boss, Bob Taylor. The king of the pickpockets spoke little of his clients - one reason Khan talked to him. If anyone knew the woman Khan sought, it was Taylor.

With his mind refocused on his personal task, Khan

hurried along the street past three drunken seamen and into the fog. Although he looked towards the ground, his keen ears picked up every footfall, jostle, cough, and laugh from the surrounding people. His shadow loomed in front of him, long and black, and he watched the bounce of his head with each long stride his gangling legs took. Streetlights became scarcer the further he walked into the poverty-stricken area, so his shadow blended with the gloom in time. Soon his echoing footsteps accompanied him and wisps of mist touched him with tentative fingers.

Before long, the sailors' drunken cursing and singing faded behind him, and private thoughts occupied his mind while the amorous vapours caressed him. London's history, steeped in mystery and hidden wonders, held many secrets, and his quest had led him here. But, those same oddities attracted more questions that piled up against him.

Terrified shrieks resounded through the narrow alleyways ahead of him. His eyes narrowed, peering through the hovering fog. It was hard to pinpoint the sound's source which seemed to move in separate directions. Then another scream. This time from another direction. The trouble with Whitechapel's streets, alleys, and lanes, was sound could echo across long distances. The pea soup fog hindered him further. He stopped walking and allowed the mist to cloak him.

The frightened voices approached from ahead. Hairs rose on his neck in anticipation. Khan stood against the wall, waiting to see who came near. Before long, the screaming became voices, and he realised it came from a group of children - the same he encountered earlier.

They raced past him, not noticing his tall frame skulking in the shadows. Their voices sounded scared, terrified even, but that meant little. They could have picked the wrong drunk's pocket, and he may have been chasing after them.

Khan paused upon hearing another voice coming from the place the children left. Another child, thinner than a toy kite's struts, raced by as though chased by the Devil himself. When he passed, Khan moved through the mist again, heading through Fashion Street past the doss houses. Dim lighting from inside the overcrowded residences trickled onto the fog to create an eery atmosphere. The aura of death mixed with the semi-darkness and his senses heightened.

Somewhere he heard a dog barking, and another dog started too; it sounded like a fight, perhaps over a scrap of food.

The sound popped through his chest, and his heart jumped with the adrenaline spurt. Another scream punctuated the air, laced with the terror of an imminent end and pitched high like a steam train's departure whistle. He cocked his head to listen, trying to catch its direction, and another scream ripped through night fog; a woman's scream. He took off, bolting as fast as limited visibility allowed him without tripping or colliding with hidden objects. Blood churned through his veins, pumped by an excited heart as he ran through the streets.

Then he spotted them. Two shadows outlined against the paler backdrop of fog lit by a gas streetlight. They circled each other in a chase - a chase of death. A tall man in a top hat and long coat that reached knee level.

A shorter woman held in the man's grip as they danced a deadly waltz. Khan's heart jumped more, pounding hard as a racehorse's hooves, and he raced towards them. His fists balled tight, thumb locked over fingers, when he reached them and struck hard.

Khan meant to shout something as he pushed hard against the large man, but he managed only a grunt. The attacker was broad, thick-set, and appeared taken aback at another attacking him. Although he couldn't see the man's face, Khan thought he tried protesting, but he ignored it. Something metallic dropped, hitting the cobblestones. A knife. Khan ducked under the man's swinging arm and hit hard at his stomach. It was like hitting a stone wall. The assailant was fit, maybe a sailor, and two strong hands reached around towards him, tried to grip, but Khan stepped away as quick as a fly.

Still ducking, Khan rammed the man with his whole body. A grunt reached his ears, and the woman's assailant dropped to the hard cobbled path. A streetlight's finger touched the woman's would-be assailant's face revealing crazed eyes glowing crimson. Khan kicked the man's hat away.

Something seemed odd. The man lay still on the ground. A rivulet of blood ran from his body towards Khan's feet. He wasn't breathing.

Khan's mind concluded the large attacker was too easy to defeat. He turned, facing the woman. The next scream that filled his ears was his own as he saw the glint of steel plunging towards his own heart. The blade sliced his chest, he heard piercing ripping of flesh, and darkness stole his vision. As he died, he realised something.

He had attacked the wrong killer.

He would deal with that upon his return.

Chapter 2

AUSTRALIA - SEPTEMBER 2016

Water, icy and interruptive, smashed Craig from black unconsciousness. His sudden shocked breath drew some inside his throat, and he coughed involuntarily. Its cold grip shook him as it slid down his skin. Another load splashed upon him and he battled to breathe. Something restricted his wrists, something thin, pliable, and it rubbed with the ferocity of harsh sandpaper. He tried kicking but his legs remained still, held fast by the same kind of rope coiled around his wrists. What was he lying upon? A table? How did he get here?

"Wake up, Mr Ramsey." The voice summoned memories, times filled with fury and hate.

Then he remembered where he was.

"Colonel Blaze, I presume?" Craig replied, keeping his voice level as he could, despite shivering from the cold water's icy fingers tickling his skin.

"I thought you'd never come visiting." Blaze's voice, hidden in the darkness, held a grim smile. "What kept you?"

Craig strained to see through the darkness. His fingers searched for something, anything he could touch, anything tangible to gain traction and information. His darkness-shrouded captor saw this.

"Searching for clues, Mr Ramsey?"

Craig knew he possessed a huge ego, and he hated it more when another's smugness reminded him of it. "No, but seeing as you need one, I'll keep that in mind."

Blaze's silence at his put-down made Craig smile. It had been some time since Blaze captured him. Back then, he and Project Gemini had lured Craig under the guise of testing and documenting psychic abilities - his supernatural talents. In particular, Craig's ability to know things by touching objects belonging to others. It hadn't taken long for Craig to learn he'd been duped, and he'd escaped because Project Gemini didn't know everything about him either - specifically his other skills known by few others. Talking to the dead is useless if they're not around to listen.

Where are you, Emily?

Even Colonel Ryan or his Spirit Force comrades would be useful to have around.

It was his own fault. Emily had warned him not to pursue Denton's disappearance yet. He knew she was right. But it was his own ego and his memories of the torture from Project Gemini that spurred him. Besides, he promised to come for the Project if they crossed his path again.

"I've a question for you, Mr Ramsey," Colonel Blaze said, almost as though he read Craig's mind. "Why did you break in here? Did you truly believe we wouldn't capture you?"

Craig didn't answer, choosing to say nothing while his foggy mind cleared enough to plan. A boot scuffed the concrete floor to his left. Someone else was with Blaze.

A cloth dropped on his face, cold and wet. Surprised, he inhaled and choked on the cold water rushing into the cloth covering his face. It waterlogged his sinuses, flooding his breathing passages, and he couldn't stop it. His lungs and mind felt tortured from the chill. It wouldn't stop rushing him. The cords cut his wrists and ankles as he fought to twist from the deluge. His mouth opened to scream but more water filled it. He choked, wanted to cough, but his lungs held no air. He was drowning.

Then it stopped. The heavy wet towel lifted from his mouth. He sucked in air like a baby guzzling milk.

Soft laughter filled the room's darkness.

Craig vomited water, turning his head to release it. At last, he could breathe more than sputter. "I thought-" he coughed "-water boarding was -"

"Illegal, Mr Ramsey?" Blaze's voice came from the same place, confirming Craig's earlier supposition. Someone else accompanied Colonel Blaze. "It's only illegal if we're caught, and as you know, Project Gemini doesn't exist."

"Yet, I found you on the same base as years ago," Craig muttered. "What are the odds?"

The cloth dropped over Craig's face again, followed by more water. He tried holding his breath this time, but to no avail. Water choked and clogged him. It even felt like it was bursting through his ears. Then it stopped. He shook his head, trying to clear it as the second person removed the cloth.

"Why are you here, Mr Ramsey?" Blaze sounded a notch away from total annoyance.

This time, Craig's fingers reached the table. A psychic vision tumbled through his brain, pushing him away from his current situation. Flashes of uniformed Armed Forces officers flicked through his mind. Pieces of conversation. One word sprang to his consciousness.

The cloth's clammy embrace caught him again. More water forced its coursing rush into his breathing system. This time it took longer to stop. How? A bigger bucket?

He couldn't take it any longer, but he couldn't tell them why he was here either.

"Wait," he gasped, hacking up oceans of water from his nose.

Water boarding was only supposed to give the feeling of drowning, but Craig knew otherwise. His joints ached from his struggles against his restraints, and the water he coughed came from his lungs, and he knew about people with psychological problems from the torture. This wasn't what he expected if caught.

"Did you hear me, Mr Ramsey?" Blaze asked.

"Are you asking the same question?" Craig responded, still coughing hard between words.

A pinprick of light brought life to the darkness. Craig thought he saw a goggled profile behind it before it faded. The smell of a cigarette's smoke pinched his water-drenched nose's tortured sensors. He heard it before he felt it, the sound of a wet towel.

He shouted fast, and he sensed the unseen man pause in the darkness.

"Yes, Mr Ramsey?" Blaze's menacing voice reminded Craig of Agent Smith from Matrix.

A knocking sound interrupted Craig before he could answer. He almost laughed. He couldn't see Blaze or the person with the buckets of water, nor could he see anyone else. But he felt their distracted annoyance.

"Yes?" Blaze called, and a door opened. The room remained in darkness and stopped Craig seeing the new arrival.

"Major Oates sent me." A male's voice. It sounded about thirty-to-thirty-five of age, but the way it said it sounded younger. Craig's eyebrow raised, wondering where he'd heard that tone before, even if he couldn't recognise the voice. "Message for you, Colonel."

"What is it?"

Light blazed through the room; harsh, white and blinding. Craig closed his eyelids against it but grinned when he heard cries of agony from three voices: Colonel Blaze and two others further from the door. So there was yet another there too!

Then thunder rocked the room.

A muzzle flared.

Craig winced at the queer squelching noise behind him. Then a man fell across Craig. Blood oozed from the man's head, just above his night-vision goggles. A plastic bucket hit the floor, splashing water. Colonel

Blaze snatched away his own night-vision goggles and tossed them aside while drawing his pistol. But the other officer, quiet until now, proved quicker.

The new arrival's pistol jerked twice in answer to the other officer's gunshots before falling, dropping his own firearm. Craig realised his rescuer had died before hitting the floor.

Colonel Blaze walked towards the new arrival's corpse, rolled the dead man over to look in his face, and his expression clouded over in shocked recognition. "Holt?"

Craig watched, words trapped behind unwilling lips, as the man who shot his rescuer crossed the room. Colonel Blaze's attention remained on the dead man at his feet, his face frozen in puzzled bewilderment. The Colonel must have placed great trust in Holt before his betrayal. The silent third man approached the Colonel and the corpse, weapon still drawn.

Craig noticed it first, Blaze not long afterwards. A hammer clicked, punctuating the silence, and Colonel Blaze looked up from the corpse into the pistol's open mouth in surprise.

Nothing prepared them for the next part. An amorphous shape, translucent and dark-grey like smoke, a smoke with seeming intelligence, emerged from the third man's nose and mouth. It gathered, billowing into clouds, hung between the man and Colonel Blaze before shooting into the superior officer's facial cavities. The third man appeared surprised. He shook his head as though waking from a dream before looking straight at the Colonel. His superior said nothing, but his eyes had changed. Craig thought they looked familiar but couldn't place them. Before Craig had time to think, Colonel Blaze lifted his own weapon, stabbed its barrel under the other officer's chin which disappeared with a loud pistol crack and a splash of blood.

Craig's heart hammered hard as he watched in horror. Flecks of blood landed on his own face. He shut his mouth to make sure nothing entered it, but the taste spread across his tongue. Imagined or not, he didn't know. His hands worked feverishly at the rope even as the possessed Colonel turned to face him. Blaze's eyes calmed, the fury dissipating, as it turned towards Craig. His smile disappeared when he saw Craig was now free from the ropes binding him to the table.

Craig wasted no time, wrapping the hemp rope around the Colonel's throat. He surmised that whatever creature inhabited the armed officers could jump by eye contact. Whatever it was, it wasn't a spirit. The dead need no eye contact to possess.

A familiar voice rasped from the Colonel's mouth as his fingers flailed at the rope. "Unc! Stop it! It's me."

Craig Ramsey maintained pressure on the ropes although he realised the Colonel had stopped fighting him. A quizzical eyebrow raised as he pushed the Colonel away. "Who are you?"

Something struck him as familiar about the personality inside the Colonel.

The Colonel looked Craig in the eye, but no smoke issued forth. Whatever was there, it wasn't after Craig's body. Instead, it lifted a finger to its pursed lips and pointed to a corner of the room. Craig didn't need to look; he knew a camera recorded everything.

"Who are you?" Craig insisted.

"Not now," the not-Colonel Blaze said. "Just get out now. I'll hold the others back from you."

Craig refused to move. "I don't have what I came for."

The uniformed man sighed, retrieved a pen from a shirt pocket, and handed it to him. "Take it. That's all you'll need. Go, before they catch you again!"

Craig raised an eyebrow. Whoever this creature was, it knew about Craig's talent for psychometry: the ability to read things about objects, their owners, their histories, and more. Assorted psychic images from the pen flashed across Craig's mind. But it wasn't enough. He needed more.

An alarm bell rang through the building

The Colonel winked. "Head out down that corridor. Follow the signs. When you hear the signal, run for the fence."

Craig felt like hanging back, but the Colonel pushed him away, lifting a finger and pointing it down the corridor away from the shouting voices. "Get the hell out of here. I'll catch up soon," the Colonel hissed at him.

Craig Ramsey turned and bolted down the corridor. The shouting voices faded behind him as he ran. One of them barked orders at the Colonel, telling him to drop to the ground with his hands on his head. Craig hurried faster towards a marked exit. He opened it, paused to look behind him. Curiosity-fuelled questions still burned his mind. More intrigue flashed through him as he noticed fewer guards than expected. Had something distracted them from their posts?

He recalled the Colonel-thing's words. Wait for the signal. What signal? Follow the signs? What signs?

Something moved to the side. Craig's head turned towards the source: a lift with its door waiting for him. Hearing no one approaching yet, he looked inside the lift. Someone had ripped the console, tearing out all the buttons except for G level. An LED display showed he was five levels underground. Intrigued, Craig read a handwritten sign next to the gutted controls. "PRESS G."

Was this a trap?

Craig remembered the voice's tone. It sounded sincere enough. So he followed the note's instructions and waited as the lift took him upwards. At last, the doors opened. Craig peered outwards. There were still no guards around!

The building's exit looked inviting to Craig. Lacking a better plan, Craig raced through the exit and stood in the shadows. Someone had killed the lights earlier on this side of the building. Glass crunched under his feet; fragments of the light bulbs.

A voice beside Craig spoke, surprising him. "Say, guv'nor. What kept you?"

With his special vision, Craig peered at the new arrival: a spirit in the form of a man. By his clothes, he appeared as a Dickensian character, someone from old Victorian London. The man possessed a stout build with a black moth-eaten overcoat draped over his shoulders and a dark wide-brimmed hat perched at a cocky angle upon his head. A dark red bandanna hung around his neck. "Turner, at your service, guv'nor," he introduced himself with a lift of his hat. "Shall we chip?"

Craig hesitated, taking in the Cockney accent. "Chip? I am supposed to wait for a signal."

"A flippin' signal?" Turner responded with a laugh. "Are you feckin' kidding?" He clicked his fingers and three explosions rocked the Army base from the other side. The air filled with shouts and sirens. "There's your signal! Now, follah me, will you?"

Craig needed no further invitation and ran through the darkness after Turner who floated a short distance ahead of him. They slipped through the shadows, avoiding other soldiers with ease. Being a spirit, Turner knew where to go before the living even emerged from their barracks. Before long, they reached the edge of the base. Craig recognised the hole he'd dug under the fence. It looked like someone had refilled it, but another had been dug next to it from inside the base.

"Who are you and why are you helping me?"

Turner passed through the wire fence before he turned to face Craig. He walked back through the perimeter until his astral features touched Craig's physical nose. "My name is Turner, an' th' young master will be wai'in faw you." He faced the other direction and floated along the ground, leaving Craig no choice but to follow through the bushland.

At last, Craig saw his faithful Jaguar. But this wasn't where he'd left the car. He looked at Turner who avoided his gaze, preferring to whistle an old tune Craig didn't recognise. Next to the car sat Emily, his spirit guardian and companion.

"Craig!" she responded, hurrying towards him. "Are you okay?"

"Yes," he answered. He wanted to ask where she was earlier when he needed her help.

Emily must have heard his thoughts. "Turner and I couldn't get into the building. Something prevented our entry," she answered with the Scottish accent he loved so much about her.

Craig kicked himself. Emily never deserted him. After so many years, he should have known better.

"Yes, you should," she responded, acting haughty, and stared Craig down. At last, Emily allowed a smile to cross her mouth. She moved forward and pulled him into a hug. "Come here. It's good to see you again."

Craig returned the hug, feeling the tingles as he touched her spirit body. Emily was like the mother he never knew and had been a good friend over the past few decades. Craig pulled back. "Shouldn't we move on before they come looking for us?"

Turner responded. "Da young master is still comin'. We can' chip wi'hou' 'im."

"Chip?" Craig asked.

"He means leave," Emily explained. "Turner's a Cockney."

"An' you're th' lovelies' lass I 'ave seen in a long time," Turner responded, doffing his hat towards Emily with all the charm of a rough nut. Emily shuddered at Turner's tone. Craig guessed she tolerated Turner.

"Who's the 'master'?" Craig asked, wondering who else involved themselves in his rescue.

Movement in the corner of his eye caught Craig's attention. The Jaguar's door opened and out stepped a familiar figure. Craig's jaw dropped when he recognised the lad of Samoan heritage.

Tyrone!

Chapter 3

Hot breath blasted the nape of her neck like a Sahara breeze. Her legs strained to carry her forward in her race. She wanted to look behind her, but she knew he was close. Looking would slow her. The thing chased her stronger and wanted blood. Hers.

"I'm coming, sweetie." Its voice thundered from behind her. She couldn't see the man, nor did she know if it was human, but it sounded male. His voice sounded familiar, too, as though from a dream - the kind that faded with the sunrise. A phantom recollection. Malevolence laced with psychopathic delight in her fear.

Then the whistling! That tune. So familiar and so old.

Gay go up, and gay go down,
To ring the bells of London town.

She tripped, and its laughter shook her nerves like a chew toy in a dog's mouth. The laugh was full of sharp teeth that would tear her to shreds. At least, that's how it sounded. She wanted to scream, but it caught in her throat, obstructing her breath.

Bull's eyes and targets,
Say the bells of St. Marg'ret's.

Her fatigued limbs dragged like blocks of lead through tacky tar. And each step tortured her resolve.

She wanted to stop, but self-preservation pushed her forward.

Again, her feet tangled each other. She tripped and fell.

The creature's laughter rolled from behind like a cheesy B-grade villain.

"It's been a long time. Did you miss me?"

A gasp escaped her throat. She tried to choke it back. Show no fear. He lives on others' dread, thrives in its grasp.

"It's been years since we last met." His voice boomed through the alleyway, bouncing off the brickwork that towered around her.

Her fingers, long and white, adorned with rings that no longer held value, clutched at a nearby bin for support. In vain, she tried to stand but fell again. She choked another scream upon realising. Her legs had vanished.

Instead, a long green scaly tail curled and twisted. It arced and flicked in time with her panicked thoughts as if it were a torturous body sock trapping her legs inside.

And from the alleyway's depths hovered two red luminous orbs. Towards her, blinking. They narrowed, and she recognised them as eyes on a face framed by blackness. This blackness wore a large top hat and a voluminous dark cape that spread through the night like death's wings.

A blade flicked outward, faster than a snake and twice

as deadly. It cut, slashed and flashed in the night. She screamed, raising her arms in defence. Blood sprayed, splattered, and filled the air in clouds. The taste filled her mouth, coppery and rich. But she didn't feel the wounds. Whose blood was it?

And when she woke, his words filled her mind.

Remember me, Sirena...

***

Brianna Cogan stepped out of the police car, a hot coffee grasped in her hand. She screwed her face up at the beverage's rough, abrasive flavour and wished she hadn't bought it. At last, she swallowed with a painful gulp. It tasted like burnt beans dipped in caustic soda. She promised herself never to buy coffee at that diner again.

She refocused and looked at the alley, its entrance adorned with police tape. It looked like she was late. Lights flashed ahead; the police photographer was hard at work.

She approached Sergeant Hohenhaus from behind, tapping him on the shoulder. He jumped with a start before turning to face Brianna..

"Jeez, Cogan, don't do that." Hohenhaus noted the coffee in her hand, its steam hitting the cold air, and he looked at her. "I'm not sure you need that."

"Same guy?"

Hohenhaus nodded. "I almost lost my stomach," he said. "It's terrible. Whoever did it really hates his victims."

"Oh?" Brianna craned her neck, looking past him towards the alley. It was dark, almost as black as the stench drifting out to them. Hohenhaus choked a strangled gasp and Brianna noted his slight green-tinged complexion. The poor guy's stomach couldn't handle it. So she handed him her coffee.

"You look like you need this more than me," she said as he grasped for it.

His hands curled around the hot cup and Brianna remembered giving him coffee other times. Hohenhaus often asked or gained a coffee from her on call-outs. Had he been conning her all the time for free drinks?

Brianna shook her head at the thought as she approached the alley. "I'm going for a look. Try keeping that coffee down, Sarge."

"Knock yourself out." Hohenhaus swallowed a sip and his eyes lit up. "Hey, this is good shit."

A camera flash filled the gloom ahead, and Brianna's coffee rose in her throat at the brief glimpse. A smell of stale urine made her nose feel like falling off her face, and blood clung to the brickwork in splashes. The spatter marks screamed the killer's passionate fury. Brianna covered her mouth and nose with a latex-gloved hand as she choked back the coffee.

Brianna's gaze zipped to the victim, or what remained of her.

The corpse's legs lay spread open with a bloody river pooling between them. Her underwear formed a dark red reminder of something terrible. The attacker had torn it apart, and it looked like something had penetrated - something sharp. A coat, perhaps made of fake fur but matted in fresh body fluids, lay underneath the victim like a macabre picnic cloth.

"I reckon it was a Liston knife."

Brianna jumped and faced the voice's source: the forensics unit's photographer. "Higgins," Brianna gasped. "You startled me."

Higgins lifted the PC tablet, aimed, and took another photo. This time, Brianna blinked before the flash blinded her.

"What's a Liston knife?"

Higgins checked the photo she snapped with the tablet's camera before turning around. "A Liston is a long surgical knife. Popular legends say Jack the Ripper used one. I've seen those slashes in pictures of the Ripper's handiwork."

"The Ripper?" Brianna scoffed. "Do you think it's his ghost doing this?"

No sooner had Brianna spoken than goosebumps prickled to her skin's surface. It sounded strange to mention ghosts. In the past, she'd fostered healthy scepticism on the subject. But, the humorous held some truth for her. Brianna had met Craig Ramsey, and his spirit companion Emily Fraser, smashing her scepticism.

Higgins looked back at Brianna. Her expression resembled Brianna's from the past, a time before ghosts were real. "What the hell, Detective?" she said. "No. But I reckon we have an enthusiast on our hands."

"Brilliant," she said, stopping again at her words. 'Brilliant' was one of Craig's favourite words. "I mean-" she paused "-what else can you tell me?"

Higgins pointed at the victim. "Do you see the incisions? It looks like a surgeon's cuts, someone looking for vital organs. That main one there-" she pointed towards the chest "-is under the rib cage. I reckon he was trying for the heart."

A rumbling sound of retching and vomiting from behind made them turn around. Unseen, Hohenhaus had returned and reacted to the scene. But Brianna noticed something else. The sergeant's wide eyes were glancing to the left, and she followed his contorted gaze. There, near a bin, she noticed a lump of something, about three-or-four inches long. Some kind of lump.

Brianna noted the wall above it showed a splattery circle, haloed by bloody specks. The killer had thrown the meaty lump at the wall, and it splashed like a soggy sponge before falling to the ground. "What is that?"

Higgins turned on her iPhone's torch, shining it upon the mass. "It looks like half a kidney."

Brianna's Armed Forces history had exposed her to many things, terrible things, and this was too much for her. But a ghoulish sense of curiosity gripped her, and she had to ask. "Half a kidney?"

The forensic investigator gripped the kidney, her face showing concentration as she tried not to drop the slippery thing, and dropped it into a zip-lock bag. She sealed it and showed it to Brianna. "Yep. A little under half." She peered at it through her glasses and then Brianna saw something she never expected. The investigator blanched and looked away.

Brianna wanted to say something but refrained. It would be hypocritical to criticise the forensics investigator's weak stomach while her own performed a double pike, twist and roll. So she waited for Higgins to recover enough to speak. "Are you okay?"

Higgins took a breath, blinked, and exhaled. She wouldn't vomit. "The sick bastard has taken a bite out of it."

Brianna's tanned features blanched at the thought. "A cannibal?"

"What's that on the wall?" Hohenhaus asked, moving his light to see better. He paused, his jaw hung open in shock. "Oh, jeez."

Smeared in blood not yet dried, thin creeks of it trickling along the brickwork, was a message.

HELLO, MY SWEETIES. DID YOU MISS ME?

Chapter 4

Brianna Cogan released her heavy breath while stretching back in her chair and looked away from the computer screen. Blinking her red-rimmed eyes, she inhaled deep, arched her back, and allowed the air to escape in a relaxing breeze. It had been a hard night. All she wanted was to curl up in bed and escape the past two months of cases away. Two months had passed since she first met Craig Ramsey, a fortnight since one killer disappeared. She felt she needed a holiday after that. But the recent murders demanded her attention, or at least Inspector Myles said they did.

The killings first started six weeks ago. She had been working on the sniper case then, so another detective took that case. But investigations had turned up nothing so far. Tonight's victim, the eighth, was the first time the killer had left a message. Brianna looked at the photograph of the killer's wall graffiti on her screen. It looked like the killer wrote it with blood. Forensics would soon confirm if it belonged to the victim. Brianna had also sent a copy to a handwriting expert in Sydney for analysis. From the message, it appeared the killer had been around before. But nothing had come up in the files she searched in the police database. Even stranger, although they could see finger marks they believed belonged to the killer, there were no fingerprints.

The only thing linking this killing to the others of the past six weeks was the method. The killer had slashed each victim in what appeared a savage matter. Brianna had seen other killings from stabs and slashes. They often showed a purpose. During her time in the armed forces, the wounds appeared to tell the story of a battle, a fight beyond mere kill or be killed. With some murder cases, they differed; some killings appeared opportunistic, taken when the chance arose. But these deaths weren't clean. The killer enjoyed it, did it for fun, like a cat playing with its food.

"Has it been a long day, dear?"

Brianna turned towards the Scottish voice. She saw no one there, but she knew the voice belonged to Emily Fraser, Craig Ramsey's spirit companion. Brianna smiled, rubbing red eyes. "You don't know the half," she answered. "I don't know if it's me, but the world seems to be sicker every day. How long have you been there?"

Emily's voice chuckled. "I arrived a few moments ago, but I can see what you're investigating. Is that why you're looking tired?"

Brianna nodded, locking the computer screen so it returned to the login page. She didn't like Emily watching the screen over her shoulder though she knew it was still safe. "What do you think?"

Emily's voice moved across the room as she spoke. "Things haven't changed so much in the past years since I last breathed, except men own bigger weapons to kill quicker and faster. The man who killed those women is brutal, but he is no different to some men in my time. We had nasty means of killing people too."

Brianna had been biting her bottom lip as Emily spoke, and she paused for a moment to think. "Someone thought this killer acted like Jack the Ripper. Was he in your time?

The Scottish lady's spirit laughed. "No. I lived and died long before he was a twinkle in his mother's eye."

Emily's voice adopted a distant tone and Brianna wondered if it was because she hated talking about her past demise. So she changed the subject. "What brings you in here, anyway? Is Craig okay?"

"Craig and Tyrone are talking with each other. I thought I'd let the boys talk things out."

"Craig's back?" Brianna sounded surprised. She hadn't seen or heard from Craig for a few days. "And Tyrone as well? Where were they?"

"We didn't want to worry you," Emily answered with plain discomfort. "Craig visited the Army base to investigate that Denton lad's disappearance from the hospital."

"Project Gemini?" Brianna's eyebrow raised. "That's two days ago since he went. Is everything okay?"

"Craig's fine," Emily responded; her tone carried a smile. "See him tomorrow. Give the lads time to talk."

Brianna nodded and silence crept in, held back by the ticking of a small clock on Brianna's desk - a birthday gift from her deceased adoptive father. After ten ticks, Brianna finished pondering. "What makes me think there's more you're not telling me?"

Emily's tone surprised Brianna who expected a defensive response. "I was thinking about Craig and Tyrone. I've never seen two lads react like this in a long time."

Brianna's eyebrow raised. She turned towards Emily's voice which came from the corner opposite her desk. Her eyes looked at the chair sitting there. An indent, in the shape of a woman's buttocks, proved the only sign of Brianna's presence. It was an average size indent, possibly on the smaller side.

"I'm sure Tyrone and Craig will sort through things," Brianna replied, opening her desk drawer to pick out some gum, which she popped in her mouth. "Why are you worried?"

"It's more than that."

Brianna picked up the tone; Emily was hiding something. "Is it also about Debra's accident?"

"Yes," Emily's voice responded, a little too soon for Brianna's liking. "That's what I mean. Debra and Tyrone were both a breath of fresh air for Craig after their parents died. You know about them, right?" Brianna shook her head and Emily continued. "Craig took them on so fast and tried to fill the gaps for them. I'm not sure who helped whom the most. Craig felt they needed him, but I think he needed them as much, especially after-"

A knock at the door interrupted Emily. Brianna glanced towards the sound and kicked herself for leaving her office door open. Another detective,

Anthony Gibbons, poked his head through to look at her. The first thing she noticed was the light bouncing off his balding scalp.

"Is this a bad time?" he asked, a grin curled into a leer at his mouth's corner. "You sound like you're talking to someone."

Brianna's shoulders stiffened at his words. "I was finishing up from revising tonight's incident." Her eyes flicked towards the chair that still held Emily's buttock prints, which seemed to be fading.

Gifford glanced in the same direction, saw nothing, and walked into the office. The grin on his face grew. "Yeah, this case has me talking to myself sometimes too. You know I've been working on it a while with the earlier killings, right?"

Brianna looked at her screen, saw it was blank from logging out, and masked a relieved sigh. "I heard. Have you got anything important I need to know?"

Gifford plonked himself in Emily's seat, his knees apart. It was a sleazy posture, which didn't surprise Brianna who had heard about his reputation. She felt sorry for Emily. Even though Gifford couldn't see her, Emily must have felt uncomfortable with a mortal passing through her spirit body - especially Gifford! "I've got a file too high for a kangaroo to jump over." He grinned again, and his eyes flicked towards Brianna's breasts. They seemed to linger and lifted towards her eyes just as she was about to rebuke him. He leaned forward in his chair, his fingers touching the desk. "Perhaps we can swap notes over some wine. What do you say?"

Brianna glanced towards the sound of Emily's cough. She knew she could handle Tony easy though she felt thankful for the spirit's presence. "Wine?" she asked, playing dumb. "We're at work."

Gifford grinned. "Wine at my place," he answered. He paused, eye glinting. "Or... Your place."

Brianna stood up from her desk, towering above Gifford. He stood, trying to maintain a dominant posture, but it didn't work. Brianna stood taller than he. This amused Emily whose laugh echoed to Brianna's ears, making it hard for her to resist smiling too. Looking Gifford straight in the eye, Brianna answered. "I don't invite men from work to my place-"

"Then my-"

Brianna continued past his interruption. "And I don't believe your mother likes you bringing women home either."

Gifford's mouth hung open a moment. "Oh, snap!" He grinned.

"And I don't date men from work," she finished. She allowed that to sink into her colleague's mind. "I'm sorry. I'm not interested."

"But-"

"Which part of no don't you understand?" Brianna continued, not allowing Gifford to interrupt. "Do I need to take this to Human Resources?"

Gifford's wind left his sails. His shoulders slumped, but Brianna could see behind his eyes. Fire, darkness and anger flourished there. Brianna had seen men like Gifford before, and she felt no remorse. He couldn't get past her.

Just as quickly, his darkness disappeared. He lifted his hands, open palms towards her, and smiled. "Hey, I'm sorry, Cogan. I didn't mean to be out of line, you know?"

Brianna made no reply, knowing he could misinterpret acceptance of his apology as an allowance for his behaviour.

"Listen, I'm heading out," he answered, keeping his voice apologetic as he backed towards the door. "We can talk about the case another day. When you're feeling better, maybe. It's been a long day and everything, right?"

Gifford edged out the door and left.

Brianna said nothing. She waited and listened to his footsteps down the hall. She'd forgotten Emily was there until the familiar voice spoke from empty air.

"Well done, Brianna!"

Once certain they were alone, she released her breath in a long breeze. "I've heard of him before and wondered when he'd come my way."

Emily laughed. "He's a grown man who lives with his mother?"

Brianna couldn't hold back her grin. She'd surprised herself with that line too. She opened her mouth to respond when a loud thump echoed down the hall outside. Brianna looked up and was about to look at the cause when she heard two more punches.

"He's hitting the vending machine," Emily's voice explained. "Little men like him haven't changed since my time either, it seems."

Brianna laughed at the connotation, but she couldn't shake the odd feeling creeping over her. Information from the past killings Tony Gifford investigated could prove useful. If he had an anger problem, she'd have to watch her step with him.

***

Meanwhile, two blocks from the main nightclub strip, someone else had also finished work. For her, it had also been a long night and Delta looked forward to arriving home and sitting in front of her television with a tub of ice cream while watching Seinfeld re-runs. Most wouldn't imagine that as an exotic dancer's off-time, but it was her plan tonight.

Delta donned her vinyl jacket and waved goodbye to a colleague. Paralyzer played loud, its back-beat vibrating the furniture in the backrooms. Delta moved her hips to its rhythms as she moved through the other dancers who shared the dressing (or undressing, as she called it) room.

As Delta prepared to out the front, a dancer hurried through the side door. Her eyes lit up when she saw Delta, and she put an arm out to stop her.

"That loser is hanging around the front, probably waiting for you again," she told Delta, raising her voice above the current show's act. "Jake said he can take you

33

home if you're willing to wait half an hour for him."

Delta sighed. For the past few weeks, she had gained a new "number one fan". Some fans were okay, but this one had that vibe to watch out for - the creepy kind. He never slid money into her G-string, but he eyed her with more than lust. His stares were cold and hungry. One of the other girls joked that he looked like actor Steve Lucsonberry, only with hair slicked down tight to his scalp. Delta had met him on a slow night and danced more for him. He looked like he had money, but if he did, he didn't part with it. Afterwards, he saw her leave the club and followed her to the bus stop where he stood and cast baleful glances at her window as the bus left. He'd repeated it a few times since then. Now he was back again.

Delta looked past Julie, the dancer, and saw Jake the security guy watching the conversation. He mimed towards her as though holding a steering wheel. Did she want him to drive her home?

She thought for a moment. Jake was a nice guy behind his tattooed features. She knew she was safe with him, a family man who worked two jobs to support his sick daughter after his wife died. Jake respected the ladies and was always ready to pull away overzealous fans. "No, thanks, Julie," she replied. "I'll take the other exit."

Julie leaned forward, kissed Delta's cheek, and wished her well before heading to her changing mirror. "Take care, babe," she called over her shoulder. "See you tomorrow."

Delta dodged her way past other dancers and

waitresses towards the staff exit, her hand clutching her handbag closer as she headed outside into the cold night air. She pulled her jacket closer to ward off the cold and hurried along the back alley towards the street. She took this direction more often after Mr Creepy first waited outside the club for her before. The alley was wide enough for her to dodge about if someone came the other way towards her. But she'd rather not meet him, anyway. His soupy lips and hollow eyes freaked her out, and she couldn't read his expression. The unknown scared her the most.

She'd reached the street before long and looked around the corner before exiting. There he stood with his back towards her. She tucked her trademark red hair under a scarf and stepped onto the footpath in the opposite direction. He'd been closer to the alley another time, but she had taken precautions this time. She had hidden her hair in case he recognised her from behind. A clear flash of her fiery locks would tip him off and he'd follow her like that other week.

Her skin crawled as she followed the footpath towards the train station. Nerves. Her imagination loved to play tricks on her. Delta stepped faster, her solid heels clicking on the ground. She had to invest in some running shoes - something quieter. He probably heard her and would turn around soon.

Her breathing quickened, and her shoulders tensed, rounding over.

The wind carried a sound to her. The station's PA system was announcing her train. She raced towards the station, fingers fumbling for her Go Card, and muttered countless wishes for the train to wait longer.

Shit!

The damned barrier wouldn't open for her when she pressed the pass on it!

NIL BALANCE.

The words mocked her, flashing the red circle with the line through it. They would achieve the same effect if the sign showed a face poking tongues at her.

Delta's heart sank as the train's engines whined and it rolled away along the track.

Shit!

She turned towards the street again, and there he waited! Vacant eyes stared at her - or did they look past her? - and he approached the train station's entrance. Her mind flashed back, tried to remember what she had seen at the gates. No guards sat at the gates to check passes. Not even behind the ticket office's glass!

Who would hear her scream? Would they arrive in time if she did?

A cold wind whipped Mr Creepy's hair aside like a dead piece of fur as he passed her. She averted her eyes to avoid eye contact. His shoes scraped the ground, his steps slowed, then he stopped.

Delta's breath caught in her lungs. She dared not let go.

"Hey!"

She froze, shoulders stiffening, and refused to acknowledge him.

He persisted. "Hey! Miss!"

Delta's better sense of judgement screamed at her. But she couldn't resist his call. Her head turned. The guy looked straight at her, wallet in hand, as he stood at the ticket machine.

"Have you got change for a fifty?" he called to her.

She hesitated. It was too long for him.

"I asked if you have change," he repeated. "Can you help me?"

Mr Creepy showed no signs of recognition towards her. Her thin disguise - a scarf and dark glasses - worked.

"Well?" He seemed to plead and paused. "Can you?"

She shook her head, refused to answer, and hurried away.

"Dumb bitch." The whispered words reached her.

She responded with a middle finger salute without looking back.

A thumping rocked the air. She jumped, her feet stepping faster through the darkness towards a bus stop. The thumping continued, some swearing, and then another voice - one of authority - cut the air. It told her number one fan to stop hitting the ticket machine. The voices were faint now, but she thought it ironic the guards arrived so late as usual.

Her feet carried her fast towards the bus station, winter's dying breezes chilling her through her tight jeans. The late hour hung an eerie silence over it. And the fluorescent lights above flickered and dimmed. If the television screens displaying the timetables hadn't been working, Delta would have thought it post-apocalyptic like the scenes from the old 1970s sci-fi horrors. The displays stared back at her, mocking her. She cursed to herself. The last buses had already left. She needed another way home.

It would have to be a taxi then, but not an Uber. She couldn't call them, anyway, because her smartphone's battery died and she hadn't charged it.

Something clattered behind her. She turned, but saw no one.

But she knew. She felt it. Something or someone watched her.

As a child, Delta hated the dark. She also hated being alone. To be alone in the dark was the worst, especially when walking down the back stairs. It was the worst thing for a six-year-old child. The stairs had no backing, and someone could wait underneath them, waiting to reach out and grasp her ankles with their cold fingers. Drag her away and eat her up. Delta used to whistle to herself back then. It was the only way to scare the monsters away. And that's what she felt like now.

She pursed her lips to blow. The first note was feeble. It wavered so much she forgot the song she wanted.

Someone's deep voice chuckled behind her, and Delta turned.

Peering into the dim gloom, she squinted to see through the darkness. But she couldn't see the number one creep. It didn't sound like him either. Someone else was there.

She wanted to call out. Tell the bastard to stop creeping her out.

An unseen boot heel scraped the ground. She spun to face its direction.

Nothing. Just some paper flying past, rolling randomly in the breeze.

She tried controlling her breathing, wanted it to slow down, but her heart hammered harder. Fight or flight? Her feet chose flight.

Delta raced back towards the street. Part of her wished she'd taken Jake's offer. If she had, she'd be home now, curled up in front of the television and watching Sex And The City re-runs. That show always cracked her up and made her smile. Delta tried thinking about it now. But the jokes were dull compared to her current situation.

At last, she reached the street. A couple of cars passed by, their tyres swishing through the water from the recent rain. It felt good to be in the open air where she could run and make a scene if possible. But a part of her wondered if it would be enough. These days some psychos, terrorists in particular, were happy to attack people in the street. It took all kinds to make the world these days. Her senses stayed on high alert, high enough to -

A boot splashed behind her. It was a heavy footfall. Deliberate.

Then she saw safety ahead. It was fifty metres away, but she'd have to make it. Delta's feet sped up, carrying her forward on panic-stricken legs. Her breath sounded hollow and echoed in her ears. The scarf wrapped around her neck felt tight, constricting, and her imitation leather jacket too hot.

With a sigh of relief she reached the orange taxi cab, her fingers feeling grateful as she pulled the handle and sat inside the welcoming warmth. The driver took the car into the traffic. Only then did Delta feel safe enough to look out the raindrop-spattered window at the man following her. There were two men: one was the number one creepy fan from the club; the other was a large Indian. Creepy guy watched sullenly as the cab pulled past him; his eyes opened wider upon recognising Delta when she removed her glasses. He mouthed something then looked around at the Indian who was running after the cab, screaming something. But the cab picked up speed and left him behind.

Behind them was something else flashing too fast for a good look. But a glance was all she needed. It was tall, shadowy, and wore a strange hat and long flowing cape. An involuntary shiver shook her all over, but it was gone.

Delta settled in the car's backseat, allowing the solitude to comfort her. Her breathing slowed and her heartbeat relaxed. Soon she would be home and watching Sex And The City. Her little Maltese Terrier, Snowy, would sit on her lap, looking at her with blind eyes and licking her hand to say, "It's all right. I love you." Delta hoped her new flatmate would be there too. They'd laugh at the silly shenanigans, comment about how true something was, maybe even discuss something deeper from its provoking stories.

The voice was deep, carrying a familiar accent.

"What?" she asked.

"I said, did he look pissed to you?" It sounded rough, tinged with ancient years.

"Do you mean the Indian or the other one?"

A chuckle, dry and earthy, laced with inviting heat. "Both."

"The other one followed me from my work," she answered. "I think he wants to date me."

The car's door locks thumped down like prison gates. Delta startled, recognising the deep voice's laughter from the deserted bus station. Red eyes blazed from the front seat at Delta as their owner crooned.

"Brickbats and tiles, Say the bells of St. Giles'. Halfpence and farthings, Say the bells of St. Martin's."

And she screamed unheard into the night.

Chapter 5

Brianna covered her yawn with one hand while the other clutched the paper bag of warm goodies. As she stepped from the car, the aroma of fresh croissants from the local bakery teased her nostrils.. An explosive sneeze escaped her; it happened sometimes whenever she looked at the sun, and she screwed up her eyes to avoid the morning glare.

Breakfast was a revisited habit for her since she met Craig. When she first stayed at his home, he insisted on her having breakfast. She hadn't done that since her days in the Army, one of the few habits she allowed to wither. She used to think it slowed her down. But after her morning Krav Maga workout, breakfast would be a welcome meal to refuel.

Voices reached her ear. She recognised Emily's voice, and Craig's, but there were also two others. Brianna guessed it must have been Tyrone though she hadn't spoken to him in some time. She'd first met him in the hospital when questioning him about his sister's road death. But that was so long back, his voice was a vague memory.

"Come in!" Emily's voice called from inside as Brianna touched the door handle. "It's open."

Emily followed the voices. It sounded like Craig discussing something important. She didn't want to intrude, but breakfast was getting cold. As she entered the kitchen area, she saw him with a solid Samoan teenager.

"Hi, Tyrone." She flashed a smile in the boy's direction.

The stormy look in his eyes soon disappeared upon seeing her. "It's the detective lady." Tyrone sat taller as he flashed a grin. "Are they doughnuts?"

Brianna laughed at Tyrone's cheeky joke that inferred the police ate nothing else. She pecked Craig's cheeks with her lips. "No, but I brought enough for you too."

Craig smiled and kissed her back on the lips. It was a quick one. He must have been cranky still with Tyrone.

Brianna glanced at Tyrone. "On holidays?"

"That's our topic of discussion," Craig said as he spread a thick layer of marmalade across his toast. "Tyrone's wants to take time out from school."

Tyrone glowered, an obvious sign he didn't want to discuss it in front of Brianna.

"I left school for a year after finishing year eleven," Brianna volunteered for Tyrone's benefit. "But I worked for part of it too. What do you want to do?"

The boy ran strong fingers through his hair, lowering his gaze. Thoughts ticked along behind his eyes and added to the room's tension. Brianna changed the subject. "Is that bacon I smell?"

Brianna jumped with surprise upon seeing the frying pan float towards her from the stove. Tyrone laughed at

Brianna's surprise, to which she grinned back.

A spatula dished up eggs, bacon and mushrooms on the plates before them.

"It sure is," Emily's voice said, from the pan's direction. The spirit must have noticed the detective's reaction and laughed. "I'm sorry, dear. I thought I'd cook something up for the boys and yourself today. You have all had a big night."

Tyrone stifled another laugh, and Craig smiled at Brianna's reaction. The mood had lightened, but tension still hung like a sharp-edged pendulum.

"I'm not used to having breakfast cooked for me," Brianna said, making light of it. "I usually have something from the cafeteria on the way to work."

Emily harrumphed. "You will do better than that here, lassie," she responded. "I taught Craig to cook and Tyrone does well enough to make a fine chef too."

Brianna looked towards Tyrone who was wolfing into his meal. Craig smiled at her and winked. "Dig in," he urged. "Tell me about last night."

"Someone's killing sex workers in Statton." She took a mouthful of eggs and mushroom. Brianna's eyes lifted, and she swallowed while loading the fork with more. She nodded towards Emily. "Great eggs, Emily." She continued. "We think it's the same killer. Same MO. They're found in alleys, a couple in the parks. A homeless guy found last night's victim. He's had to find another place to sleep."

A thoughtful look crossed Craig's face. "Inspector

Myles asked for my help with something like that before Debra's accident." He mentioned his deceased adopted daughter, Tyrone's sister, with hesitation. Tyrone flinched too. Some things were still raw there as expected. Tyrone finished the demolition of his second helping. Without a word, he took the plate to the sink and left.

The two adults watched the teenager stalk away to his bedroom. Craig said nothing for a while.

Brianna wondered if there was more to Tyrone's taking time off school than said, but she didn't get the chance to ask. Craig spoke first. "Would you like help with your case?"

Swallowing the last of her eggs, Brianna replied. "Craig, I need not run to you every time I take a new case, you know." She said it with a smile to veil her annoyance.

Craig must have felt tired. Instead of firing back in defence, he nodded. "That's fair enough."

"But if it happens I do," she added, smiling into his eyes, "I know where you live."

Craig grinned. "You're planning on ravishing me in my sleep?"

"Any more?" Emily's voice chimed in before Brianna could reply. A dish of scrambled eggs floated near Brianna who shook her head with a "No, thanks. But they were good."

The dish floated away, accompanied by Emily's ts-tsking. Brianna turned her attention back to Craig. "I think you should concentrate on Tyrone now he's returned. That's what's been on your mind since that night on the bridge, anyway."

Craig's red-rimmed eyes blinked. He nodded. "True." Something stirred behind his eyes. He was gearing up to say more. "Do you know what he was up to while away?"

"What?"

Craig drew a slow deep breath. "When he and I talked last night, he gave me a piece of that surfboard over there."

Brianna followed Craig's gaze. Standing against a sofa was a piece of Tyrone's red-striped surfboard. "What the hell happened to that?"

"Tyrone wanted to stop the pain of Deb's death." Craig paused and took a breath. "He wanted to paddle so far out that he couldn't return, and a shark attacked him."

Brianna's jaw hung open, partly shock at Tyrone's suicidal wish but also the story's other half. "The shark ate him?"

A laugh from beside them caught their attention. Craig looked across at the voice's source, invisible to Brianna but not to him. "No' bloody likely," the voice answered, carrying its Cockney tone.

Surprised, Brianna looked at Craig who smiled in response and explained. "Brianna, meet Turner. Turner, this is Brianna."

"Pleased 'o make y' acquain'ance," Turner's rough voice responded. Brianna tingled as she felt something like a callused hand lift her hand and kiss it.

"Give Brianna's gun back too," Craig laughed. Brianna felt her holster, shocked to find it empty, and looked about her. Her pistol floated beside her.

"Ah, shit!" Turner grumbled. The gun turned around, pointing handle-first towards Brianna, who took it back as Turner apologised. "Old habits, y' know."

Brianna's eyebrow raised, questioning, and Craig explained. "Turner's a spirit now, but he lived in the Victorian years in London. You can guess his profession."

"I saved young Master Tyrone from t' shark, I did," Turner added. "I 'appened walkin along on 'he wa'er when i sees 'he youngster flip in 'he air. Da shark was jumpin up af'er 'im. I persuaded 'he shark 'o chip, picked 'he boy up from 'he wa'er, an' 'ook 'im back ashawe. 'e'd died bu' i' wasn'' 'is 'urn ye'."

Brianna paused, processing everything, and remembered something. "That day when I was shot up," she said. "I woke up later and heard Emily talk. Did I die?"

Craig nodded. "You suffered a Near Death Experience, I'm guessing. It happened to me too, but that's another story. It gave you the ability to communicate with spirits, yes."

"And has that happened for Tyrone?"

"Well," Craig started, stretching the word. "Kind of.

Tyrone could always see and hear spirits. It's linked to his cultural heritage, I think. But, yeah, he's been affected."

"How?"

"'e saved Mr Ramsey's life las' nigh', 'e did," Turner spoke up. "An' Mr Ramsey should cu' 'he boy some slack, I reckon."

Brianna heard Emily make a similar sound from the side and wished she could see her spirit friend better. Seeing her at all would be better because she was only limited to hearing Emily. "What happened?"

Craig's features hardened. His mouth tightened and his jaw was rigid.

"Go on," Turner insisted. "Speak 'he 'ru'h an' shame 'he devil, will you?"

"I was caught and knocked unconscious at the Army base last night," Craig responded. "I was about to escape when -"

"Da boy can 'ake over people's body's," Turner interrupted, sounding annoyed with Craig's slow response. "S'op playin i' down. The boy possessed a few soldier's bodies so 'e could sneak in wi'hou' bein caugh'. 'e go' fur'her 'han I could because 'hey 'ave shieldin aw some'hin 'ha' stops spiri's like me en'erin. I 'hink i''s acciden'al meself. Bu' 'e go' 'hrough an' broke Craig ou' ov 'here."

"That's enough," Craig said, focusing his vision on an otherwise empty space.

"I'm goin' anyway," Turner's voice responded, fading as it moved towards the bedroom areas. "Thee need ter cut da boy slack, Mr Ramsey."

Craig took a deep breath, his face reddened by Turner's words, and he looked at his cup of untouched tea. Brianna couldn't help noticing the silence filling the air. On the one hand, she agreed with Turner; Craig showed more thought of Tyrone and what could have happened to him than gratitude for him being alive. Yet Craig, a free spirit himself, didn't realise how much that could suffocate the boy.

"I know you disagree with me," Craig answered.

Brianna's eyebrows raised. "But you weren't touching-"

Craig allowed a small grin to cross his face. "Just because I'm psychic doesn't mean I lack common sense," he winked.

Brianna smiled back, wondering what to say when she realised something. Craig wasn't asking her, but he wanted to confide in her. He wanted her opinion. "You grew up as an only child, and so did I," she started.

"I had my cousin. She was close like a sister."

"Close. But it's not the same thing," Brianna responded. "Tyrone lost his sister, and that's hit him harder than you know." Craig opened his mouth, but Brianna continued. "Sure. You can touch him, feel his pain, but it's not the same. His pain is his pain. Let him feel it. And be there when he needs you."

"But it is my pain," he answered, his tone harsher

than usual. "I lost family too. We should go through this together as a family."

Brianna sat back, undeterred. Maintaining her composure, she answered in an even tone. "I didn't say you hadn't lost family. I attended the funeral, so I know you did. Each of you is feeling the grief in different ways. It's natural to feel the way you do. But look at the bigger picture. You need to respect each other. Give him space when he needs it. He'll come back. He's come back already. Don't push him away."

Brianna's phone rang, cutting Craig off from replying. She looked at the display with a disappointed sigh and answered the phone.

"Hey, Cogan," a voice said to her. She took a moment to recognise its owner; Gifford. "We had another one last night. Corner of Hartley and Grange. Inspector Myles is sending me down too. I'll meet you there."

Craig leaned forward as Brianna hung up. "Another murder?"

Brianna nodded, pulling a face. She couldn't handle Gifford this morning. She looked at her croissant, cooling but still hot enough to melt the jam.

"Take it on the road," Craig offered. "Do you want help on this one?"

Brianna smirked, one hand holding the croissant and the other brushing Craig's cheek. "I'm sure I can handle this one," she grinned, pecking him on the cheek, and hurried out the front door.

Craig's brow crinkled as he watched her leave. "Okay,

catch you again soon."

He sat and leaned back in the chair and wondered. When Brianna touched his cheek, he picked up a mental image of a sleazy guy. The man looked like moved from one woman to the next, leaving them used and wasted in his wake. Another image slipped into the vision. The man's name was Tony, and he was kissing Brianna, running hands down along the curves of her buttocks. She seemed to reciprocate! Was this a memory or a fantasy?

For a moment, Craig felt something clutch his chest. Anxiety. Could that revelation have been real or fantasy? And, was it Brianna's fantasy?

He shook his head, still feeling the effects of the previous night's torture. A yawn escaped his mouth. Was fatigue distorting his psychic visions?

Or were they manifestations of something deeper?

Chapter 6

Death's stench hung in the air and assailed Brianna's nose as she slipped under the police tape. It was blood; stale blood. And no matter how often she saw it, Brianna never got used to it.

This time, the murder was in a car park accessible via a narrow entrance between the tavern and the abandoned TAB. The hotel and three other businesses used it for their employees' cars. And having only one entrance, any breeze that entered didn't blow the stench away.

The second thing Brianna spotted, besides the civilians gawking from the verandah, was Detective Gifford strutting around like a leather-covered peacock in his shiny jacket. Polished to a shine, his boots reflected to a shine. Brianna reckoned Gifford did that to spy up women's skirts with the reflection.

Sergeant Hohenhaus noticed Brianna first and hurried to her. Brianna handed him her coffee before he uttered a word.

"Thanks, Detective," he said. "You're the -"

"I know. I won't want it, anyway, right?"

"It's putrid down there," he confirmed, waving a waft from his nostrils. "Like a bloody abattoir."

Brianna wondered if Hohenhaus meant the death stench or Gifford. She couldn't help grinning at that, and Gifford mistook her smile as a greeting.

"Cogan!" Gifford's tone dripped with excitement as he strutted with his arms pumping and chest puffed. "This guy's getting cockier, I reckon. Check this out."

Brianna took in the scene. Besides the darkening blood stains, she noticed the killer had ripped the body open again. She couldn't help wondering. Was this man a fan of Jack the Ripper? The real Ripper would have died a long time ago. But he lived in London. Would he escaped from England to Australia and sired murderous children?

A flash popped nearby. Brianna glanced in its direction and spied something else.

"Is that what I think it is?" Brianna pointed at something hanging nearby.

Gifford looked where Brianna pointed and ducked under the stairs for a closer inspection. It looked paper-thin, curled up with diamond-shaped patterns along its length. "It looks like a snake's skin," he exclaimed, his voice filled with surprise. "Spring must be closer than I figured if they're coming out now." He poked it with its foot to stretch and open it. "That's a big skin! The snake must be as big and thick as -"

Brianna gathered it must have been a large snake, but she didn't want to hear or think of Gifford comparing it to himself or hinting at his own anatomy. Thick as his head, she could agree with, but that was it.

Gifford waited for the police photographer to finish

her task before stepping closer to scrutinise the body. "It's the same MO as the other one," he commented. "Just like the others last month too."

Brianna noted wounds on the victim's wrists, red and rubbed raw. "Rope burns," she murmured, looking around her. "I don't see any rope around here."

Gifford snorted, with a knowing smirk that crossed his face. "They're job-related injuries."

Brianna cocked an eyebrow and reached for the victim's handbag. It looked good, but it was cheap.

"She was a hooker," Gifford explained. "Worked in the Valley and doubled sometimes as a stripper at Gilroy's. You can't tell, but she was a real looker too. Fine piece of -"

"A regular there, were you?" Brianna muttered under her breath as she found the victim's wallet and searched for ID.

Although a sexist idiot, Gifford was right. The girl had been an attractive sort.

The ID photo showed her with blond hair, but now it was a crimson red. Patches, untouched by the pooled blood, shone in the sunlight. But the victim's address was in an older neighbourhood where she didn't expect the girl to live.

"It's got to be the same killer as the past couple of months," Gifford said, loud enough for everyone to hear. "But we all thought your boyfriend helped catch him. I guess Ramsey's not the psychic he's cracked up to be, huh?"

Brianna ignored the urge to punch Gifford in the throat. But she wouldn't let it go either. She stood up to face Gifford. "You still haven't given me those case notes, have you?"

Gifford's face reddened, and his stance tightened up like he was ready to lash out. He chomped hard on the gum in his mouth. "You'll get them today."

"Good. I look forward to that." Brianna narrowed her eyes, picking out Gifford's five weak spots where she'd like to strike the arrogant tosser. Gifford was the first to look away by turning to face the dead girl.

"Whoever the killer is," he said around his gum. "This guy hated her... or he loved doing it."

***

An hour later, Brianna stepped out of her car and surveyed the block of units before her. Delta, the victim, used to live in one, according to her identification. Brianna never associated this neighbourhood with exotic dancers or prostitutes. From her experience, they lived in lower income areas, unless they did well for business. This was an area associated with young families and older retirees. Known as a quiet living area and safe place, it was a block from the suburb's shopping centre with a school nearby.

After locking her car, Brianna walked along the cement path lined by garden beds filled with burgeoning blooms. The body corporate ensured a good gardener tended them and the strips of grass well. The sounds of playing children floated to her ears, and the air smelled clean. What a lovely neighbourhood.

Brianna stopped at the door and paused upon seeing the intercom system for each unit. A camera peered at her from above the door. Rent here would be higher than she expected someone like Delta could afford.

Brianna pressed unit 12's intercom button. Delta's unit, according to her identification. The buzzing speaker cut the hair. All other sounds ceased as though listening. Brianna waited. Perhaps Delta had a room-mate who could be home?

"Can I help you?" The voice from behind startled her.

Brianna turned her head, seeing an older woman standing there with plastic grocery bags in her hands. They looked heavy, and Brianna stood to the side so she could pass. "I'm looking for Delta Brown," Brianna said, adding an upward lilt to her words to make it sound like a question.

"Delta?" The woman paused a moment, her hand poised to press button 11. "She should be at home now. Hasn't she answered?"

Brianna shook her head. "I'm not looking for her so much as I'm looking for any family of hers. She's had an accident."

The woman removed her hat, adorned with a single flower she had picked from the garden, adjusted it, and placed it back on her head. "Oh," she said. "An accident?" She looked stuck for words.

"So I'm looking for her family. Do you know if they're home?" Brianna repeated her question.

"Who are you?" The lady peered at her from behind her thick glasses. Something about her movements and gazes distracted Brianna's attention for the briefest moment. Then it passed.

Brianna showed the woman her badge. "Detective-Sergeant Brianna Cogan from Statton CBD Police. I would appreciate any help you provide." She waited a beat as the woman hesitated. "Can you tell me?"

The woman shook her head, a thoughtful light in her eyes. "No, Delta doesn't live with family. She does live with a friend, but she's not home now. Is Delta okay?"

Brianna pondered her reply. Such news was for next-of-kin's ears, but something about the woman hinted she might have been closer to Delta than she said. "It's not good. Do you have her friend's contact? I need to contact next-of-kin."

The lady's mouth formed an O of surprise, which she covered with her mouth. "Oh! that doesn't sound good, does it? Do you have a card I can pass with a message?"

Something tickled across Brianna's scalp when she noticed the woman's eyes shift. Did they change shape? She was uncertain, but the pupils appeared almost diamond-shaped. Brianna stepped back. "No." She shook her head. "What time do you expect her housemate to return?"

The woman offered a faint smile. "After work, dear. You can come back then."

Brianna checked her watch. It was still the middle of the day. She would check on other things before returning. But the notion nagged her intuition. The old woman knew something, probably even lied about Delta. On the surface, she appeared fine apart from the nosiness. But something else niggled at Brianna's mind.

Brianna glanced over her shoulder as she crossed the street to her car. The old woman was inside the building, watching from behind the tinted glass door. It might be anything; old people are naturally nosy, but what was she hiding?

***

Meanwhile, Tyrone wanted to be anywhere but his uncle Craig's place. Thoughts popped in his head, crowding his mind with conflict. With a bulky backpack slung over his shoulder, he listened for a moment. Satisfied the coast was clear, he tiptoed towards the front door. He jumped at the sound of Emily clearing her throat behind him.

"Tyrone! Where are you going, Mister?"

"Out," he replied, turning to see the spirit standing with her arms crossed and tapping an annoyed foot. Emily's gaze burrowed into his and he lowered his eyes. Tyrone hated fighting with Emily. "I have to get out of here."

Emily's forehead softened, but she remained stern. "Out? Away? More like you're running away from your problems."

The teenager shook his head. "I need to think. Uncle Craig has it stuck in his head that I have to finish school. Just because he can carry on as though nothing happened to Deb, he thinks I should too." Tyrone crinkled his eyes to hold back a tear. "What would he know?"

At that moment, Turner appeared, his large coat's collar raised around his ears. He floated past Emily and stood between her and Tyrone. "Would yew lay off da boy, Emily? Sometimes a geezer needs space, a place ter fink and-"

Emily's eyes flashed sparks as she turned to face Turner whose face dropped when cutlery and jewellery clattered to the foyer's tiled floor. Emily, Turner and Tyrone all looked towards Turner's feet at the pile that fell from Turner's pockets. "You don't need silverware if you're roughing it, lads," Emily reminded Turner. "And Mr Turner..." Emily pointed her finger into Turner's astral chest and pressed again for each word she spoke. "I respect men's thinking space, but I don't respect men who teach boys to run from their problems."

Turner grunted, grabbed Emily's wrists in his broad hands and held them fast. "Blimey! Runnin' away? That's not what i' is. Don't yew forget where I came from an' what 'appened after I died. Horace Turner ain't a runner, but I understand lads well. It's only been a little over a 'undred years. Nuff said, yeah?"

Emily, who had pulled her hands away, snorted. "Mr Turner, all you know about lads involved teaching them to rob and steal from a young age. When I first met you, you -"

"Gawdon Bennet! When we first met, yew was workin' wiv what secret society, da same as I was," Turner boomed. "And I still am. Okay?"

Emily's mouth hung open, her words stopping as she measured Turner's words. She paused. "You're-" Turner winked at Emily with a slight nod. "Really?"

"Now," Turner said while Emily digested his words. "Excuse us, Hairy Knees, so we can go camping. We 'ave work ter do. Nuff said, yeah?"

Emily stood there, still shocked, as Turner led Tyrone out the door. Turner's words floated back from outside, explaining that Hairy Knees means Please; he hadn't been rude to "the old busy body". But Emily ignored the words as their voices faded into the distance. At last, she about-faced and headed back to the living room where she rearranged items and muttered to herself.

"The poor lad." She shook her head, tutting to the air. "Having a guardian spirit like Turner. What is the universe thinking?"

Chapter 7

Brianna parked the car and surveyed the block of units. Children were playing "street cricket" down the road with one of them standing in front of a wooden box that served as wickets, his cricket bat ready for the ball. The bowler threw the round missile, and Brianna laughed when the ball exploded into juicy pieces as the batter slammed it. They weren't using balls. The kids were throwing mangoes instead, creating a shower of fruit salad with each blow. Perhaps she should say something to them, stop them from littering, but Brianna had another agenda.

A woman's voice answered when Brianna pressed the door's buzzer. "Who is it?"

The door's lock disengaged when Brianna identified herself to allow her to enter. Inside, the building's interior looked better than she expected, too, with stairs sporting better carpet than she had seen in some motels. Spongy carpet cushioned her shoes as she ascended the stairs towards Delta's unit. Fresh paint covered the walls. They weren't plain brown brick like her home's apartment building. What money did Delta make to afford to live here?

"Down here," someone said, and Brianna paused, her breath taken by the sight.

The woman was beautiful. Deep eyes, the colour of

earth and framed by raven-hued tresses, regarded Brianna as she approached the apartment's open door. The lady appeared no older than thirty, yet she moved with a majestic posture more graceful than most well-trained in finishing school. Yet another part spoke of femininity tempered with strength, a person comfortable in her skin, someone conscious of other people's gazes but ignored them the same. Brianna couldn't take her eyes off her.

When Brianna reached the apartment's door and saw the lady up close, the sight mesmerised her more. She couldn't believe someone of Delta's profession lived in this building, not on her money.

"Detective Sergeant Brianna Cogan." She noted the woman's smooth skin and her professional manicure upon shaking hands.

The woman replied, "Melody Kostas", with a slight accent and regarded Brianna with dark brown eyes. Something twinkled there; was it a change of shade? Brianna wasn't certain.

"How can I help you, Detective?" Melody's eyes shifted, and Brianna glanced and saw the old woman from before duck into her own apartment. Brianna guessed the two neighbours had spoken with each other. Melody wanted details without tipping her hand.

"May I come in?" Brianna moved forward slightly. At first, Melody stood still but changed her mind and allowed Brianna to enter.

The apartment's interior spoke of wealth, too, but not opulence. Melody was obviously a person happy with wealth but didn't go overboard into tackiness. Melody walked her through the entry hallway into a large open plan space that comprised a large kitchen and living room, separated by a long wooden dining table and upholstered chairs. A large vase, at least seven-to-eight feet tall, stood to the side; its designs resembled something Brianna would expect on Grecian urns. The whole layout seemed to appear a mix of ancient history through to present day, yet the interior designers must have been an artist to pull it off so well.

"You have a beautiful apartment." Brianna admiring it. Compared to Craig's home, this was Buckingham Palace!

Melody thanked her, motioning towards a leather couch and offering her a seat. "I'm about to have a coffee. Would you like one?"

"Yes, please. Black, one sugar."

Melody poured the boiled water and mixed it before handing it to Brianna before seating herself opposite. "I understand you have news about Delta. How can I assist?"

Brianna placed her coffee on a nearby coaster after taking a sip. She hated this and knew it could go either way. "I need Delta's next-of-kin. Can you help?"

Melody's face dropped. Although the news hit hard, Brianna guessed she already heard or guessed. Perhaps the neighbour told her enough to fill in the blanks. The woman's dark eyes focused on Brianna, a tear forming around the reddening lids. "Delta's mother died years ago, and she fled an abusive father. She has no other family. I guess that makes me her next-of-kin." She paused, tapping her foot a while before sniffing. "What happened?"

Brianna released a breath she'd been holding. "Delta was murdered last night on the way home from work."

The coffee cup, which Melody had picked up, dropped from her fingers, smashing into pieces on the tiled floor. Her eyes hardened and flickered to her right. Brianna moved forward, but her host waved her away and picked at the coffee mug's pieces, which she carried to the kitchen and dropped in a bin. A moment later, Melody returned with a cloth for the mess. "Have you caught the man who did it?"

"What makes you believe a man did it?" Brianna wanted to know. "Did she have enemies?"

Melody shook her head while wiping the mess. "Delta's an exotic dancer. They don't have enemies, but her profession attracts all kinds of men. Some of them are obsessive stalkers."

"Did Delta mention having such a stalker?"

Melody finished mopping the coffee from the tiles and faced Brianna. "Not exactly. She mentioned a man who came to the club, a regular, I believe. But most of the workers knew him. They think he's harmless. You could try asking them."

***

Earlier that day, before speaking with Melody, Brianna had spoken with Delta's club manager. Their stories matched Melody's. Delta had no enemies, but she had a stalker. A man they nicknamed Jagger because his voluptuous lips resembled those of the British singer.

Ever since Delta, who her workmates described as having a heart of gold, paid him special attention during a dance routine. Why? Because she felt sorry for him. But it backfired on her. The lonely-looking man with the sad eyes had asked for her phone number, said he wanted to buy her a drink. Instead of giving her number, she compromised by spending a little time with him in the club, drinking to the side. No sexual contact happened. They sat to the side, shared drinks, and that was all. Brianna had asked if this was normal practice. The manager admitted he never liked the idea, but it sometimes helped when the girls acted as the club's ambassadors. Patrons often came by, developed protective feelings for the girls who entertained them and took their minds off everyday worries. Spending time with the clients helped foster a "family feeling" and patron loyalty.

But sometimes that backfired.

This customer appeared harmless, but he developed a "lost puppy" connection with Delta. Gifts arrived by messenger, addressed to her. Sometimes a card. There was nothing malicious in them, and he always remained quiet.

The manager conceded that sometimes they have to watch out for the quiet ones. The extra attention embarrassed Delta. She didn't want to lead "Jagger" on, and she even told the other dancers he was sweet, not just creepy.

But then he asked her to dinner and maybe a movie.

Delta's refusal was nice, and "Jagger" took it well enough. But he kept coming back always in time to see Delta's dance routines. After another week, the staff realised "Jagger" knew Delta's shift times, so she changed them. But he kept coming back.

On Delta's last night, "Jagger" was there again. But with her workmates' help, she escaped through the back exit and out the alley.

That was the last they saw of her.

Now Brianna sat at her computer, poring over footage from the city's security cameras.

The video followed Delta's passage from the alleyway towards the railway station. The subject's pace quickened as she approached the station like she was in a hurry. Had she felt that someone was following her or was it something else? Delta's head bobbed, the way someone does when they curse, and she walked away. Why? Brianna looked closer and realised Delta's pass hadn't let her enter the station. What rotten luck.

Ah! There! Someone was following Delta. Brianna zoomed in on the short man, trying to see his face. But he didn't look vicious. Instead, he looked lost, forlorn, and lonely. Maybe that's how some stalkers start. Brianna recalled a boy from high school days who used to sit on the edges, watching her and her friends. He'd been a nice guy although weird in his hand-me-down clothes. Later she found he had a crush on her; he'd told one of his mates who blabbed. Brianna never saw the boy again, probably due to embarrassment, but the man on the screen could have been another version of him. Lonely, seeking love, maybe a knight in shining armour complex who saw beauty and cherished the girl who possessed it, blind to all other faults. Or maybe the video would prove her wrong?

Brianna noted another man appearing behind Delta at the train station's turnstiles. He clutched something resembling a wallet. They exchanged words. Delta looked frightened but made no response, only walked away and gave the man the finger. He took offence, calling after her, but continued towards the ticket booth before walking towards the platform. In the meantime, Delta was hurrying down the street.

Brianna played the video quicker, watching for anyone else. The soupy-lipped man the club staff mentioned appeared but didn't seem to notice her as he headed towards the train station. So she ignored him, following Delta's movement towards the bus station, where things became interesting.

The woman in the video seemed nervous. Her limbs appeared stiffer and her shoulders rounded in a defensive posture. What scared her? Brianna could see nothing out of the ordinary, even when Delta looked over her shoulder. What could be wrong? The dancer read the times on the bus timetable, mouthed something that could only be a curse but unheard without video sound, before heading back towards the street.

Now she hurried, lifting her hand to hail a cab. There was "Jagger" again, just behind her. He looked like he was hurrying to catch up, but he missed her. The girl stepped into the cab which soon drove away.

But Brianna kept watching soupy-lipped "Jagger". His

shoulders slumped as he watched Delta's cab pull away into the darkness and speed down the road. Dejected, he waited until the car disappeared around the corner before he walked back towards the train station. He seemed in no hurry. But before long, he passed through the turnstiles towards the platform where he waited for the next train.

She needed another lead. The cameras on the street near the alley were her next bet. But what about the taxicab? Brianna zoomed in on the cab's registration and identification number. That would come in handy later.

The street with the alley where they found Delta's body had no cameras, therefore she had no other footage to check. No leads.

Then Craig's voice came to mind. It's not what you see. it's what you don't see that matters.

So she replayed through everything again, but this time, in reverse. Sometimes playing or reading things backwards highlights special points. However, Brianna noticed nothing until she played it forwards again.

What was that?

Rolling the mouse, Brianna zoomed in on the strange flash she saw. Perhaps it was a flash of reflection, or maybe her growing fatigue was playing tricks on her eyes and mind.

Or. Maybe. Not.

Two pinpricks of light shone, reflecting from the passenger's side mirror of the cab a few moments before Delta opened the door. Brianna froze the video frame and zoomed in. Then she stepped back a frame or two, checked, and repeated until she gasped at the sight. It was the cab driver. His eyes either reflected street light or burned like coals in the dark.

Brianna rubbed her eyes and was about to look again when a knock at the door distracted her. She looked up and saw Gifford.

He smiled briefly and said, "Hey, Cogan. I'm heading home. Are you ready to come?"

***

Craig's chest tightened, and he breathed with difficulty. The anticipation of the unknown gripped hard. A sickly coloured tinge of crimson covered everything he saw as though it was lit by a dying sun. But where was he?

The round lumps of cobblestones he stood upon made standing hard. And the clatter of distant wheels reached his ears. This happened so long ago.

Manic laughter rocked and echoed from behind. Craig turned, facing it, clamminess brushing his face like a deviant as his eyes searched the half-light for anything among the darkened buildings. The scene reminded him of a time so long ago, but he couldn't place it.

Footsteps, clicking and hurried, approached from another direction. Craig whirled to face them, sensing the woman's fear before he saw it painted on her face. She ran straight for Craig, not seeing him as she looked over her shoulder. Too late, he tried avoiding her. She passed through him like he was a ghost. Craig was an expert with astral travelling; the experience was nothing new, but this still startled him because he knew he wasn't out-of-body.

Loud mocking laughter rocked through the air, echoing off the buildings. The woman gasped, turning to face the lane from which she had come. Craig followed her gaze. Shadows grew from around the corner, morphing and melding, joining and billowing like clouds before taking form. The lady turned and ran, her frightened footfalls disappearing down an alley. The demonic laughter rolled towards Craig who ran after the woman. Perhaps if he followed her, he could at least comfort her, let her know she wasn't alone.

Words of a song filtered through the air to him. Something familiar, but its name escaped him.

Pancakes and fritters,

Say the bells of St. Peter's.

Two sticks and an apple,

Say the bells at Whitechapel.

Craig's feet dragged as though weighted with lead. He struggled to move, grunting with the effort until finally, in the blink of an eye, he crossed a great distance to appear beside the woman. The laughter came closer. The woman breathed hard, half-sobbing and half-screaming, as she wheeled about in terror upon finding herself trapped by a dead-end. Craig tried to calm her, but she wouldn't listen. Did she even hear him? He couldn't tell.

The woman dashed back the way she came but took

another turn into another lane. The unseen pursuer's laughter still echoed off the brick walls, but now Craig heard footsteps, slow, confident, and arrogant, approaching. Craig's words caught in his throat, nothing but a mute's protest. His feet dragged, following the woman, hoping to hamper the attacker. Craig wasn't sure he could stop the man.

Then he gasped.

Crimson eyes, brighter and colder than Lucifer's own, blazed through the fog, pierced Craig's eyes. A heavy but lithe figure cloaked in clothes of shifting mist and shadows moved through the pea-soup, carrying a long knife that scraped against the walls and creating sparks. Craig strained. The man's shape changed in the half-light.

Once again, Craig tried shouting. And this time, the creature stopped in its tracks. Did it see him, just five feet away? The thing, whatever it was, paused and looked in his direction, right through him. For a moment, it sniffed the air, snuffling the thick air. The woman's gasp echoed from the lane. Turning towards the sound, the creature bounded through the fog. Craig clutched at its black cloak, but something sharp cut his hand, and the creature laughed.

Craig ignored the surprise. He dashed after the creature. But he could only keep up, not overtake. A high-pitched noise deafened him; he covered his ears and realised the sound never stopped; it emanated from within his mind.

Now the woman's screams cut through his consciousness, filling his ears. But Craig heard another sound too. Children's screams. He turned to see tiny shadows darting away through the shifting passages. Damn! He headed towards the woman's screaming and saw her under an archway, struggling with a large man in a large stovepipe hat. Was that the same demonic creature? He couldn't be certain from the distance.

Dragging his feet, he arrived at last to see the man fall to the ground. A blade flashed, reflecting distant gaslight, but wait!

That wasn't the woman he saw earlier.

No!

Brianna!

Craig's chest threatened to explode. His heart hammered harder as he pushed against the unseen force delaying his efforts to hurry to her side.

An explosion of blood hit him in the face, geysering across the bricks and cobblestones; thick, hot, and tantalising. But the horror inside Craig controlled him. He caught her body as it slumped and noticed Brianna's garb looked over a century old. Brianna's dead eyes stared at him, lifeless and unblinking, her mouth open in a painful grimace. He choked tears and tried to staunch the crimson flowing from Brianna's throat.

Laughter rocked, and a face appeared before him, familiar yet unseen for years. Too late. The other man's sword plunged through Craig's heart as he wondered.

Why? Why, Khan?

Craig woke with a start, swimming in salty sweat and

his heart hammering. The banging was so loud, he could hear it through his chest.

Bleary-eyed, Craig realised he was in his own home, having fallen asleep on the couch in front of the television. A fleeting memory occurred to him. He'd crashed in the lounge after arriving home from his corporate show. It was late 2016, not the late 1800s.

Craig coughed, unable to find the saliva to swallow, and cursed the hammering in his ears. Then he realised. It wasn't his heart. Someone was at the front door.

Emily floated towards the door, passing Craig with a clucking sound and muttered something about having to do everything. Craig shook his head and hurried ahead of Emily, passing her and unlocking the door.

Craig's jaw dropped open upon seeing the large framed man standing before him, sunken eyes and prominent bald head. The same man from his dream. "Khan?"

The visitor bowed to Craig, his brow crinkled with concern. "Craig Ramsey!"

Craig shook his head, feeling consciousness return and a horrible premonition coming over him. "What are-"

"Craig," Khan interrupted, his deep voice infused with urgency. "This is important. Jack is back!"

A wave of dizziness passed over Craig as the world slipped away from him. He tried clinging to the reality as it dissipated like butterflies scattering upon the breeze. Only it wasn't a cloud of beautiful winged insects. It was another dream that left his heart pounding and a nagging premonition's voice.

***

The vagrant pushed his grime-infused hands deeper into the dumpster, sifting and sorting. The pungent aromas would have crinkled anyone's nose, but not his. To him, this was his life, a constant scrounging for a delicacy. At his feet sat a buffet of treats: half a squashed banana and its peel, a mouldy piece of fruit cake, a fast-food restaurant's cup of warm lemonade, and a dead rat for protein. All he needed now was something sweet for dessert. He fingered the grizzled stubble on his sandpaper chin and snorted back on a trapdoor booger. A grumbling sound reached his ears, and his eyes shifted. That wasn't his stomach; what was it?

Trying not to show panic with any fast moves, he edged away from the rubbish. His foot slipped, flattening the rat under his shoes made of duct tape and cardboard.

A spitting sound reached his ears accompanied by a cat's mad dash through the rubbish tins six feet past him. A ginger figure dashed past him towards the street. What spooked it?

Squinting, he peered into the darkness to see a shadow standing there. "Get ya own dinner!" He stood between the unknown visitor and his paper plate of treats. "You 'af to find your own food."

His eyes opened wider, larger than saucers, as he saw the curves of the shadow. Feminine curves. Sexy. They reminded him of some movie star, someone he'd seen when he was a kid. He couldn't remember her name. But this wasn't a woman. This was someone or something else.

Yellow orbs flashed where the eyes would have been. And then he saw the shape of breasts. Young breasts. They looked firm, good enough to grab and-

Something whipped his legs from under him. Something strong. The creature floated towards him. Then he saw it. A tail; long, supple, scaly, and twice as thick as a man's arms.

Fangs glistened, dripping venom from the woman's triumphant grin.

The scream gurgled from his throat as the serpentine body coiled around his torso, quicker than a whip.

Chapter 8

A bleary-eyed Craig rose from his bed the next morning and rubbed his eyes. Remnants of a dream stuck in his mind, but he felt so tired his mind couldn't sort them. The image of a black-haired woman with tanned features flashed, but too fast to make sense. There were others too, but the memory faded fast, replaced by Emily's voice from the kitchen.

"Wake up, sleepyhead! You slept in, and you don't want to be late."

A glance at the clock revealed the time. Six-thirty. Most people would think about stumbling out of bed. But to Craig, this was sleeping in. He'd missed his workout with Yong in the kwoon; the ancient master would punish him for that later. Craig staggered out of bed, his head swimming with tiredness, and trudged towards his en-suite. Five minutes later, after a hot shower followed by a frigid shower, an invigorated Craig stepped out to choose his clothes for the day.

Wearing black dress jeans and a royal-blue Ralph Lauren shirt, Craig strode into the kitchen where Emily was flitting about at the stove. The Scottish spirit hadn't noticed him as she hummed a haunting tune that Craig didn't recognise. He picked up a triangular piece of toast, crunching into it, relishing the warm, buttery texture mixed with marmalade. Emily turned to face him.

"You will be late," Emily chided him.

Craig lifted his watch. "But it's only seven o'clock. I've plenty of time before the shop opens and -"

Emily rolled her eyes. "Did you forget you're meeting Brianna? The poor lass will think you stood her up, and I'm not covering for you this time."

Craig's mouth dropped open. He spun towards the calendar on the refrigerator, saw the date and the reminder, and muttered an expletive. "Thanks, Emily. I had forgotten. What would I do without you?"

"I wonder the same." An amused smile crossed her lips as she watched Craig make a mad dash for the door.

Craig had opened the door but an inch when someone knocked on it. He looked at a deliveryman with a long parcel in his hands.

"Parcel delivery," the newcomer answered, appearing surprised at the door opening so soon.

Craig didn't waste time on niceties and took the pen to sign for the package which he placed on the foyer's floor. He mumbled a quick "thank you" before hurrying towards his Jaguar. The deliveryman grumbled something in return and jumped in surprise when the front door slammed.

From inside the door, Emily watched Craig's Jaguar roar down the street towards the motorway. A sly grin crossed her translucent features as she turned and looked at the clocks in the kitchen and living room.

With a wave of her hand, the clocks stepped back an hour, and she giggled. How long would it be, she wondered, before Craig realised she had turned the clocks forward an hour to get him out of the house so she could watch a movie?

***

Craig's stomach rumbled with hunger as he changed lanes on the motorway. Breakfast would have helped, but he could have that at Brianna's place. But with Craig having slept in, Brianna mightn't have time to eat. He sighed. Brianna was a great lady: strong, without losing femininity, and adventurous. He liked that. A life without adventure would bore him. And he couldn't forget how personable she was. Despite their friction upon first meeting, they had forged a friendship alongside their bristly partnership on the case a couple of months ago.

What was that?

Craig checked his watch, its display reading eight o'clock. But his car's clock read seven am. His eyebrow raised in consternation as he pondered. That was odd. He turned the radio on and listened. There was the announcer, Sally Green, reading the news. And now...

"It's seven-oh-eight on STQFM."

Craig's eyes narrowed as he checked his watch. Somehow it had jumped an hour, and so had the clocks on the stove and kitchen wall. How could-?

"Emily," he muttered with a grin. "You old interfering woman."

At least he wasn't late. That meant he had time to collect breakfast on the way.

With Craig's lifting wakefulness came memories; flashbacks of a dream. Blood, pools of it; a knife blade and gleaming fangs; darkness and a finger of light touching a beaten, blood-blotched face. Brianna's face. Tyrone.

***

After picking up breakfast at a bakery, Craig arrived at Brianna's place. The first thing he noticed was the other car. Since Brianna's Skyline's unfortunate end a month ago, the detective had been driving a marked police car from work. But it wasn't there this time. Craig's eyebrow raised with curiosity at the Holden Statesman as he parked behind it. Brianna must have changed to a different vehicle. This car attracted less attention, standing out less than her marked police cruiser had.

Craig grabbed the bags of croissants, locked his Jaguar, and allowed his hand to sweep across the Statesman's surface as he walked around it. The expected psychic vision came to view, overlaying his physical vision. The Statesman belonged to another man, not Brianna, who worked at the police station. An air of familiarity washed over Craig; he knew the man but something wasn't right about him. A faint impression of Brianna came to mind, but she hadn't driven it here.

Craig shook his head. Was it jealousy or fear of loss? No, it couldn't be. And Brianna was a big girl; she could decide for herself. Craig chided himself and decided it was fatigue playing tricks on his mind. The dreams had all but faded from consciousness, apart from some faded images and emotions, but they must have meant something to linger so long.

The front door opened and out stepped a man dressed in a leather jacket shiny enough to compete with his balding scalp. An unlit cigarette dangled from his lower lip. As soon as his eyes fell upon Craig, a surprised expression turned to recognition, and he leered at Craig.

"Well! Craig Ramsey!"

For a moment, Craig was at a loss. The man knew him, but oh! now Craig recognised him. How could one forget that shit-eating grin and the masked eyes of jealousy? "Detective Tony Gifford, right?"

Gifford lit his cigarette with a shiny lighter which he shut with a flourish. "What brings you here?" He blew a plume of smoke into Craig's face.

Craig cocked an eyebrow, having noticed Gifford's posture. Gifford's actions were more transparent than a windscreen. Craig brushed the detective's attempt aside as he raised a hand to open the front door and walk in.

But the door swung open first and Brianna emerged, and her eyes took in the scene. "Hi, Craig," she half-smiled, closing the front door behind her. "What have you -" Brianna paused, her eyes catching the brown paper bags and the faint aroma of baked goods brushed her nostrils. To the side, Gifford leered, a chuckle escaped with a waft of smoke as he ground his cigarette out on the grass, and he eyed the couple.

Craig's breath caught in his chest, aware of Gifford's

peacocking, but it was what Brianna held in her hand that caught him off-guard: two key-rings. One, he recognised as Brianna's. The other set, Brianna handed to Gifford, saying, "Don't forget your keys."

Craig followed the exchange, a sinking sensation inside him which he fought back as he stood taller. After Brianna pulled the front door shut, he cleared his throat to attract her attention. "Breakfast?"

Brianna glanced again at the paper bag then at him, an apologetic look on her face. "I can't. We received a call-out."

Craig heard nothing much past the "We". The bags were heavy in his hand.

"You snooze, you lose, Craigie," Gifford chortled, holding a hand out towards Brianna. "Come on. The bodies will be putrid soon."

Craig forced himself to return a smile for the one Brianna gave him. "I'm sorry."

"It's all good," she replied, taking the paper bag he offered. "Me too."

Their fingers touched for a moment.

Another vision.

Craig's eyes lost focus and he looked as though from above the scene. Gifford and Brianna, both pursuing a man in rags. Their quarry's laughter pealed and echoed through the alley. Then handcuffs on his wrists.

"Brianna."

She turned around.

"Yeah?"

"You will catch the killer soon," he mentioned in an almost off-hand tone. "Very soon."

Brianna's eyebrow raised as though questioning, but a car horn beeped and distracted her.

"Come on, hurry up," Gifford called from the car and revved its engine. Brianna hustled herself and into the passenger's seat. Craig approached Gifford's side of the car and fixed a hard stare upon him that caused Gifford's sleazy grin to subside.

"What's up?" Gifford asked, his jaw bouncing while chewing a piece of gum. Craig leaned forward, his hand outreached. Gifford snatched his own hand away but not before Craig managed to touch his skin. "What the hell are you doing?" Gifford looked at Craig, ready to complain more, and his face slackened, the gum dropping from his mouth.

Craig leaned forward towards Gifford, aware that Brianna said something but choosing to ignore it. "Tony," he whispered loud enough for only the detective to hear. "Stay alert when you meet the killer this week. Your distraction had better not cost her life."

Gifford's face remained stunned, his tough guy mask gone as he gazed into Craig's cold eyes. At last, his lips worked out a weak voice. "Whatever, Trevor." He hit the accelerator pedal, completed a U-turn, and drove the car away towards the intersection.

Craig watched, trying to forget his vision of Brianna

in a pool of blood.

83

Chapter 9

Brianna looked across at her work partner as he shifted gears that groaned at his touch. Gifford's jaw clenched hard enough to make his temples pulsate.

What had Craig said to him? It sounded testosterone-charged, protective of her. The idea intrigued Brianna because Craig didn't appear the jealous type. And being a psychic, he must realise he had nothing to fear. The past few weeks would have cemented that for him too.

So whatever Craig said had driven Tony into a dark cave.

Tony's free hand extracted a stick of gum from his jacket's inner pocket, unwrapped it, and stuck it in his mouth. His gaze appeared focused but lost in black thoughts.

It was time to draw Gifford from his cave.

Brianna coughed. "What's going on?"

Gifford glanced at her then at the road and shrugged. "I don't know what you mean." His voice carried defensive claws.

Brianna forced back a wry smile and bit into her croissant and enjoyed its soft texture. The way it melted in her mouth brought back memories, good ones of when her adoptive father used to take her out for breakfast on school holidays. She was close with him before Death ripped him away from her and his wife. An image of Craig slipped through her mind again.

Gifford muttered something, taking a corner too hard so Brianna felt herself forced towards the car door.

"Pardon?"

Gifford took another fleeting look at her. Did his eyes flick towards her boobs? "I said I think you should be careful of the guy."

That caught her attention. "Why? What's he done to you?"

"Listen, Cogan, be with whoever you want." Gifford brushed a hand over his shiny head and across the back of his neck. His tone changed, sounded almost nice, but Brianna sensed the undertone. "I worked with Ramsey for a few months before you started at the station. I thought he was a fruit loop or a great con-artist. He convinced the Inspector to let him tag along with me, don't ask me how, and then he puts his hands all over everything. I tried to say something because he was messing up evidence. The Inspector ignored me just like he ignored you in the beginning. Sure enough, we caught someone who happened to have a similar weapon on him. And he fingered another murderer too. Even helped the Burglary Unit with capturing a robbery suspect."

The car passed a woman walking at the side of the road. Gifford stopped talking to scope her shapely legs and large backside. It didn't matter that Brianna sat next to him.

"So what's your concern?"

Gifford threw Brianna an exasperated look. "Are you kidding me? I don't believe in any of that shit. The guy's a tosspot. He's made a lot of money out of the gullible too. How do you think he affords that Jaguar of his? Or the house? You can't tell me he makes that from his magic act and palm reading, can you?"

Brianna quelled the anger rising in her. Yes, she once doubted Craig too. When they first met, Craig had visited her office after his niece died in a traffic incident she investigated. He'd attacked her scepticism straight away and told her things no one else could know. At first, she believed he had researched her online. But her own Googling provided nothing that could lead to the things he told her. Then she found out just how real he was. That was the day she found she could talk to Craig's spirit companion, Emily.

"Maybe he doesn't need to," Brianna replied.

Gifford laughed. "Dead right there. I checked him out. The man's full of secrets he won't tell others."

She recognised her partner's gambit. Tony was goading her to absorb her in an argument by painting dark pictures. Brianna finished the second croissant but wished she had butter or marmalade for it.

Gifford was like a pit-bull terrier grabbing its victim and wouldn't let go.

"Has he told you how he makes his money?"

"I reckon you will tell me, anyway."

Gifford snorted, ignoring Brianna's tone. "I didn't think so." This brought a smirk to Brianna's face as she realised Gifford's capacity for storing manure had reached his nostrils. But Gifford followed up with another statement. "That's not all though."

"Let me guess," Brianna drawled. "He's a spy for a secret government organisation who knows far too much about you."

Gifford's eyes crinkled. "What the hell are you talking about? No. He lost his marbles years back. He spent time in a mental ward in Brisbane."

Brianna's jaw dropped before she realised it. Surely not. She would have picked up on something like that. Gifford didn't look at Brianna, but he must have sensed her surprise. "Yeah, that's right," he added. "It happened about ten years ago. He was in an accident. Authorities think he was at fault. Two people died, and he had their blood on his hands. He kept talking about spirits and demons and a few other whacked out phrases. The guilt must have been too much for him. He admitted himself into the loony bin where he stayed for about a year. Not sure how he got out. They should have kept him locked-"

Gifford had stopped the car at their destination to finish his tale. All the while, Brianna fumed. Why hadn't Craig told her about this before? Was Gifford telling the truth? The way he looked at her while he told the story showed he enjoyed making her squirm.

Then Brianna remembered her own experiences with the spirit world and how she came to meet Emily, Craig's spirit companion. Her features softened as she turned towards Gifford. A smile spread across her lips and she gazed at her work partner. "Thanks for telling me about that. It's confirmed something that's been on my mind."

She leaned over towards him. Gifford noticed too and grinned, licking his lips in anticipation.

"And what's that?" he wanted to know, ready to take her mouth with his.

Brianna's head darted forward to butt the sleaze-bag's mouth. He screamed, jumped back and lifted a hand to his mouth to staunch the bleeding from his swelling lower lip.

Brianna gazed into Gifford's tear-rimmed eyes. "You're an arsehole. Thanks for reminding me."

***

The mobile phone's ring cut through the air. Craig reached into his pocket to retrieve it and read its display before answering.

"Brianna," he answered. "Is everything okay?"

Something was strange. She should have arrived at the murder scene by now. Why would she be calling?

Brianna Cogan's voice filtered through to his mind, filling him. "Everything's fine," she answered. "Listen, I want to ask you something. Do you remember how I said I didn't want your help on this case?"

Craig's eyebrow raised as the hand not holding the phone adjusted itself with its own separate load. "Yes?"

"I've changed my mind. Can I see you today?"

A smile crossed Craig's face. He couldn't touch her at the moment to pick up what was happening, but he didn't need to. Gifford must have tipped Brianna over the edge. "Yeah, sure," he responded, checking the time on his watch. "When and where?"

"My office," Brianna answered. "Eleven?"

"I've a few errands to run first," Craig answered, looking at the flowers he held in his other hand. "Some people to see. How about eleven-thirty?" He nodded into the phone at Brianna's affirmative response. "I'll see you then."

Craig's practised fingers disconnected the call as he knelt to place the blossoms on the ground.

***

By the time the two detectives arrived at the new scene, Gifford's lip had swollen until it looked like a miniature sausage. A trickle of blood oozed from its cut, which he dabbed at with a tissue, wincing. It looked redder than a baboon's backside and twice as sore. It would be awhile before the sleaze attempted anything else with her. Brianna couldn't help smirking to herself as she put her mobile phone away. The male detective cast furtive glances in Brianna's direction as he parked the car and hurried out of the car towards the taped-off section.

Sergeant Hohenhaus nodded to Gifford, who was stepping over the tape, and snapped a glance at the detective. Then he saw Brianna approaching. A smile cracked open on his round face. "Gifford's looking

89

better than usual," he murmured with a sly wink to Brianna. "Do you know why?"

Straight-faced, Brianna's merely shrugged. "Someone gave him a mouthful."

Hohenhaus snorted back a laugh and stopped in case the detective took a shot at him too. He pointed down towards the lane. "Another one. Same everything. I'm off coffee now."

Brianna slapped Hohenhaus on the back as she stepped past the barriers. "Nice to hear, mate. I brought none for you."

Nothing surprised her when she approached what the forensics team were photographing. Another half-naked woman, her body sliced and another half a kidney against the opposite wall. Brianna's stomach curdled and grumbled, but she pushed back the initial cramps and the urge to evacuate her breakfast. Gifford retched this time, the taste of his own blood on his mouth mixing with the sight. That would be enough to make him think more about the entrails scattered about the place.

Boldly written in the victim's blood, the killer's graffiti shouted from the brick wall. "So many years later, so many deaths. Have you learned nothing?" Whoever the killer was, he (or she) had issues and felt they were trying to teach society something. By leaving a message, they either hoped to be caught or loved taunting authorities.

Brianna took a cloth mask from her pocket, something she'd prepared earlier, and clipped it on.

Thank goodness for the drops of aromatic oils she put on the cloth mask to block the stench of death. Although it didn't eliminate the putrid foulness, it helped suppress it. She removed a short piece of thin dowel from a pocket to poke at the kidney on the ground. The teeth marks looked the same. She spied a nearby scientist. "Jenkins, has anyone run a dental check on this bite?"

The forensic scientist looked in Brianna's direction at the organ and shook her head. "Yes, but nothing came up. Maybe the tissue didn't take a good enough impression. Or the killer's records aren't on our databases. It happens. I'll bag that soon and check later though."

Tony Gifford dashed out of the alley, a hand over his mouth, and slipped on a patch of blood. One leg slid ahead of him, another flew into the air, and he dropped in the mush. He picked up a hand, saw the patchy coppery tones of the body fluids, and vomited.

Brianna looked away in time to avoid the geyser of puke. A few seconds later, once certain Gifford had left the alley altogether, she opened her eyes again. What was that there?

A large piece of snake skin, thin enough to appear membranous with scales, lay on the ground near a cardboard box - probably a homeless man's abandoned abode. Brianna lifted it with a pair of tweezers, examined it in the light for half a minute, and fumbled for a plastic bag large enough to hold it. "Have we got a snake problem in Statton?"

Jenkins shrugged. "Not sure about the city, but there

are plenty in the suburbs. A snake handler I know says this year's breeding season came early." She snapped another photo. "That partner of yours is a bloody klutz. I'm not sure how much he contaminated with his upset stomach. I noticed blood on his mouth and a bruise. Do you know anything about that?" Brianna feigned deafness, but Jenkins continued. "I've heard how he's tried being on everything but the Titanic. Good work, Cogan. He had it coming."

The scientist's words warmed Brianna who realised how widespread Gifford's sleazy reputation was. She smiled behind her mask and stopped when she spied something else.

A piece of card.

Brianna gripped it with tweezers and held it to the light. Hey, hey, hey! A photo identification with a company name on it - Statton Cabs. This was the best break she'd received. Craig's words floated through her consciousness as she recalled what he said earlier.

He may have been right.

***

Behind mirrored glasses, across the road from the alley, another pair of eyes watched. The distance did little to hinder the watcher from zooming upon Brianna who remained oblivious to him as she scrutinised the piece of card in the plastic bag. A smile crept across the dirt-encrusted face to reveal brown stained teeth.

The woman looked tasty. How would her kidney taste? Would her coppery blood slake his thirst while her organs sustained him? And who was that man with her with a stomach weaker than her? The woman's companion vomited again into a nearby rubbish bin, eliciting a laugh.

A grimy hand reached for the ignition key, turning it to coax the vehicle to life. Such a wonderful feeling to bring this invention to life, charging its heart with energy and power.

The observer's eyes never left the pair as the taxi cruised past the police, melting into obscurity with the traffic. Humming the tune.

Gay go up, and gay go down,
To ring the bells of London town.
Bull's eyes and targets,
Say the bells of St Marg'ret's.
Brickbats and tiles,
Say the bells of St. Giles'.

Chapter 10

Craig Ramsey appeared at Detective-Sergeant Brianna Cogan's door a full minute before promised. A smile radiated from his mouth when he poked his head through the door. "Am I too early?"

Brianna looked up from the computer. She had just finished her report for the morning's observations. "No, you're on time. Come on in."

Craig's eyes settled upon the Out tray on the desk. It was smaller than the In tray; the overflow, perhaps. "You mentioned you needed my input," he said, removing his jacket and hanging it on the back of the chair opposite before sitting. "What do you want to know?"

Brianna swept her hand across both trays. "These are the murder reports I mentioned to you before. All of them are women. Some prostitutes, a few strippers, and a couple we think homeless." She frowned for a moment. "Gifford," she snorted softly, "says they follow the same MO as the killings Gifford worked on with your assistance."

Craig remained quiet and impassive.

Brianna nodded towards several reports on the other side of her cluttered desk. "Gifford wrote these reports, yet I found no mention of you in them. What can you tell me?"

A blank look sat on Craig's features, his eyes unfocused as though he were elsewhere. Brianna clicked her fingers. "Is Emily here? Are you talking with her?"

Craig started. "No, sorry. I didn't sleep well last night. I need to refresh my memory. May I read through one of Gifford's reports?" Brianna tossed one across to Craig who looked at it in wonderment before comparing it with one from Brianna's other pile. "That's a thin file. How -?"

Brianna waited and watched Craig's expression transform into a lost in space look. A few seconds later, he dropped the file back on the desk.

"Well?"

Craig breathed in, sitting back in the chair, and steeped his fingers. "It's coming back now."

"But you hadn't even opened the file to read it."

The psychic investigator allowed a cheeky grin to cross his face. "But I touched it. That's all I needed." Brianna nodded, recalling Craig's ability. "Gifford's scepticism created barriers for me," Craig admitted. "He wouldn't allow me to check the evidence, saying I might taint it. That's fair enough. Still, I found a few things by touching the brickwork and ground after the forensics people trampled over it all. It wasn't easy."

"What did you find?"

"Back then I found the killer has a mental illness. Part of him believed he was a demonic creature, an ancient one. And he only attacked on nights when no moon came out."

Brianna scribbled this note down. "And what else?"

"I told Gifford that after April 2016, Jacob would kill no one else." Craig paused, looking upwards. "Jacob Cherry, if I remember correctly." He watched Brianna added that to her notes.

"So what else can you tell me about Jacob? Where does he live?"

Craig took a deep breath, held it, and exhaled in a long stream. "You'll never catch Jacob."

The words threw Brianna's recollections back to June when she had visited Craig's nephew Tyrone in hospital after his sister's death. Those were Tyrone's words, except he said Craig would be the only one to catch the killer.

A wry smile crossed Craig's face. "I can't catch Jacob either. The bullet got him first."

Brianna's shocked expression spoke volumes. "Gunshot? Why?"

"He felt it was the only way to stop the voices and the singing in his brain." Craig reached over for a recent file, saying, "And my bet is we have another murderer; a copycat."

Then his face dropped. "What?"

"What?" Brianna asked. Had this Jacob returned from the dead? Was he possessing someone else perhaps, like Emily did with me?"

Craig dropped the file, its contents scattering on the floor. He muttered something, his voice changing pitch, and a spasm ran through his body as he fell to the floor where he continued convulsing. Brianna choked back a scream and hurried around the desk to where he lay in a writhing mess. Craig's limbs were stiff at the joints, twitching, when she reached him. Despite this, his hands fought her away when she tried rolling him on his side into a recovery position. All the time, she spoke to him, asking if he could hear her. Was this a vision or a seizure?

After what seemed ages, Craig's body relaxed, and with a sigh, he lay there.

Brianna hesitated. What could she do? Craig's face no longer held the tortured expressions. Was he epileptic? Her eyes darted around the office, searching, until they fixed upon something. Her gym bag. Quickly, she whipped off her jacket, rolled it up to form a pillow under Craig's head. The towel was wet with water from her drinking bottle, and she wiped his sweaty brow with it.

At last, Craig's eyes fluttered and opened. "How long was I out?"

Brianna released a tense breath. "Long enough to give me heart failure. I have to ask, are you epileptic?"

Craig shook his head and struggled to sit up. He took her water bottle, sucked a mouthful for his dry mouth, and tried to stand. Brianna helped him up to his chair. "I'll be fine. Just had a vision." Brianna opened her mouth but Craig stopped her talking. "Let me get my head in order first."

Brianna opened a desk drawer and pulled out a bag: her secret stash of jelly babies. "Do you want some sugar?"

Lifting his eyes, Craig replied, "From you? I might." A cheeky grin shone from his dishevelled face.

Brianna chuckled. "Yep, you're okay. Here you go," she said, handing him the bag. "Don't say I never give you any."

***

The screaming tore through the air. Melody's heartbeat threatened to burst from her chest as she sprang upright in the darkness. A voice called from elsewhere in the building; concerned voices and banging on her front door. But the dream's afterimages remained strong, pushing at her memory. After some fumbling, she found the switch, clicked it, and the blackout curtains withdrew.

"Melody!" The voices called out.

"I'm fine," she shouted back. "Just a dream."

But what a nightmare it had been. She had been following a man. The way he ran from her, his breathing heavy with effort as he hauled his large bulk through the darkness. The man's eyes were large as fists, bulging with the whites shining. A large thump came to her ears as he tripped and fell to the ground. Even his fingers clawed at the ground, anything he could grip in an attempt to stand and hobble away from her. Never in her life had Melody known someone to be frightened of her. Such an alien feeling.

Melody rested her face in her hands as she attempted clearing her head. Get those thoughts and images out. But they persisted.

Her arm jerked involuntarily as she recalled slashing at the man. His blood spattered across a brick wall as his head rolled. A queer sound came from his windpipe. Were those words? Were his dead vocal chords saying something?

The door smashed open, and she looked up to see her neighbours. They'd broken the door to come in.

"Melody!" Old Mrs Boyd exclaimed. "Are you all right, dear?" Then she stopped, a look of horror crossing her face. "Oh, child! What happened?" The old woman hurried over to the Melody and took hold of her hands.

It was only then that Melody became conscious of the stickiness coating her hands. A tacky coolness remained on her face where she rested on her palms. Then the smell she had noticed but never registered.

Blood. But not her own.

Mrs Boyd turned to one of the other women who had entered. With a wave of her hand, she sent them away. "Out! I'll look after her."

Out they went, one of them lingering a moment to take in the sights before shutting the door. Old hands, gentle but firm, lifted Melody's face by the chin and grey eyes gazed into hers.

"For how long have you been having the dreams?"

Melody shook her head. The images were returning. She whimpered at the memories, vivid and painful, as though they had happened.

The neighbour lifted Melody's face again. "Look at me, Melody." Their eyes met. "How long?"

Mrs Boyd sighed, her head bent as she thought. What was that on the floor? More blood! A trail of boot prints led from the side window to Melody's bedside, stopping at a pair of boots. Old fashioned boots. Mrs Boyd's eyes opened wide in surprise, but she didn't mention them.

Melody followed her neighbour's gaze and released a shocked sound. "What happened to my boots?"

The old woman pushed them aside. "Come, dear. It's nearly midday and you've been sleeping still. I think we need to get you some help."

***

A knock at the door interrupted Craig and Brianna's conversation. Gifford entered and, upon seeing Craig in the office, stopped himself from saying anything. A look of shock crossed his face.

Brianna looked up. "What's up, Tony?"

Gifford glanced at Craig who gazed at him with a serene expression. "Um. Yeah, there's been another call out. You know the cab driver's identification you found? Well, it turns out the guy hasn't turned up for work in some time. But we've tracked down the car."

Brianna stood and grabbed her jacket, pushing past

Tony to leave the office. "Let's go then. I've got to visit the loo first."

Tony and Craig remained alone in Brianna's office; Tony standing near the door, checking his fingernails, and Craig about to exit. The police detective appeared uneasy, and Craig guessed the reason.

"Did you have that bruise this morning?" Craig asked, trying to remain subtle.

Tony shook his head and returned to chewing a fingernail. An eye shifted far enough to see Craig, but not to appear obvious.

Craig approached Tony so the police detective couldn't avoid seeing him. "Do you remember what I told you this morning?"

The policeman eyeballed Craig while chewing a piece of fingernail. "You said we would catch the killer, yeah. That's great. I hope it's today." Then he resumed chewing his fingernails and turned his head away. Craig caught a flash of a bruise on the homicide detective's mouth and wondered if that was why.

Craig suppressed a chuckle and persisted, refusing the detective's ignorance. "I said you would find the killer, not catch. It's a warning." His voice hardened. "Tony, you must pay attention. Your life depends on it. So does Brianna's."

"Why don't you tell her then?"

"Because you're the only one who can do something about it, Tony." Craig fixed a stare on him. "I saw him stab you and Brianna both. It could be today if the taxicab leads you to him. That part I don't know. But it will happen this week." Tony squirmed, but Craig persisted like a pit-bull terrier that wouldn't let go. "You, Tony. Keep your eyes open and stay awake. Got it?"

Tony snorted but Craig persisted. "This is not funny, Tony. If you won't do it for yourself, do it for Brianna. She's your work partner, right?" The policeman remained still as an Easter Island statue and as expressionless.

Both of them stared at each other like wild animals sizing the other up. Brianna approached from the doorway.

"Are you two finished with the lovey-dovey eyes? Tony, we better go check this lead now."

Craig turned to Brianna. "Tony and I were just discussing the case," he answered, checking his watch. "Do you want me to tag along?"

Dark, undisguised thunder crossed Tony's face. Ignoring it, Brianna shook her head. "No, I think we'll be fine for this one."

Craig nodded although every fibre in his body wanted to be there too. Anything could go wrong, and he didn't trust Tony to be awake. But what else could he do without appearing like a worry wart? Resigning himself to destiny, Craig replied, "Okay. I have something to check, anyway, so I'll leave you to do your job. Watch out for Toomey. He may seem a harmless man, but it's the quiet ones you have to watch." He reached to squeeze Brianna's hand, but she pulled him closer to deliver a quick kiss to his lips.

"Thanks," she replied, a cheeky look on her face. "I'll see you tonight."

As the two detectives hurried down the hall, Craig placed his fingers to his lips where Brianna kissed him. Mixed visions. He still saw the red-eyed stranger plunge a knife into Tony after slitting Brianna's throat. But he also saw a vision of himself in bed with Brianna. Was it a memory, fantasy, or plain wishful thinking?

Chapter 11

After a workout and meditation with Sifu Yong, Craig's head had cleared considerably. The dreams and visions still sat in his mind, but concentration on the day came easier now. Even his concerns about Tyrone seemed smaller now. A shower helped complete his return to humanity

So a refreshed Craig Ramsey entered the kitchen to find Emily bustling about in the living room. The television was on, playing an old movie with Liam Neeson and Jessica Lange. Craig guessed Emily must have been watching it, and upon hearing him, bustled back to her duties. Sometimes she did that and would turn the television off to hide the fact, but this time she was too late. On the screen, Liam Neeson emerged from a lake as naked as a newborn baby - only cleaner with less goo.

"Is that Rob Roy?" Craig asked Emily who was dusting the already-spotless shelves.

The Scottish lady looked up towards Craig, a smidgen of red glowing on her otherwise pallid features. "Who?"

Laughter escaped Craig's mouth. "Don't tell me you don't know who Rob Roy was."

"Of course, I never knew Rob Roy MacGregor," Emily responded with a pout. "Not well, anyway." She winked. "Old Rob was in his sixties when he died, and I was but twenty. But he and my Daddy were friends. But that Liam Neeson reminds me of my husb-"

The phone's ringing interrupted Emily, leaving Craig intrigued. The Scottish lady spirit rarely spoke about her living existence before becoming a spirit. But the insistent phone's tone demanded his attention. Perhaps it was Brianna ringing? He grabbed the phone and sighed with relief upon seeing Brianna's caller ID.

Brianna's voice came through the phone, controlled but shaky. "Craig?"

Emily noted the worry lines crowding Craig's face and hovered closer as he responded.

"Yes? Are you okay?"

Brianna's voice remained composed with the slightest tremor. "I'm okay, but I need to talk to you. Are you busy?"

Thoughts fluttered through Craig's head. Whatever happened must have been terrible. Brianna would have seen horrors during her military career prior to the police. For something to upset her now, it must have been horrible.

"Yes, of course, you can."

Brianna replied that she would be around in twenty-to-thirty minutes before hanging up.

"What happened?" Emily asked. "Is Brianna hurt?"

Craig shook his head with a slight shrug as he headed towards the refrigerator to check inside. "Not from what I can tell."

The spirit floated around in front of him. "Is it that horrible detective Gifford? Has he done something?"

"Tony Gifford?" Craig raised an eyebrow. "What do you know about him?"

A knowing smile emerged from Emily's face. "I met him the other night when I visited Brianna in her office."

Sensing Craig's curiosity, Emily added, "He seems to have taken a shine to your lady friend. Who knows?" Her voice changed to an enigmatic tone. "He's persistent." The words hung in the air, silent but cunning as a shithouse rat, as Emily hovered away towards the lounge area again. "The Universe has a way of giving us things and testing if we truly want what we wished for. What do you want, my boy?"

***

A dishevelled woman stared back when Brianna checked her reflection in the rear-view mirror. Tremors ran through her hands as she attempted pushing her hair back in place. And a quiver escaped her lower lip. Hold on, she told herself.

She had booked to speak with a counsellor in the morning. It was the best they could do, but it wasn't good enough. She needed to speak with someone, and it had to be someone she trusted. Craig.

Brianna blew her nose, pushed her hair in place again, and stepped out of the car. Craig's front lights shone like a lighthouse beacon for a returning ship. Comfort and familiarity.

The door swung open before Brianna could raise her finger to push the bell. A shudder ran through Brianna, making her jump, when she saw a translucent shape that resembled a human woman. She couldn't stop the startled cry. The shape froze for a moment before floating forward, and a familiar voice spoke.

"Dear Brianna! It's me."

Brianna scrunched her eyes. A relieved smile broke her rampant stress' fog like a sunbeam through storm clouds. "Emily? Is that you?"

"In the ectoplasm," Emily responded, her spectral arms wrapping around Brianna. "Can you really see me now?"

"You're faint, like looking through cellophane wrapping." Brianna rubbed her eyes before looking again. "Are you making yourself visible to me?"

Emily's arms felt comfortable to Brianna as the spirit led her inside Craig's home. The gentle aroma of Italian food - pasta, bacon, and something else - teased her nostrils and calmed her more. Craig's cooking.

"You experienced something shocking today, didn't you?" Understanding and knowing filled Emily's sentence. "Your psychic senses are still developing, and sometimes shock brings them on faster. The ectoplasm in your blood system is still working on you. One day, who knows, you may see me much better."

Emily's words flew past Brianna's mind. Her psychic abilities were still developing. That explained it. The kitchen was homier than Brianna's and lifted her spirits, reminding Brianna of her adopted mother's home in Banksia Grove. Things were so different since she left home to join the Army so many years ago.

Craig looked up from the stove where he was taste-testing what smelled like carbonara. His eyes lit up upon seeing her and returned the spoon to its pot before approaching and holding her in his strong arms. Comfort. There it was. His warm breath on her neck soothed her more when she returned the hug. "Hey," he said, smoothing her hair with his fingers. "You're shaking. Come and sit down."

He placed a glass of Gavi di Gavi in Brianna's hand. She drained it before she realised it.

Craig turned to glance at Emily who nodded and left the room while he looked at the wine bottle on the bench and again at the depleted glass.

The buzzing in Brianna's head was fading. Her shoulders relaxed as she sat back among the cushions, and she remained quiet, her mood calming, until Craig spoke in a gentle voice.

"Are you feeling better?"

Brianna nodded, conjuring a smile from somewhere that threatened to unseat her shock. Shaky fingers placed the glass on a coaster strategically set by her host. "I'm okay. Shaken, not stirred." A laugh escaped at her joke.

Craig watched with patient eyes and remained silent. Those eyes. Brianna had seen them before, looked into them, but now they held another light. Had it been there, or was she seeing things differently, just like she could see whispers of Emily's spirit form now? Perhaps. Maybe it was something else. Shock. Yes, it must be. An encouraging smile from him.

"Do you want to talk about it?" Craig asked.

She didn't have to talk about what happened, did she? Hadn't he seen what happened when he hugged her? Couldn't he touch her and know? That was his psychic power. But Brianna understood; Craig's insight told him Brianna needed to talk. Of course! Talk. Get it all out so she could heal. He was her counsellor before the meeting the next morning.

Brianna nodded. "You were right, you know." Her fingers curled into a fist. "We found the killer."

***

"When we left the station, the first thing I noticed was Gifford stayed quiet until we reached the car. We were halfway to the river bank near Royal Park where the homeless people hold a camp by the time he said anything. But I had to speak first." Brianna swirled the wine in her glass, watching the light play and bend in the liquid.

"I asked Tony about the taxi cab. What else did they know about it? He said, "Toomey the Confessor has it.""

"Confessor?" Craig asked.

Brianna nodded. "Whenever we have cases attracting media attention, George Toomey comes out of the woodwork. I first met him when I joined the police

109

service here. It was my first day. Hohenhaus was desk sergeant and Toomey was telling him how he had committed the Crime of the Century by stealing jewellery from Myers. Of course, he hadn't."

"He sounds like a lonely man," Craig responded, sipping his own wine and sitting back into his own chair. "How do you handle people like him?"

"Hohenhaus asked him for the loot, saying he'd let Toomey off the hook if he gave it back." Brianna managed a small grin. "No robbery happened. Toomey cooked it all up in his head but handed over a heap of tiny pebbles. Hohenhaus collected them in a plastic bag as 'evidence' and told Toomey to stay out of trouble."

Craig chuckled and Brianna continued.

"Toomey even confessed to being Denton the sniper," Brianna added. "Did I tell you about that? No, I don't think I did. So when Toomey came in three weeks ago and told the new desk sergeant about killing the women, no one believed him. His story matched what the media knew, and we took no notice. Why would we? Toomey has been such a fixture of everyday life for us, we didn't believe him!"

Brianna's eyes dropped, contemplating the glass sitting on the coaster. "I never expected Toomey to steal a car, not even a taxi. But here's the kicker. Gifford also gave me the other news. They found the cabbie who owned the taxi dead last week. Dr Kroot had found evidence of the driver having sexual activity just before he died, and something with fangs had bitten his throat."

Craig's eyes opened wide for a second before narrowing in suspicion. "Blood sucked out?"

Brianna cast a look at Craig, a mixture of impatience and incredulity. Blood sucked out? Was he kidding? Maybe not.

"No. He died from suffocation or heart failure. Something had squeezed the life out of him. I'd say Toomey found the empty cab, maybe with its keys in the ignition, and taken it as a mobile home for himself."

Craig excused himself and left his chair to serve up dinner. Rather than set places at the dining table, he set place mats on the coffee table before serving up the aromatic pasta dish. Brianna must have gathered a significant appetite and licked her lips.

"We parked the car away from Tent Town," Brianna said, once Craig sat opposite her. "And by the time we reached it, we were sweating like pigs. Ha! Did you know Tent Town, a place where homeless people camp together, has its own 'mayor'? Neither did I. But a group of them approached, and the 'mayor' spoke with us. Webber is his name. Webber told us Toomey was still out. Perhaps we should have listened closer when he mentioned Toomey's behaviour had changed. But he mentioned the taxi cab, and I assumed Webber meant that. About thirty minutes must have passed while we waited, and then we saw him."

"The Toomey I recall from the past walked about like a mouse with his back hunched, ready to jump at the slightest sound. He lacked confidence in his walk, only showing it when telling stories. But this Toomey was different. He resembled him by features but not posture. The man we saw approaching Tent Town walked like he owned the place. Even the mayor had commented earlier on Toomey's changed behaviour, from a wallflower type to a confident man, although he kept to himself. Webber guessed 'owning a car' did that to Toomey.

"Seeing a man and a woman together in Tent Town seems odd, considering its inhabitants are all male. Maybe we have that air of cops around us, but Toomey noticed us straight away. He's damn fast. When he ran off, I had to run at a full sprint to come within twenty metres of him as he dodged through the trees and bushes. Gifford puffed something about him taking off like a wild animal. I know what he meant because Toomey bounded like a deer. Instead of crashing through one bush, or dodging it, he bounded over it like a kangaroo. The whole time, he chattered with his high-pitched voice.

"At last, we saw where he was headed. The taxi cab was ahead. I would have tackled him as he unlocked it, but Gifford had other ideas. He removed his gun, aimed and shot out two tyres. The discharges were loud, cracked like thunder, and I heard screams from nearby civilians. Gifford shouldn't have done it, not with them around. Maybe he'll hear about it later from above,

"Toomey turned to face us and dashed straight for us. He'd always seemed shorter before, but this time he seemed bigger, heavier, and more powerful; not the weak little guy I remember. Surprised by Toomey's attack, we hesitated, ready to tackle him. It was a ploy. The confessor about-faced away from us and dashed straight for his car again, and as he reached it... he jumped over it!" Brianna's face matched the astonishment in her voice. "He didn't even slow down as he bounded like a gazelle. Gifford muttered something but I couldn't catch it for his heavy breathing.

"Meanwhile Toomey continued dashing without stopping and dodged in and out of the afternoon traffic. We kept following on foot. Too far back for the car and the road was thick with vehicles.

"We battled to keep up. Toomey always looked weak and pasty, but as a human mouse, he did well. We chased him for three blocks before we caught him, and it was only because he ran into a blind alley.

"Gifford made a comment. Both of us were panting, puffing and sweating from the run. Toomey wasn't even sweating.

"He stood there, his feet taking an even stance, and waited for us to catch our breath at the entrance. There were no exits at the other side. A brick wall stopped him, and so did the building's locked doors. The place looked dead.

"I called out to Toomey, told him we wanted to ask questions. But he remained like a statue. I thought he made a small smile, but it disappeared. Maybe it was exertion from the recent running. But I'm not sure now. I approached him slowly. We really wanted to ask him about the cab, how he found it, where, and so forth. Confessors always want to be caught but not him.

"I moved forward, my hands in front of me with

palms outward and showing me unarmed. Toomey narrowed his eyes and his head leaned forward so he looked up through his eyebrows at me. Despite the running, he barely puffed. Homeless people must be stronger than I thought, and more resilient. I was within ten feet of Toomey when he reacted. One moment he was there, the next he was to my side. After one shove, I fell hard against the brick wall and he slapped me hard. Tony was already moving and jumping on Toomey. Both fought hard, hard enough for me to see a splatter of blood (Tony's?) land on my feet.

"Then Tony screams a scream I last heard in Timor. The same sound a man makes when he's in mortal pain. I caught a flash of something, a blade. And it's a long one. Shock filled me. Tony dropped to the ground. Blood pooled around him. But he was still alive.

"Toomey was about to run, and he takes a step. I tripped him, pushed him to the ground, and stomped on his knife hand. Then I knocked him out. It happened fast and I cuffed him. After kicking the knife away, I approached Tony. He's holding his hand over his stomach wound, but his blood seeped between his fingers. So much blood. I haven't seen that since the military. Tony's face was white from shock and he had trouble breathing without screaming.

"But it didn't end there.

"While I'm trying to slow Tony's bleeding, a scraping sound comes to my ears. Panic hit me. Was Toomey up and after us? But, no. He was up on his feet, contemplating the cuffs holding his hands behind him. In one motion, he jumps, lifts his feet in the air, and moves his restrained hands under him like a skipping rope so they're now in front of him. Then he runs!

"Maybe I should have run after him, but I couldn't leave Tony there, bleeding and dying. Toomey was out of the alley, running into traffic and out of sight. Horns blared and brakes squealed, followed by a sickening sound.

"Toomey had run in front of a bus which couldn't stop. He died on impact."

***

Brianna paused, eyes unfocused. While talking, she had finished the plate of food, which pleased Craig. He had worried Brianna might have lost her appetite.

"How is Tony?" Craig asked.

Brianna glanced towards him. A fleeting thought passed her mind, visible in her eyes, before vanishing. "He's in hospital now. The knife missed his vitals, but he's going to be sore for some time. Very lucky guy. By the way, the knife is really old. The design on its handle looks like something from ancient days, thousands of years ago, but the blade is keen."

Craig nodded. He didn't like Tony, but he wished no harm either.

"Craig, tell me the vision you had when you said we'd find the killer."

Not the question he expected from Brianna. Craig took a deep breath and let it go. "My vision involved you and Tony in the alley with the killer." Craig's voice trailed away.

115

"Your words are truth," Brianna replied, her face hard with focused certainty, "but there's something else you're not telling me. Tony told me in the hospital that you saw something happen to me. If he hadn't pushed me out of the way... What did you see?"

Craig paused, realising how things looked. Tony Gifford was still working his way to Brianna, it seemed. "The truth is," he started, "I saw you both killed."

"Tony and I both died?" Brianna's face whitened. "Why didn't you tell me?"

Craig's eyes closed. "I saw the vision multiple times, Brianna. Sometimes, but not always, I see the vision in different perspectives. It's like watching a DVD with different movie endings. If an action changes, it produces a different reaction."

"Gobble-de-gook," Brianna said. "What aren't you telling me?"

"I had to look at it in different ways. If Tony had done nothing, Toomey would have sliced you up before Tony could jump in, only to be killed as well. If Tony went first, he would have been stabbed through the throat before you were cut from your genitals to your sternum." A stunned look perched on Brianna's face at Craig's words; her lips moved to speak, but he pressed further. "If I'd told you instead of Tony, he would be dead, but you would have been seriously hurt too, dying hours later."

"But you-"

"But I offered to come along and to help," Craig added, picking up Brianna's empty plate and stacking it with his own on the coffee table.

"And you would have saved us both, I suppose," Brianna quipped.

Craig remained silent, picked up the dishes and took them to the kitchen where he rinsed them. Brianna watched his face and must have realised something. Lifting a hand to her lips to cover her shock, she inhaled. "Oh, my God. Neither Tony nor I would have received injuries or died, but... you would have died instead, wouldn't you?"

Craig stood from the dishwasher after stacking the dishes and shut it. "Dessert?"

"No!" Brianna responded. "I mean, yes, dessert would be good, but you're not changing the subject. Would you have died or been hurt instead of Tony and me?"

"Yes, let's change the subject," Craig replied. "You need to gain another perspective for which you're missing the point. You are alive. Tony's alive. We are all alive, and you're bloody welcome." He tossed Brianna a Cornetto which she caught. "There's your dessert."

Brianna looked at the Cornetto, turning it in her hand. Looking up, she said, "So you were really looking for the best possible outcome?"

Craig took a bite from his ice-cream, crunching into the chocolate top, and nodded. "You would have done the same, wouldn't you?"

"I would hope so," she answered, "but you could have fought harder to come along, you know. Tony would have appreciated the chance to have me for himself."

She fought to disguise her smile, but her eyes laughed too much and released her broad grin. A pillow flew through the air, missing her by a foot.

Craig replied, rolling his eyes and polishing off his dessert. "Just can't make you happy, can I?"

Brianna moved closer, leaning closer. "Up for some makeup sex?"

***

Their lovemaking flowed easily, taking them from the living room to the bedroom with clothes trailing their migration. For both of them, the primal dance was necessary to break the tension in a way where actions speak louder than words. At last, after the dirty talking, the kissing and fondling that led to them joining in frenzied earnestness, they came to the same conclusion. Then gave more of themselves again before exhaustion left them asleep in each other's arms.

After a delicious dream that possibly drew inspiration from their recent nocturnal activity, Brianna's eyes opened. A smile played upon her face briefly as she watched Craig's face as the moonlight caressed it the way he had caressed her earlier. Even in sleep, he held that expression: a hybrid of confident cockiness overcoating a strong sensitivity to others. He reminded her in ways of her past love Tom, the only man for whom she could give love. At times, particularly when she fought with Craig, Tom seemed to shine through his eyes. Craig may have been thinner than Tom, but he held the same swagger and was just as capable. Another smile appeared on her face as she remembered the brief rivalry between Tony and Craig. Memory came to

Brianna of when she had reached towards Craig's hand before leaving with Tony to the murder scene. She had seen how Tony was peacocking, trying to psyche out Craig and make him jealous. Rather than create an embarrassing scene she wanted to touch Craig's hand, knowing he would pick up her thoughts and intentions. Although Craig wasn't the jealous type, she wanted him to know how she felt. But he had seen more. Brianna's mind flipped back to Tom, then to Craig. Then she knew.

Brianna sighed and attempted to move without disturbing Craig's arm which lay across her in a loose but protective embrace. He stirred slightly, and she kissed his lips, whispering, "I love you."

Although sleeping, he responded in kind, rolling onto his back as he mumbled. "I love you too, Celina."

Brianna's eyes flipped open.

Celina?

***

"Celina," he whispered, fear and abandonment flowing through him as he watched the willowy blonde fade away before his outstretched hand.

But he couldn't stop her. Darkness swallowed him. Something gripped his arms and ankles, pulling him in different directions. Enemy hands threw him upon a table, hard as a rack, and secured his limbs in cold steel. A sense of déjà vu staggered his thoughts as he realised where he was. Craig jumped as the cold dry material draped across his face. He wanted to scream, but it was to no avail.

Cold, icy water drowned his cries and screams as Blaze's laughter echoed in the blackness. "I found you, Mr Ramsey. This time you can't be helped."

But Blazes voice changed, and the dripping towel whipped away from his mouth. Craig choked back water, peering through the darkness at the shadow. It wasn't Blaze standing there. This creature also looked familiar, but from where? Eyes of coppery amber glowed like coals dipped in hellfire from a face wrinkled like mildewed brown paper. A top hat perched above them, black as the ace of spades and cold as obsidian. From the shoulders billowed a cape, blowing in a breeze that he couldn't feel.

Slash! The blade sang as it cut through the air. A curious sound and a strange numbness took his body as blood ripped through the air from his chest. Again, the dagger plunged into him, slicing him from the chest to his pelvis. Then something grabbed his privates, stretching them out as the blade hung in the air. The laughter that rolled deep from the bowels of Hades stifled his will.

Now another person, similar in appearance but this one he knew. The face was young although the eyes were centuries old. "Craig, listen to me. Jack is back!"

The knife stabbed downwards again, slicing him as he woke.

Sweat dripped from Craig's nakedness as he peered up at the ceiling in the comfort of sudden wakefulness. Khan and the Ripper's voices still filled his consciousness. His chest heaved another breath as he looked beside him to check on Brianna. She was still there, her chest moving with each breath of silent sleep, and he allowed himself to relax. Everything was okay. It was just a dream.

Chapter 12

Three weeks had passed since Toomey had stabbed him, but Tony's wound still hurt like hell. Daggers (for want of a better term) of pain fired through his abdomen whenever he sat up in bed, and he felt sick whenever he sat on the toilet. He particularly felt it around the point where the staples rejoined the wound. Those itched like blazes, and he had to scream to himself to stop scratching them. But the doctors had removed those after about ten days.

Because the wound was deep, barely missing vital organs, the police service had given him two months off. Deep stab wounds require long-term treatment and follow-up outside the normal emergency room. The body needed more time to heal from the trauma.

Gifford examined the crimson wound in the privacy of his hospital room's shower. The water stung as it ran over the area. Ah! that'd form a nice scar. Something he could show the next girl, assuming he could land one.

A flash of angry disappointment dribbled from his mind in a juicy dollop of self-pity. Gifford would have loved to show the scar to that Detective Cogan, maybe use it to bed her, but pity sex didn't seem her thing.

Indeed, the bitch still hung out with the "sick-ick guy" Craig Ramsey. What did she see in him, anyway? The guy looked like a poofter, dressed like one, and even spoke like one. How could he be man enough to give Cogan what she needed from a man?

Gifford snorted. The bitch was probably a gold digger chasing after Ramsey's money. That explained what she saw in Ramsey!

The disabled detective mulled over things. Why had he stepped into the knife? He could see it a mile off, just as Ramsey said he would, but he didn't need the psychic to tell him that. Now he'd saved Cogan and handed her over to that nancy-boy.

Destiny!

The word rang and echoed through his head so much Gifford could have sworn the speaker stood next to him. He glanced up towards the source. No one there. Just him, the running water, a painful wound, and a sorry-looking bastard looked back at him from the mirror.

You own me five farthings, say the bells of St Martin's.

Gifford jumped, turning around and wincing from the pain in his abdomen from the movement. Someone spoke to him, singing, but he saw no one there. What the hell was that? It sounded like a nursery rhyme but none Gifford recognised. He whipped the shower curtain aside, but no one was there either, and no one was in the hospital room either. "Must be crazy," he told himself. "No one here."

Only us, my lad. You and I.

Gifford startled and stood with his back against the

cold tiles of the ensuite's wall and shower water cascading down him. A sound like a heavy bellows heaved louder. His breathing.

Then a voice chuckled around him. His eyes widened, swivelling in their sockets as he scanned the room. Where was that coming from?

Come now, Tony. Are you a man or a woman? I am here to help you get what you want.

"To get what I want?" Tony's voice was a whisper. The invisible man made no response so Tony repeated himself louder. "What I want?"

Yesss, Tony. You want that Detective Cogan bitch, don't you? I know you dream of having your sexual way with her. Don't you?

"Who are you?" Gifford's lower lip trembled like a shaken rat while tears mingled with the shower water as he looked around with wild eyes. "Where are you?"

Footsteps, the sounds of near-silent soles scuffing the carpet in the main room, reached his ears. "Tony?" A female voice floated from outside. "Are you okay?"

Gifford recognised the voice. The nurse! "Stay away," he called. "Someone's in here. Get out before he-"

The shower whipped away, Gifford screamed and so did the nurse upon seeing his maniacal, naked personage facing her. The nurse took a step back and regained her composure before pressing the bathroom's call button. She lifted her hands, palms out towards him, and lowered her voice with shushing sounds.

"Relax, Tony," she sing-songed. "What's wrong?"

Gifford muttered, appearing to wake from a dream, and cast glances around the room. A befuddled expression crossed his face as he saw no one but the old nurse. "What? Someone else was here."

The nurse looked around and saw no one else in the bathroom. Only a bed, trolley and associated furniture stood in the bedroom. "When? There was no one else here when I arrived."

A male nurse appeared at the door and stopped at the bathroom entrance. His eyes noted the scene. "What's happened?"

"It's okay, Peter," the female nurse responded, finding Tony's towel and wrapping it around him. "Mr Gifford thought he heard someone else in the room and panicked. There's no one here now. Come along, Tony."

"Looks like he's running a fever, Judith," the male nurse said, finding another nearby towel and helping dry Tony off.

The female nurse, Judith, felt Tony's forehead. "He is. How long have you been feeling hot?"

A cocky grin crossed Tony's face, his twinkling eyes glinting as he eyed off Judith's feminine assets. "Who are you calling hot, babe?"

"Okay." Peter hurried Tony along towards his bed. "That's enough. You have a fever, and we need to check that wound. Hey! Have you been in the shower? You keep that area dry, or it will get infected."

Tony barely felt the needle's sharp kiss pierce his bum cheek. The room rolled in his vision like an old television screen's out-of-control vertical hold, and he tipped backward as hands guided him towards the bed. But he still heard the other man's heavy breathing in his head - the breath of someone waiting like a patient hunter.

The room darkened around him and choked off the sunlight streaming through his bedroom window. The gloom was so thick that it gained substance. With an unearthly knowing, it gathered around him as though with arms and held him secure. He limbs stiffened, refused to move, and something appeared in the darkness.

Two burning, red orbs. They flickered once or twice as they approached. Tony gasped upon realising they were eyes. Staring embers that narrowed, studying him before widening with a raucous laughter.

Be a good boy, Tony. I'm here with you. When you help me, I will help you get what you want - and more. But first you must rest. I will help you heal better than those primates can.

The voice frightened him at first. But the more it spoke, the more he listened, and the more he listened, the more he relaxed. Above the red eyes, he spotted a tall hat, similar to something seen in an old black and white movie. A magician's hat or something like that.

Yes, Tony, a magician, but it's not the kind of magic you've seen before. Now, sleep. Relax. I will have you out of this hospital soon.

***

Melody Kostas sat up in the darkness, her screams echoing in her head, and choked back another cry upon realising where she was. A hammering sounds filled her head, pumping a cocktail of adrenaline and life juices through her throbbing ears. She looked at the clock, seeing the time, 10:30am, and groaned as the pillow accepted her falling weight. Her clammy forehead chilled her hand as she brushed the hair from her eyes and calmed herself.

The dreams were back again. But how? What caused them?

Melody rolled out of bed and stretched. A finger of sunlight poked through the curtain which she pulled back. The gardener stood out the front with his shears clipping the hedges. Children made noises that floated on the winds to her ears from the nearby school. Life continued as always outside her unit, but something told her more was happening.

A memory teased her conscious thoughts. A tall, dark stranger with a voluminous black cloak that billowed behind him like a cloud. He had appeared in her dreams. Always, he followed her. At one time, she dreamt of kissing the stranger, but she couldn't see his face. Yet a part of her imagined him with eyes like jet or obsidian, polished orbs that knew her soul. As much as she felt in tune with, and in love with this stranger in her dream, a part of her felt she had to run. Then there was the other man, the one before. He dressed similar but his eyes were like coals, burning red with rage, anger and hunger; psychopathic and murderous; hate incestuously mingled with a sick blood lust. Heat radiated from his mouth when he taunted her. Evil had created him.

The latter man haunted her dreams before and stopped just three weeks ago. A part of her recognised him, but Melody didn't know how. Perhaps it was the dream memory. Sometimes dreams act funny, making us think we remember things from the past that never happened. Like the time she thought a friend, long dead now, gave her a batch of books. They were antique books and held something, some hidden treasures that could reveal her secret. Information she required. Yet when she looked in the shelf, it wasn't there. She even questioned someone else, one of her friends, if they had seen them before they last moved homes. But, no, they didn't know of them.

The murderous man was a figment of her imagination from somewhere. Maybe she had seen him in a movie as a little girl? Children's experience have strange ways of reoccurring in nocturnal dreams and appearing real. Just like the other man whose soul seemed pure and light. He was most likely a fantasy, someone created perhaps as a saviour from the psychotic killer. But even her saviour, her enemy's enemy, wanted to capture her, maybe to kill her. What did all her dreams mean? Something pulled from the back of her mind, tapping like fingers on a window, but she couldn't place it.

Melody shuddered again and reached for a silk robe to cover her glistening nakedness before heading to her kitchen. A cup of chamomile tea would help settle the nerves before she prepared for work. The kettle rumbled as its water boiled. To the side, she hunted through the refrigerator for breakfast before grabbing a mushroom, eggs and a tomato. Just right for an omelette.

Then she saw it.

A card on the refrigerator door. Delta must have stuck it there before.

It was a black business card with silver letters embossed on its surface: Craig Ramsey, Psychic Investigator. A psychic? Yeah, Delta must have placed it there. But something drew Melody to look further. The man's photo appealed to her: a strong jaw and eyes that looked deep into the viewer's soul. He didn't look like the run-of-the-mill psychics who dressed in royal blues and deep amethyst purples, such a cliche that held no substance to her. Mr Ramsey's eyes may have stared, but they held intelligence. Deep intelligence. His smile appeared genuine too with a posture that commanded rather than begged attention. He looked handsome too, nice eye candy.

Having forgotten the omelette for now, Melody poured her tea into a mug and carried it to the living room while examining the back of the card. So, the man was more than psychic. He was a hypnotherapist too.

So many others claimed the same, but something told Melody to check this man out more.

***

His host slept the sleep of the healing. But he didn't. Work needed doing, and after 5,000 years, the end was approaching. Perhaps this host was the right one after

129

so many before him.

Inside his host's mind, he browsed memories. Such a short life these humans live. But no one survived as his host long, anyway, because that's how his life rolled. You can't scramble eggs without breaking them first.

But this host proved interesting, almost as interesting as his last one over a century ago. Previously, he had inhabited a doctor, a surgeon from a London hospital close to the Whitechapel murders. But this man. What a windfall! The man was a policeman. Who would suspect him? His previous host, a homeless man named Toomey, worked well: anonymous, almost invisible as part of the scenery. But this man, a man of the law, what a find! People would look at him and suspect nothing. He could cover evidence, replant it elsewhere, and place the blame on someone else while he followed his mission. The mistress would be so pleased with him.

Corrupting Toomey had been easy. All the man wanted was status. A car stolen from the host before Toomey, a Pakistani cab driver, was all it took. But this man Gifford reminded him of the surgeon from the 1880s. He relied on base instincts: hatred, lust, and ego. Gifford held a hatred of anyone doing better than him, people who had what he desired. The pitiful fool believed the world owed him something. But he also hated women and liked them for their sexual flesh.

Well, that was understandable. But his own hatred of females stemmed deeper.

The creature's eyes widened upon recognising a man in Gifford's memories. The strong jawline, the spiky hair, and the confident gait rang bells, almost like St

Stephen's in his head. A psychic man, powerful and intelligent. And the stranger had stolen this Gifford's woman.

I know this Craig Ramsey.

Perhaps Gifford would prove more valuable than anticipated.

Chapter 13

Craig Ramsey woke with a start from his dreaming. A thumping sound filled his head, which ached as though crushed under a truck. What kind of dream was that?

But the knocking didn't stop from waking, and he realised it was someone at the front door. Craig rose from his bed, rubbing his weary head, and trudged out to answer. Who the hell would visit at this time of night?

Emily, too, appeared and waited near the front door as Craig approached it. "A visitor from the past," she said. "Friendly."

With a nod, Craig unlocked the door and opened it to see a tall man he hadn't seen in nearly twenty years. "Khan! What -"

"Listen, Craig, this is important," the mysterious stranger replied. "Jack is back!"

Who? What? Craig's head still felt muddled.

Khan pushed past Craig without waiting for an invitation to enter, striding straight to the lounge-room. In a fluid motion, he whipped off his leather jacket and tossed the garment neatly upon a nearby coat-rack without looking.

"Make yourself at home," Craig intoned, a wry smile

crossing his lips as Khan flopped into an armchair. "Would you like a drink?"

Khan nodded and looked towards Emily. "A double schnapps, please, madame."

The phantasmic lady glared at Khan and refused to move. "Do I look like hired help to you?" she retorted. "Get it yourself, you great ape"

Khan scowled back with dark eyes piercing Emily. Craig held his breath, waiting and wondering, until both Emily and Khan laughed aloud at each other. Emily floated forward, giving the large man an ethereal kiss upon the cheek while Khan stood to hug her back. They couldn't connect physically, but Craig realised something he didn't know.

"The two of you have met before?"

"Yes," Khan responded as Emily floated away towards the liquor cabinet. "Decades before your birth, Craig. But I dropped by six weeks ago too."

"Don't you remember me telling you, Craig?" Emily confirmed, returning with a large bottle of Schnapps and a glass. Khan took the bottle, twisted the top off and drank loudly from the vessel.

Craig shook his head. "Perhaps. But I was busy." He took the glass from Emily, found a brandy next to his own armchair, and poured himself a measure. "Khan, who is Jack?"

"Jack," Khan responded, "was the scourge of Whitechapel. I had a run-in with him, or I should say 'her', many years ago in 1888. At the time, we thought he -"

Craig shook his head, uncertain if he heard Khan correctly. "Her? And how can he, I mean she, be back?"

Khan's annoyed glance silenced Craig. "If you would allow me to continue, I can tell you." He slugged some Schnapps. "Years ago, while on my way to visit a particular contact, I chanced upon a man and a woman fighting in a Whitechapel alley. Her screaming was loud enough to summon the police, but no authorities could hear her. The fog was thick enough to distort the sound. And the streets were dark." Khan took a breath and another swallow. "Well, when I ran to aid her, it turned out she needed no help. Indeed, the man did. She had killed him with a large Liston. By the time I realised that, she -"

"She killed you," Craig answered, his voice trailing as he recalled parts of his dream. "Is that right?"

"You must quit interrupting me, Mr Ramsey," Khan responded, raising an eyebrow. "It's rude. As I was saying, she killed me. You know I'm immortal and can spring back to life, but the resurrection takes time. By the time I awoke, the authorities had taken me to the local morgue. A doctor was about to cleave me from sternum to stomach. The poor chap dropped in a dead faint when I asked if it would hurt."

Craig smiled having witnessed firsthand Khan's ability to regenerate himself, thanks to a wish granted centuries earlier by a rogue genie named Azriel.

"Are you telling me this woman is Jacqueline the Ripper, not Jack?" Craig asked.

Khan finished the bottle, burped, and set the empty bottle on the side table. "Not only that, Craig," he answered. "The bitch is as immortal as me."

"Have you seen her?" Emily asked, glancing towards Craig and at his eyes. Her telepathic voice spoke in Craig's mind. The poor man. I wonder if he wants to catch her for another reason.

Craig nodded, understanding Emily's point that Khan was a lonely man. Immortality wasn't a blessing for him. Azriel's granting of the wish proved as much a curse as Khan had endured watching his loved ones die many times, never seeing them alive again.

Khan smiled, watching Craig and Emily, and his face turned grim. "You doubt me. I suppose it's natural. I've met no one else who lived for more than my one thousand years. But I swear to you, by my soul, this woman is still alive today." He stopped to look around, his gaze fixing upon the liquor cabinet; Craig nodded with a "Help yourself" expression, and Khan rose from his seat to walk towards the drinks.

"But first, when I resurrected in the morgue, I noticed another cadaver next to mine. It belonged to my friend, Turner, the Cockney I needed to - Yes, Craig? I see you want to interrupt. What would you like to know?"

Craig was apologetic. "Did you just say 'Turner'?" He looked at Emily who shrugged non-committally. "Did he happen to be a pickpocket and raise children in his gang?"

Khan thought for a moment. "Why, yes, I believe he taught children the art. And he inspired such loyalty from them. Do you know him?"

"Perhaps," Craig leaned closer as Khan returned with a large bottle of vodka from which he drank straight.

"As I was saying," Khan continued, "when I saw my dead friend, I realised something more. This was the man I saw fighting the woman in the street. She had killed him a moment before I struck him down. I immediately felt saddened for selfish reasons... He promised information that could lead to curing my affliction."

Craig remained silent. Khan swigged more vodka before sighing and gazing at the bottle's contents as though lost in thought. Craig wanted to tell him about his dream and his connection with Turner, but waited. Did this relate to the present murders and, if so, how? As far as Craig knew, the psychotic killer killed women - not men.

Khan continued: "My only chance lay in his cohort, Bosworth, who could take me to their gang leader. Perhaps he could lead me to the information Turner's death denied me. So, being naked, I liberated the unconscious undertaker's person of his clothing and hurried back to Whitechapel where I'd last met the gang."

"Bosworth accommodated me and had heard of Turner's demise through the urchins. Nothing happened in Whitechapel, or anywhere else in East London, without the Workhouse Swig gang knowing. They and a rival group, The High Rip gang, came under blame when one of the Ripper's victims, Emma Smith, met her demise. This came about because Emma had visited a doctor before her untimely death and mentioned being attacked by a group of youths. While the High Rip gang could have attacked her, I find it unlikely as they usually attacked sailors and dockers of the time; their three R's involved random violence, robbery, and revenge killings. Their main weapon of choice was knives, which brought the authorities obvious blame in the beginning, but they also used leather belts as a lethal weapon. But, as I said, I doubted the High Rip gang's guilt in the deaths of all those women because they were family.

"Bosworth's gang, almost as well known as a gang of delinquents known as The Lemon Street Gang, weren't known for their violence. Most of the Workhouse Swiggers gang comprised urchins, children of prostitutes who either abandoned them or couldn't look after them because of their work. They dealt with smaller crimes - pick-pocketing mostly and burglary. Much of their loot came from strangers in the streets, but on occasion, they specialised in grand theft and acquired many pieces from wealthy citizens, including esoteric items.

"That is how I came to approach the Workhouse Swiggers. As you know, I've been searching the past five hundred years for two special items: a mask of Egyptian origin and a lamp that King Solomon owned. Legend says the mask can undo time, reverse things that happened, and the lamp holds the Father of all Genies. Either one of those artefacts can reverse my immortal affliction, caused by my foolhardy wishes with Azriel.

"Bosworth knew as much about the items as Turner,

it seems, and he pointed me towards an address on the other side of London. There, he said, I would find the mask. A fence named Darling who lived in the unlikely area of Marylebone; Gloucester Place, if I remember correctly. But I could be wrong. As immortal as my memory is, some things still escape me.

"But I remember the house itself. Behind its short brick wall fence with the decorative wrought iron piece on top stood a stunted tree, naked of leaves for London was approaching winter. The gate was on the property's corner, and rosebushes lined the path that ran alongside the house's front windows. The interior drawing room's lights blazed, but I saw no one. But I knew someone had to be home. No one left the lights on, and if Mr Darling wasn't home, surely a servant would be present.

"When I reached the front door, tingles ran up my spine. Most long-lived men tell me their longevity came from listening to such a premonition. To me, it means as much. Danger. For when I saw the door sitting ajar, a black cat standing in wide-eyed startlement at my appearance, that sensation nearly overcame me.

"In those days, I often carried my faithful sword or a smaller one, but that night I entered unarmed. The door squeaked on its hinges as I pressed my way in, but I continued anyway with my ears pricked for any noise. No sound reached me, save for the terrified cat's hurried passage into the cold night.

"Inside, everything seemed fine. A tall clock stood nearby, its pendulum dutifully counting time like a metronome. Was the master of the house home?

"No. My senses told me something else. Someone was there, besides me, and he or she was intruding too. The sound of their hushed breathing whispered through the air, tempered with my heartbeat's excitement. My fingers found the welcoming texture of polished wood and wrapped around an umbrella. Although not as effective as my faithful sword, the umbrella's solid handle could prove useful for striking a temple, and the tip as a stabbing point. A master of swordplay could turn it from an inefficient slapping device into a decent weapon.

"With my brandished umbrella, I waited outside the door and listened. The intruder was searching for something. Had he heard me too? Curiosity gripped me. Who were they? Did they have the mask in their possession? At last the person stopped searching. A faint voice reached my ears; the words escaped me but sounded remorseful. How puzzling.

"Throwing caution to the wind, I stepped from my hiding place around the corner to stand in the corner. The intruder caught the sound of my boots on the carpet, the squeak of the floorboard, and whirled to face me. I'm not sure who was most surprised. Me... or her! What was she doing there?

"Yes, it was she who had killed me. I recognised the soulful brown eyes, deep as mysterious pools and filled with menace. Dressed as a man, her speed astounded me. In a fluid motion, her lithe figure reached to her waist and flung a knife towards my throat. But I caught it by the handle, its blade less than an inch from my throat, and threw it back at its owner.

"She moved fast. The knife sliced through the air,

vibrated as it stuck in the wall, and a piece of her long raven tresses floated to the floor. I've seen no one move that fast before. In a moment, she advanced upon me, throwing exotic punches and kicks at me. Through all my travels across the world, I had never seen such martial art moves. Judo, Kenpo, even Ninjutsu. It was all of these and something else, something more. My own reflexes saved me from some blows, but more often than not, she connected with me. Luck, however, was on my side, and I circled around her and manoeuvred her towards the wall. But she saw through me and dropped to her knees, aiming a punch where even my immortality can't protect me.

"The pain in my groin startled me, I wanted to vomit, and my assailant took the advantage. Somehow I flailed a hand out to catch her, tripping her foot, and her shoulder hit the door on the way out. No sooner had I stood, I saw the woman dashing down the hall towards the front door. It slammed and her hurried footsteps vanished in the night.

"All I had were the bruises from her blows to my face, shoulders, and torso to remind me of her. The memories of her athletic display and exotic looks. I've never seen a woman in Britain fight like that.

"Perhaps I should have chased after the woman. But I wanted to check on Darling. It didn't take long. There, in a pool of blood, lay the poor man. He was sitting up in a corner of the room, on the floor, with his legs before him and his head on his lap. A long dagger, its handle engraved with ornate pictures of something resembling Greek gods, protruded from his chest. Exotic weapons were nothing new to me. But the likes of this, I had never seen before. I pulled hard on the dagger, expecting resistance from the body's suction, but it came away easily, thanks to holes and grooves in its blade - part of its design.

"A gurgling sound bubbled from the corpse's severed neck, making me jump in surprise. The body twitched, and a thick grey cloud erupted from it, swirling and turning in the surrounding air. For a moment, I felt as though eyes watched me from the smoky mass before it passed through the wall and disappeared.

"How strange! It reminded me of the first time I encountered Azriel in the bottle. But it felt worse, forbidding. The horrible sensation lingered over me as I watched the body drop back to the floor in a heap.

"Knocking at the front door jolted my senses. Voices reached me, calling out for me to open the door. Footsteps moved around the front of the house, and I heard a whistle blowing with urgency. The police!

"The dagger felt warm in my hand, and I felt a guilty surge overcome me. I couldn't open to door for the authorities who would ask too many questions. Their logic wouldn't understand since the media was howling for answers to the Ripper cases. And I was a stranger in London. Easy to blame.

"So I rushed upstairs, ignoring the incessant banging and whistle-blowing, and found a window. But it was no use. While a tree stood outside the window, five officers stood at its bottom. They didn't know I was upstairs, and I could have surprised them into submission, but not before they called for help. I had only one other option.

"The fireplace. It took me five minutes to scale from inside the flue up the chimney, being careful not to drop the chimney pots and alert the officers below. And there I sat in the cold darkness, mist billowing from my mouth and nose as I waited and listened. A full hour passed. I cursed the woman, the magnificent warrior who had evaded me twice now. And I wondered about the dagger now fastened to my belt with a cord.

"I needed to investigate it, learn more about the curious blade, its power and what it symbolised. And I knew just the man to tell me."

Craig had been leaning forward while listening with rapt attention to Khan's story. In the years he'd known Khan, Craig had rarely heard accounts of the immortal's past; this was a treat. Eight empty bottles sat beside Khan's feet. If there was one thing the tall man loved, it was a drink while story-telling.

"And what did you learn about the dagger?"

Khan peered into a bottle that once held Southern Comfort and sighed before tipping it upside down above his upturned open mouth. A solitary drop fell upon his waiting tongue, and he placed the bottle on the floor next to its other fallen comrades. "I took it to a friend of mine, a man whose name you may know: Reginald Ramsey the second."

The eyebrows on Craig's face raised in surprise. "An ancestor of mine?"

A smile crept across Khan's face along, contrasting with his narrowing eyes. "By your reaction, I believe you never guessed my previous involvement in your family."

Craig shook his head, curiosity growing. In all his life, Craig had heard little about his father's side of the family, having been raised by his mother's sister. He looked towards Emily, who was taking an interest in some dust on the DVD library, brushing it away with a rag. The ghost cast a quick glance at them before resuming her task. Craig glimpsed Khan in a thoughtful expression watching the Scottish lady too. Sensing Craig's gaze, Khan turned back towards him.

"Yes, Reginald is your great-great-grandfather and was active within a particular society interested in, shall we say, exotic items and history," Khan explained, casting another glance towards Emily who was now hurrying off towards another part of the house. He opened his mouth, as though to say something else, paused, and turned towards Craig. "Reginald was beside himself when I showed the dagger to him. He recognised the symbols in an instant, which surprised me. But a lot of things surprise me about humans. For instance, I have lived since the eleventh century and possess time in abundance. I have witnessed many things, even some events not recorded in history despite their importance and influence upon everyday life. Yet some mortals, having lived for only fifty-to-sixty years accumulate knowledge rivalling my own. Reginald's knowledge staggers me."

"And what did you learn about the dagger?"

Khan sighed, eyeing off the liquor cabinet, his thoughts trailing. Despite having imbibed enough alcohol to kill an elephant, Khan's speech and actions had not suffered. "Not a lot. Reginald told me the symbols on it were old, older than those found in Sumerian ruins. I wonder if it's as old as Azriel's bottle, maybe older. Although I think differently today, we concluded the woman may have been an adventurer or archaeologist. Or something else. The question came into her involvements in the killings."

Craig eyed the clock on the wall and saw it was a quarter to midnight. Khan wasn't ready to slow down; he stood and walked towards a bookshelf, fingered the spine of one, and turned back towards his host and said, "That is until nearly a century later when I saw her again."

"The search for my immortality's cure had taken me around the world three times in those many years. Two world wars each delayed me, including a time when Adolf Hitler's men captured me in Poland. I'd been imprisoned for a few years while his scientists studied my affliction. I could have escaped sooner, but part of me thought they might succeed in finding a cure. They didn't, and when the Allies released me, I had the devil of a time destroying all evidence of the research. But that's another story.

"In 1971, my journey took me to Yorkshire. Once again murders were taking place, and yes, you can guess the name. The police believe it was a man named Peter Coonan, also known as Peter William Sutcliffe. The press came up with the name of The Yorkshire Ripper. If there's one thing I learned while watching human civilisation. Their imaginations have declined since the heady heights achieved in the 1700s to 1930. They can think of nothing original and have to rip - pardon the pun - names from the past.

"Such an incredible coincidence though. The murdered women were prostitutes again. Coonan used their services regularly, it seems, but I know he wasn't the only one.

"One night, while walking the streets to clear my head, I came across another mugging. Can you imagine my sense of déjà vu? The screams, the scuffling in the foggy darkness, the sickly sound of a blade penetrating flesh. Muggings in English towns are common, particularly around Liverpool and Leeds. I would have let it pass if a turning car's headlights hadn't shone upon the scene.

"There she was! Just as lovely a picture as I remembered. Long, black, wavy hair in a style common to the time. Her high cheek-bones and smooth skin. The clothes were different. In fact, she wore something like leggings and a long coat. As the headlights passed, she glanced in my direction and the recognition upon her face told me everything.

"I shouted, but she had already dropped the person to the ground and run in the opposite direction. The thrill of the chase excited me nearly as much as my other thoughts. The woman had not aged a day since I grappled with her in 1888. Amazing. Was she immortal too?

"Pausing long enough to ensure the victim was indeed dead, I dashed after the lady, following her echoing footsteps through the foggy streets. Her feet flew fast, tapping quick staccato steps in time with her hurried breathing. My heart hammered too as I gained ground.

"It took me five blocks before I dared reach my finger

for her collar. I felt her hair graze my hand, but I missed. All I grabbed was her long leather jacket as she escaped into the darkness like a will-o'-the-wisp.

"Despite my failure, I couldn't help smiling. Yes, the woman had vanished again, but I knew I wasn't alone in the world. But such a shame. Why did I share my immortality with a soulless killer of victims in the dark alleys of England?

"The police were already at the murder scene when I returned. One of them stopped me upon sight, asking my name and identification. Rather than create suspicion, I answered their questions. Yes, I did hear something. Running in the opposite direction. No, it looked like a woman. I gave her details but otherwise kept myself out of the picture as much as possible. If the police were looking for her, perhaps they may lead me to her and I could learn the secret of her immortality. Had she stolen the item I wanted from Mr Darling nearly a century ago? If so, I needed it, and any help would prove valuable.

"Nothing came of it though. Sutcliffe came out. Something tells me he's just a confessor. Yes, he'd been involved with the women murdered by the 'Yorkshire Ripper', but he would have confessed to anything, and he still does today. What I haven't figured out is how he knows so much when I'm certain that woman is the killer."

Craig's eyelids threatened to collapse and surrender his eyeballs from their sockets. The dry redness on the edges stung, and his head hurt from fatigue. But his mind ticked. "How do you know the woman killed the women?"

Khan's right eyebrow raised as he looked upward. Craig wondered if Khan had even considered that question before.

"My point of asking," Craig explained, "is her appearance could be circumstantial evidence. If you see a bloody knife next to a dead man, you can't assume the knife killed him; it might be his enemy's blood on the blade."

Khan shook his head in disagreement. "There is more, my friend. Just a week ago, here, in Statton, I learned more. You may be aware of the media's reports of recent murders in this city?"

Craig nodded, thinking of Brianna's work and their discussion the other day. He glanced at his watch.

"I will not keep you too much longer, Craig," Khan promised. "On this particular night, I was in your nightclub district, for my pure pleasure this time." He took a breath allowed a smile. "I'm immortal, you know. Not dead. I had left the nightclub on Bank Street when I chanced to see one of the dancers leave her workplace. My eye was upon her when something else caught my attention. Another man was following her. I knew of the killings and thought I might be of assistance. But I hung back too, in case it was pure coincidence, or circumstantial as you suggest. Then something occurred to me. The man, who was dressed in a long leather jacket, didn't have the stiff-hipped walk of a man. Instead, the person's hips swayed like one of those Victoria's Secret models one sees strutting the catwalk. The first woman walked through an alley, probably as a shortcut, or maybe she intended to escape her pursuer.

"A bus drove by then, obscuring my vision for a second, and when it was gone, the stalker had vanished too. So I ran towards the alley, and there I heard a commotion from the alley. Stabbing sounds, the ripping of the blade's withdrawal from the flesh, struggling against the vacuum. A man shouted, two women screamed. Struggles. Then a sound like something spitting in anger, a large cat perhaps. Another scream.

"When I reached the source of the calamity, it had all finished. My immortal heart could have stopped. There, before me, she stood, wiping her blade upon the man's corpse. Nearby lay the female dancer's body, legs spread in a disgusting pose. But that's when I saw the oddest thing. The female assassin glimpsed the woman's body and hurried closer. A curious wailing left her open mouth, and I fancy sobs reached my ears. I've never seen a person wantonly kill another and mourn over their victim.

"In a sudden fit, the killer convulsed. Her back arched as though electricity coursed through the spine and a guttural moan left her throat. The seizures continued, contorting her body and causing her to jump back in the shadows. Whatever the mad fit, I hung back and waited. Perhaps I should have moved then. The lights and darkness created strange shapes on the walls that awoke a primal fear inside me. These things were best seen from a distance.

"At last, the scene quietened, and I watched the lady emerge from the shadows. Craig, it was strangely terrifying, even for me, but I managed to summon the will to step in front of her, barring her exit.

"Upon seeing me, she stopped still, a look of fright

upon her face. This amused me and I couldn't stop the laughter. How arrogant I was, and foolish. I lost my opportunity.

"In a flash, she leapt and grabbed the uneven brickwork, scaling towards the top. I jumped, tapping her ankle enough to jar her from her handholds. Anyone else would have fallen in an ungraceful heap, but not this woman. She landed on her feet better than a cat, even kicking me in the face, before running out the alley. The blow surprised me. By the time I recovered, she had disappeared."

Khan relaxed back in the chair and gazed at Craig who was fighting hard against sleep. Oblivious to his host's condition, Khan cleared his throat. "The reason I came to you, Craig, is I require your help."

"In finding your girlfriend?" Craig grinned, attempting to stifle a yawn and failing miserably, but his host remained still as an Easter Island statue, only fleshier, and stared.

After a moment, the immortal broke his stare, and his baritone voice filled the room. "Fatigue has its claws in you, my friend, and I fear I have imposed upon your time. But I must know. Will you help me find this killer?"

Chapter 14

Meanwhile, where the city's traffic had quietened, a lone figure glided through the shadows. He walked with the stealth of a rodent. Despite the quiet and solitude, the homeless man's pricked his ears for danger. Few people saw the neighbourhood the way he did. Every nook, every crack in the pavement. Henry identified them all better than the back of his hand - if that was possible. Nothing escaped his attention.

Every day he wandered these streets fixing up these things. He hated change. Stray litter on the streets always upset him. He'd grumble or mutter about it as he bent to pick it up with a dirty hand and stuff it in his canvas bag.

There was another one now. His eyes, as keen at night as in the day, had spied a cigarette butt. Henry bent forward to pick up the cigarette butt. Ah! Marlboro Red.

Henry could identify thirty-eight unique cigarette brands and four cigar types by smell.

Cigars were rarer. Only a few people smoked them here, but he knew them now. He knew them all after fifty years of collecting rubbish from the streets.

Thirty years ago, Henry's sister Claudia took him to visit the doctor. And she told him about Henry's obsession: collecting rubbish, collecting and arranging it. Whenever she moved it, he always reacted angrily.

The doctor asked him questions, made him look at pictures. He said Henry was an Artistic Sad Ant. Henry wasn't sure why the doctor called him that when he just liked order. Things had their place, their harmony. He once read the Chinese invented Feng Shui - the art of placing items in a home to improve the energy. To Henry, his cleaning of trash from the streets was like that. He created order in the streets that no one else seemed to care about. He did not understand why. Didn't they like their streets clean and tidy? The rubbish trucks took the rubbish to the tip. And Henry picked up the things they missed.

Henry didn't live with his sister anymore. She told him he couldn't keep storing beer bottles under the house where he loved collecting them. But he did it because he loved how the sunlight refracted through the glass. It created brown light and glinted from the bottles' necks.

It reminded him of the sparkly crystals and stickers his mother used to hang around the house. Claudia hated those too and threw them away the day their mother died. Henry had fought with her over that. He even visited the rubbish bin to re-collect them and hid them in his room. But there was no room under the bed. He had so much rubbish under it that the bed's feet couldn't touch the floor.

At last, after so many years of enduring Henry's habits, Claudia flipped. She shouted and yelled at him. Henry hated loud noises and covered his ears. He ran and hid. Claudia often yelled at him, but this time was worse. She used words starting with F and S. Even a C word. They were naughty words. His mother used to hate naughty words and had even spanked him when he repeated one. Claudia would be in so much trouble if their Mum had heard her say that. He told her. But Claudia punched him for it. Hard. So he ran away, lived on the streets, and collected his treasures in the old dirty canvas bag with the CSR logo on it.

But it hadn't always been fun on the streets. Two months ago, he started hearing a voice in his head. It was soon after he found the knife, the sharp one that nicked him. And he bled. But he used the old hanky an even older man had dropped to staunch the flow. The bleeding soon stopped, but the cut had hurt worse than a paper cut. Worse than Claudia's hand slapping his face.

The blade sang to him an old nursery rhyme about oranges and lemons. His mother used to sing it to him before she died. Henry loved the knife for that. For a short time, it was as if his mother was with him. Then the other one came. The one with the hard-to-say name. Henry didn't like him. He scared Henry.

At first, he seemed nice because he made the knife sing to him through the cut. But then the singing changed. The words were different. They talked about killing women. Henry didn't hate women, but the bad man did. In particular, the man wanted Henry to kill certain women. He said it had something to do with their blood. The Bad Man led Henry to one of those places where women take their clothes off for men who give them money. Henry liked those girls. They were always nice to him. One even took him to Hungry Jacks and bought him a hamburger meal there. Stacy was her name. Bad Man wanted Henry to kill Stacy. But Henry said NO. That was not manners.

Bad Man yelled at Henry for that. He was angry. He told Henry he was a useless piece of a Bad Word. And he kept shouting in Henry's head, which made Henry sad.

But Henry tried a new trick. He sang another rhyme about Baa Baa Black Sheep to drown out the other song. Bad Man hated that and left his head, saying he couldn't work with such a simple mind.

The Bad Man may have left, but the knife blade still sang to Henry. It sang of oranges and lemons, and it sang about killing too. Even when Henry held his hands over his ears. He thought hiding the blade would do it. That's what you did with things you didn't want. Claudia often said that, but Henry didn't want to throw away his comics, his bottles and other treasures. All he wanted to throw away was the knife. So he hid it in the rubbish tin.

Such a silly place. The rubbish men didn't empty it in time. Toomey from the riverbank took it first. He found it while hunting for Chinese food. It smelled of cabbage and everything else the Chinese ate in their restaurants, but that's not what Toomey found there.

Henry felt bad about Toomey finding the knife because he used to like Toomey. But he didn't like him so much since Henry cut himself on the knife while foraging through the bin. The Bad Icky Feeling felt Henry, the same kind as when he accidentally pushed Claudia over when they were children and she had hurt herself. Henry didn't mean to do that, nor did he mean to hurt Toomey with the knife.

Toomey turned nasty, and wouldn't bring him comic books anymore, so he couldn't read about Spiderman and Batman. Maybe Toomey knew Henry had put the knife in the bin and thought he did it to hurt him. Henry wasn't sure. But Toomey must have known something because now he called Henry the same names as the Bad Man did.

Toomey must have been bad too. Girls were dying again after he found the knife. Maybe the Bad Man told him to do it too. Henry was certain about that.

Ever since Toomey died in the car accident three weeks ago, the singing started in his head again. And the voice of the Bad Man returned. He sang louder, called Henry new names filled with black and hatred. Henry tried singing his other nursery rhymes, but they didn't work. The Bad Man sang louder. The voice stayed in his head, making it hard for Henry to think straight or do anything. And it came from inside his head. Holding hands over his ears wouldn't work.

And now Henry sat in the alley, crying hot tears like a Big Baby. The voice had stopped for now, but Henry knew the Bad Man sat there, watching and waiting like a monster in the darkness. The quiet time allowed Henry peace.

A sound caught Henry's ear, and his eyes flicked towards it. A shape stood there, one that he knew. Was it Stacy?

"Henry Twiner?" The voice was female, but it wasn't

Stacy who sounded like a Christmas angel. This woman sounded kind but spoke like a mother too.

Henry nodded fast, darting his eyes about for a place of escape.

"There's no need to fear me."

The woman's shape moved in shadow, just a silhouette. Henry could not see her features, but her shape revealed beauty like the dancers from the club, like Stacy. But this woman was proud too. Her confidence was not the show of a stripper. It was the strength of someone else, like the ladies who wore suits in the street.

Henry's mind remained indecisive. Should he run or should he stay? Something told him he was in trouble, but her voice said otherwise.

"I need your help, Henry," the woman said, her voice soothing him.

It's the bitch! Kill her!

Henry started, shocked by the Bad Man's voice. "No!" His scream filled the air. "I won't!"

The woman stopped in her tracks. Her features stayed in the shadow, but something glinted from where her mouth was. "You won't help me, Henry?"

Henry said nothing, covering his ears as the Bad Man shouted more B words in his head.

"You can hear him, can't you, Henry?"

What? Henry's jaw dropped. How did the Super Woman know?

"Is that right, Henry?" The woman's voice dripped like honey laced in salt and made Henry feel calmer. "I can help you. Would you like me to help you?"

Run, you fool! She's going to kill you! The Bad Man's words sounded genuine. Henry had to run. In a flash, he scampered further into the alley. *That's it! Go! Don't let her catch you!*

The woman called after him, but Henry wasn't stopping. Not for her. He had seen how her eyes glowed yellow in the darkness and the flash of white from her mouth. That looked like a long tooth. Two long teeth, like Dracula had in the movie Claudia made him watch on TV as a boy to scare him.

From somewhere behind him, a sliding sound like paper rubbing on the ground reached his ears. What was it? Henry had never heard that before. It came fast, approaching and then overtaking him. Through the corner of his eye, Henry saw the woman's shape pass by like he stood still. Then she stood there in front of him.

Henry ran too fast to stop before he crashed into her arms. He felt her hot grip, her breasts against him. Hot air blew on his throat, and it felt good, made things happen down between his legs like when he was a kid watching movies with a man and woman kissing. The kisses used to make him grow hard enough he poked through the hole in the front of his pyjamas. That used to embarrass him then because his mother said it only grew big if he played with it. And he never played with it. No. That could make him go blind, and Henry liked seeing colours and patterns and things.

"Henry, stop." The woman's voice was gentle, and her hair flowed about him. It felt soft against his cheek. "I know of the demon in your mind. I can help you get rid of it. Do you trust me?"

Henry quit struggling against her tight grip. The woman comforted him like a mother, but she wasn't his mother. And her embrace felt good. But he knew. Looking at her eyes, he saw the golden glow's iridescence. It looked good and relaxed him. But he knew.

"I didn't kill any of them," Henry muttered, his head rocking back and forth. "I promise, I didn't do it. He asked me. But I sang. I stopped his voice. He shouted bad things at-"

"Relax, Henry. I know. Do you want me to stop him for you?" Then he felt the woman's arms rubbing his back, relaxing him. Henry wondered how he could feel that when something else was holding him close.

He sobbed with a slight nod. "I have to die to stop him, don't I?"

"Yes, Henry, but you will go to Heaven and meet your mother," she answered. "I promise it won't hurt."

Soft lips took his mouth, a sliding tongue flicked inside. Henry knew this was a grownup kiss. His first one. And he loved it. Henry liked it so much that he didn't care as the life left his body, not even when he saw the end of a snake's tail through dying eyes.

Chapter 15

Paperwork. Reports. Administrative work. Brianna hated it. Her fingers danced a wonky tango on the computer's keyboard with the faded letters. At each paragraph's end, she stopped to pause, trying to keep her head in order.

On the one hand, she felt good about clearing up the serial killings. She and Gifford had caught the killer with the knife in his hand, so to speak, and although he hadn't confessed, everything worked out. Blood droplets on Toomey's clothing matched the blood of the victims. Toomey hadn't merely found the bodies and come across the discarded knife. Toomey had held the knife and carved the victims himself. But some things didn't add up.

The killings showed a knowledge of human anatomy. Toomey didn't have that knowledge. He hadn't even worked in an abattoir. But maybe he'd picked the know-how up by watching others or talking to someone. Perhaps he was a natural.

As soon as the dental work came back from Dr Kroot, Brianna could match it up to Toomey's teeth and the marks in the human kidneys discarded on the ground at the scenes. Maybe even the-

"Hello, Brianna dear."

Emily's voice made Brianna jump with a start. She turned around, faced the shadowy figure, and sighed. "You scared the crap out of me, Emily. The details of these murders are damn creepy."

"Thank heavens you caught the man," Emily responded. "How are you today?"

Brianna's eye flicked towards the clock. Was that the time already? "I'm in a hurry with this report," she replied. "I need someone else to do it for me, but that's impossible. It has to be me."

"That is a shame." Emily's voice lacked the usual compassion and mirth with which Brianna was familiar. "Is that all that's on your mind, dear?"

Brianna released a sigh and leaned back in her chair. "Why does this remind me of the lectures my mother gave me?"

"I overheard something this morning that disturbed me," Emily responded. "You sounded upset about something, and I want you to explain it to me."

Brianna paused to recall the day's earlier events. Craig had been explaining a few things about the house for when she moved in. Security details. How the house was protected from outside attack. And yes, Brianna was in a mood.

"It's not your," Emily glanced towards Brianna's lower body, " menses, is it?" Emily's tone showed she knew it wasn't, but Brianna answered anyway.

"No." Brianna thought for a moment. "At least, I don't think so."

Brianna glanced towards Emily's shape and jumped, startled, not by what she heard as much as what she saw. Emily's shape appeared thicker, more visible, than before. A white face framed by red hair long enough to flow over her shoulders to her chest regarded Brianna through brown eyes. It was the countenance of a young woman about thirty-two years old with a mouth that looked like it often curled in a smile at the ends. She may have been young, but the eyes reflected centuries of experience. The eyes and mouth weren't smiling so much now though.

"Then what is it?" Emily asked. Her voice carried a sterner tone. "Why are you grumpier than two Scotsmen fighting over a penny?"

Brianna was normally a strong woman herself and had physically fought for her worth, but Emily's tone was motherly enough to unearth Brianna's words. "Craig's keeping secrets from me, isn't he?"

Emily's voice remained strict. "What man doesn't? He has a right to be himself as much as you deserve to be yourself." Then the spirit hesitated. "What kind of secrets are we talking about?"

"Do you remember three weeks ago when I came over after we caught the serial killer?"

Emily nodded. "You were one shaken lass and needed that good -" She paused, giving a wink.

Stunned that Emily knew about her and Craig's lovemaking session that followed that night, Brianna paused. "You don't stand there watching, do you? Do other spirits do the same?"

Emily shook her head with a slight grin. "No, we have better things to do. But for all three innings, you were both loud." Brianna's mouth dropped open in surprise for a second before transforming into a smile. "But," Emily said, waggling a finger at Brianna. "You're avoiding the story. What happened?"

"Do you mean our lovemaking?"

"No!" Emily responded, her countenance fighting back a laugh. "You were talking about Craig's secrets and somehow brought up the lovemaking yourself. What secret?"

"Correction," Brianna answered in a firm, authoritative voice - the kind only a police officer can muster. "You suggested I needed it back then. I wanted to talk about what happened after that."

A cheeky smirk crossed Emily's face. "Yes, I did, didn't I? What secrets do you think Craig is keeping from you? I'll tell you if you're right."

Brianna's eyebrow raised. Did that mean Emily might be keeping something from Brianna too? She asked anyway. "The other night, he called me Celina. Is there something I should know about her?"

Emily raised a hand to her mouth, covering it. "Oh, dear. Did he?" The Scottish spirit turned away, muttering to herself. "Oh, that's not good. The poor dear."

Brianna reached out to touch Emily's shoulder but it passed through the ghost. "Hey, stay here, Emily. Who is this woman? Do I need to worry about her?"

The concerned look on Emily's face faded as she faced Brianna again. "Craig hasn't told you about Celina before?"

Brianna shook her head and Emily appeared lost in memories, a thoughtful gaze plastered across her face.

"On New Years Eve of 1999, Craig first met Celina. She used to be a dancer and they met while both working at the same party for the Royal Perth Yacht Club. This was the night people expected planes to fall out of the sky and computers to blow up or something because of the Y2K bug. You remember that, I expect. I liked her even though I knew she wasn't right for the lad. But he loved her terribly." Emily shook her head and sighed.

"Without all the details, they soon fell in love and moved in together. Craig thought it a good thing because they both worked as entertainers. He had his psychic ability then too, but he persisted in using other parlour tricks with his magic and mentalism. On some occasions, he also worked as a private investigator, but that's beside the point. The two of them soon moved in together and even started a mind-reading act between them. Craig loved showing her new tricks. I think it was her laugh and her innocence when they worked. Then two years later, she gave him the news. He loved hearing it. A baby! His baby.

"And when the little girl was born, even I fell under her enchantment. She was so gorgeous, the perfect composite of her Dad and Mum. Julia, they called her, and she had some of Craig's innate abilities. Most children do, but her ability to see me was well-developed. The little girl could see spirits and always smiled whenever she saw me."

Emily paused and drew a breath as though about to release a sigh in the memory's wake.

Brianna had sat back from the computer to listen, her face a picture of thought and realisation. "What happened to them? Does Craig still see them?"

Emily's features reflected a phantasmic tear that glistened from the office light. She wiped it. "They died, Brianna. About this time eight years ago, just shy of the little girl turning seven months. They died in a traffic accident on Mount Lucrapana. The roads are so twisty there, and the corners are blind. Celina had been visiting her mother with Julia and was on the way home when something made her swerve the car. No one knows what it was. Perhaps a kangaroo or a wallaby on the road. The car broke through the rails." Emily's voice trailed away.

Tears were streaming down Brianna's face by the time Emily finished her tale. Sniffling, she wiped her face and cleared her nose with a tissue. "Was Craig there?"

"No," Emily replied. "And that's one of the reasons he blames himself. It was Celina's car, and she never serviced it. Before she drove the little girl up there, Craig had suggested she take his car which he always looked after. He was in Brisbane for a show and didn't need his car. Craig was beside himself when he heard the news. The two of them had argued about something, nothing important, but they never kissed and made up. He had stormed off to the airport to catch his flight. He'd kissed Julia goodbye, but neglected Celina. The news arrived on his phone as he was about to walk on stage. You should have seen his face, Brianna. I have never seen a man's heart break as his did. I, too, wish I could have been there. Perhaps I could have saved the little bairn."

Brianna remained quiet, looking at the computer screen. The words on its screen no longer carried meaning as she imagined the scene. "I feel so bad now," she admitted. "That's terrible! I -"

Emily shook her head, hugging Brianna. "None of us can afford to leave our loved ones while angry. I don't know why we do that." After a moment, the Scottish lady moved back to regard the detective. "He visits the cemetery on their birthdays and the anniversary of their death. If you noticed he turns secretive or quiet, that's when he's torturing himself."

"Tony Gifford told me Craig was admitted to the mental hospital," Brianna said. "Is that true?"

Emily's features fired to life with anger. "That little man is lucky to be alive. No, it's not true. Not completely, anyway. Craig admitted himself a year later, but only as part of a case; an unrelated case."

Both women, the body and the spirit, remained silent. One pondered the story while the other regarded her with a thoughtful gaze.

"Do you have any other concerns about Craig's secrets?" Emily wondered.

Brianna shook her head and wiped away a stray tear. "No, not at all. I think Craig's talking in his sleep to Celina. That and the appointment he's taking with an attractive-looking brunette today built up on me."

"Oh, yes," Emily responded with a nod. "I can understand that. But you have nothing to fear. Craig is only interested in you, dear. He wouldn't have cooked for you, otherwise."

"I know. It's not like me to feel jealous."

Emily's eyebrow raised. "It's not?"

Chapter 16

Craig was sitting in his home office, a room accessible by a different entrance, when the doorbell buzzed. Memories of the Brianna's strange words and actions that morning disappeared from his mind at its sound. He needed to keep a clear head with clients, especially when they paid healthy fees for his psychic services.

His chin almost hit the ground upon seeing the vision of feminine beauty waiting for him to answer. Sex on legs was the first thought to cross his mind, followed by Keep Cool. The woman reminded him of classic beauty; the kind seen in paintings of classic antiquity; a mixture of exotic sensuality and modern sophistication. Deep brown eyes regarded him with mild curiosity while soft-looking lips curled at one end with knowing amusement. As quickly as they curled, they straightened. "Mr Ramsey?"

Craig nodded. "Melody Kostas?" He offered his hand which she took in a grip that revealed nothing to his psychic senses. It was as though she shook hands with many men but would give nothing away about her thoughts or intentions. A business person's touch. Craig searched Melody's eyes. Where most people would look away, Melody's eyes held confidence and power, and never wavered. Something else appeared too, but as soon as Craig focused, it vanished without a sign. "Come in," he answered, standing aside to allow her entry.

Melody's body described its own rhythm as a picture of grace. Her absorbent eyes surveyed the office with a cursory sweep. Most times, new clients would eye the photos on the office wall, especially the one of a younger Craig standing with Oprah and Mel Gibson. While Melody's gaze paused on these photos, they did so with a casual interest. Her eyes seemed to take in the exits: the door through which she entered, and the other that was closed but could open to the main house. Her gaze shifted towards the comfortable-looking couch to the side and lingered.

Craig diverted his gaze from Melody's shapely derriere to her eyes when she looked from the couch to him. "Would you like something to drink?" Had she noticed his eyes?

Melody assented with a nod.

"Tea? Coffee?" *Me?* Craig chided himself for the naughty thought, knowing he was happy already. But it was a delicious thought.

"Tea, please," Melody responded, seating herself on another chair. "Milk, no sugar."

Craig poured black tea from a teapot he'd made fresh a minute before Melody's arrival. As he handed it to Melody with a saucer, her eyes flicked towards his.

"Mr Ramsey, you asked if I wanted tea or coffee, yet you had tea freshly made..." Craig smiled, suppressing the huge cocky grin he wanted to release. "How did you know?"

Craig shrugged as he sat opposite her at his desk. "Some things I'm lucky with, I guess."

"How often do you get... lucky?"

Redness crept up Craig's neck from under his collar. The desk hid other bodily reactions, for which Craig felt thankful. His chest hammered like a baby with a new toy as his mind raced to change the subject. Melody's eyes smiled at Craig's silence. "Forgive me. That came out the wrong way. How lucky do you get?"

Craig shook his head, fighting to remain professional. He cleared his throat. "How can I help you, Melody?"

Melody's cheeky smile wavered. "Yes, the reason for our appointment. I came across your card through my house mate, Delta." Melody's voice sank in volume, her gaze clouding. "She's -"

"I know about Delta," Craig answered, offering a box of tissues from his desk. "The dancer, right?"

Melody nodded, dabbing her face with the tissues. "It's been nearly a month since she died. That homeless man."

Craig allowed a compassionate expression to cross his face, but behind them his business mind ticked away. From when he shook Melody's hand, he realised she was a woman of means. He didn't know how, but money was no object for her. The labels on her clothing showed she wore the latest fashions, but she also dressed for power. Fingers manicured by a professional told him that Melody was a person who took pains with details, but she could easily delegate menial tasks to others. "You own the club Delta worked at, right?"

"Yes! How did you -?" Melody's surprise burst through her voice. For a moment, she regarded Craig with a sceptical but wondering look. "Delta was a client of yours, wasn't she? That's how she had your card. Did she tell you about me?"

"That's not important," Craig replied. "Let's cut to the chase. You want to know about your dreams?"

A surprised expression crossed Melody's face, dampened by another as though she expected it. Curious, thought Craig, but he took it in stride by allowing the silence to absorb.

"Yes, Mr Ramsey- ("Craig.") I'm sorry, Craig." She paused. "Before Delta... Before she passed, I had dreams of a man." Melody waited, took another sip of her tea and shook her head at a biscuit Craig offered. "It wasn't any particular man, but he returns to my dreams often. Sometimes I am stalking him, following him across the world. The streets are always dark, and most times very few people walk them, but not always. Other times, he is following me or someone else. He talks like he knows me, and although he seems familiar in my dreams, I don't know who he is."

Craig looked across steepled fingers at his client. On the outside, he showed patient and empathetic understanding through his listening posture. Inside, he felt rumbles of shock tightening his stomach. Could it be? "How often have you had these dreams?" As the word left his lips, Craig realised a hint of foreboding overshadowed his question.

"They started four months ago," Melody responded. "At first, they were once a week, then every two or three nights. Now they happen every night. But there was a point where they stopped for a couple of weeks before resuming three nights ago."

Craig leaned back in his chair for a moment, his brow furrowed. "You mentioned the man and said he wasn't any particular man. Does his appearance change or does he look like anyone you know?"

Melody frowned, her eyes switching to the side. "This is the strange thing. Sometimes he looks different, as though he's another man, but the same. His voice is always the same."

Craig nodded. Should he ask the next question? Probably not. But it begged investigation by a different means.

"Melody, have you undergone hypnosis before?"

She shook her head and lifted a hand to brush aside a strand of black hair from her face. "No, is it real?"

Craig nodded. "Yes, it is real. Just as," he nearly said Delta's name, "the others told you. I use several techniques and none of them require needles or watches." Craig pointed towards the corner. "I can video it if you want to watch later too."

She paused as she regarded the nearby camera. "That would be interesting to watch later."

Was that the hint of a smile and a cocked eyebrow? He couldn't be sure, but again Craig felt the erotic energy radiating from Melody's body. There was something about the way his client moved on the couch, settling herself for induction. Never had he felt like this before. The sensation in the pit of his stomach brought quivers below to which his body responded further. Sexual arousal. What the hell?

Craig turned around to look at his desk, took a deep breath and exhaled in a quiet stream. All the time, he told himself it wasn't right. What was going on? What was he doing?

Then he spied the video camera. He reached up, flicked its switch, and turned to see Melody looking back from the couch. She was in a supine position upon it, looking back at him with her soft, dark chocolate eyes, which looked deep as the oceans, mesmerising. Hypnosis! Was she hypnotising him?

He closed his eyes, focused within, and -

"Mr Ramsey, what are you doing?"

Craig allowed his eyes to open and saw her there. Yes, Melody still looked as beautiful and seductive as before, but he felt nothing now. "Just clearing energy before I start with the hypnotic regression," he explained, sitting down near her. He noticed, only by virtue of being a red-blooded male, her breasts pushing up against her top as she lay there. But that was all. No overwhelming sexual desires. Interesting, Craig thought, noting to himself he would look into this. "Have you undergone hypnosis before?"

Melody shook her head. "Not that I remember."

"Okay. The best I can describe what's about to happen to you is this. I will ask you to close your eyes and guide you into your subconscious. We will probably go back into your childhood. You may not remember much when you awaken afterwards, but you will wake feeling refreshed and better than you were before you arrived." Melody nodded, gazing up towards him. Craig felt another wave of desire cross him, but he countered with another mental block. Was Melody aware she possessed some degree of psychic ability that allowed her to charm others? It was more than physical although she held a perfect score there too.

"This is a team effort between you and me," Craig added. "I won't make any suggestions against your values or morals." He paused, wondering what they were. "But if you were, you would awaken immediately and leave the hypnotic state. Okay?"

Melody nodded again, and Craig began the hypnotic induction.

Craig directed Melody through the beginning steps, asking her to close her eyes and concentrate on her breathing. Upon seeing her steady breathing in his rhythm, he spoke again. "As I count from fifty down to one, you will feel yourself relaxing. The more you breathe, the more you will relax, and the more you relax, the better you will feel... and the closer I am to the end, the closer to a deep relaxed state you will be. Nod your agreement."

Melody did.

"Fifty... forty-nine... forty-eight...."

Craig counted down, with an occasional stop to check her progress.

"Five... four... You're so relaxed. Three. Two. One."

He spoke the last one with finality. "You're now in a dark room, lit only by two candles. It's warm here, relaxing, and you're safe. Ahead of you is a door, a large door made of wood with a big iron door knob. Do you see it?"

She gave an imperceptible nod.

"Behind this door are your memories. This is the place you keep them safe so you can look at them any time you wish. Are you ready?"

Melody remained still. Fifteen seconds ticked on the clock sitting on Craig's office wall. His eyes flicked towards Melody's collarbone, which was visible above her top. The skin was smooth and flawless with a tint of tan. Attractive, yes, but Craig noted he no longer felt sexual signals from her. Nothing tempted him. What had happened earlier? Then Melody took a deep breath, her chest expanding, and she nodded. She was ready.

"That's good, Melody. Reach out, grab the knob, and turn it."

Melody, her eyes still closed, lifted her hand, reaching out with her long, graceful fingers and gripped what must have been a large door knob in her imagination. The fingers seemed to touch it lovingly, as though caressing it, or having second thoughts before tugging the door open. Craig smiled at this and continued.

"As you look through the open door, Melody, you will see a corridor filled with paintings. Pictures of significant times in your life. Allow yourself to talk through the hall and look at them. When you find one that relates to your dreams, tell me."

Craig waited, watching Melody with trained eyes. Her eyeballs moved under her eyelids which barely fluttered. Occasionally, her face changed as though stopping to admire certain pictures. At last, Melody stopped. Her arms lifted to hug closer to her. Her breath came quicker.

"The painting is only a representation," Craig reassured her. "It's not real; just a hologram or artificial recreation of what your saw and heard. You are safe. Please nod if you have found the one related to the dream."

"There are many paintings," she murmured. "Different paintings. One for each time I dreamed."

"I see," Craig replied, his voice smooth as silk and warm as though fresh from the sun. "Look beside the picture and you will see a button. See it?"

"Yes."

"Press it and you will find yourself inside the painting. You are safe there and able to see it as a third person." Craig paused and gauged Melody's reactions. She appeared relaxed. Confident. "Press it when you're ready."

Without a pause, Melody's finger reached upward and pressed an invisible button.

"You're now inside your memory, Melody. Let's see what we can find."

***

Melody's memories came in fragments. An air of

confidence washed over. She hadn't felt like this in a long time.

Her clothes were different. Old. Leather covered her, tailored to match her body's contours, and decorated her body with its tanned hues. A cape, black as night, draped from her shoulders reaching her knees. A charged scent filled the air, the metallic aroma of blood. She hated it but something told her to follow it. Instinct drove her forward through the drifting pea soup.

The scratching and rustling of the nocturnal drifted to her ear: a cat foraging for food; its meal, a scrawny flea-bitten rat, waited and listened with its nose twitching in the air. From deeper in the fog, she heard something else: the footfalls of heeled boots. The person's gait was steady, confident as though it owned the night. But she heard more. Children, from a gang, she believed. Unlike the children of the privileged, the street urchins of this area showed no fear of the night. Dangers may lurk in the darkness, but it hid the children too. They learned to use that advantage.

Memories of children, her own, perhaps, flashed through her mind. But the images remained faded as though aged by time. Memories so old, they could be dreams.

A shadow flitted past. Tall, dark, and malevolent. A hunter's instinct rose in Melody's chest, urging her heartbeat to quicken and pump blood hard as she hurried after it. She must find it, catch it.

Something rocked Melody as though the ground shifted under her feet. But nothing else moved. Dizziness overcame her. Pitching forward, she caught herself and dropped to one knee while the world stopped its rocking. She swallowed back nausea, took another breath and opened her eyes.

Everything had changed.

Yes, she was on a dark street again, but this was different. The buildings were cleaner, newer, with fresher bricks and mortar. Some were made of different materials with new designs. Less grime covered them, replaced by writing and messages by some illiterate. She saw a symbol: three lines crossing like a sloppy triangle or rough letter A inside a circle. They represented a Proudhon quotation: Anarchy is the mother of Order. Other painted scrawling stood out too.

A sound attracted her attention. She turned and saw two black youths spraying a brick wall. The whites of their eyes seemed to glow from beneath their hooded heads. The nearest one turned his head towards her, revealing a teenager's face filled with acne and scarring. He scrunched his eyebrows at Melody, decided she posed no threat, and turned back to his work.

Melody didn't know her mission. But her feet did, and they carried her down the street.

The familiar scent wafted to her sensitive nostrils again. And two words blazed in Melody's mind. Another one.

Melody didn't know what "another one" meant. But she hurried, following the smell carried by the salty ocean breeze. She compared herself to a dog chasing a car. Something in her mind told her, but she didn't know what it was.

A flash of black. Two shining, red eyes that blazed like fire appeared from within it. The shape laughed and disappeared around the corner into the darkness.

Melody reached the corner and peered through the alleyway's gloom. Trained fingers reached inside her long flowing jacket and touched the hilt of her weapon. And her nostrils flared as she sucked in air to catch the scent. He was here. He was always close by. Slowly, she slid the dagger from its scabbard with a gentle sound that her ears alone heard. But it still sounded loud.

She ducked before she heard the blade whistle past her ear. Instinct guided her. The offending blade clunked against hers which she lifted to block. Melody punched outward with her free hand and connected with something soft and warm. A grunt came from it. Melody's attacker stabbed again in her direction. Missed. But she felt the metal's cold kiss. By the time the attacker pulled the blade back, she rolled to the side.

Laughter in the darkness.

With her heart bashing against her rib cage, Melody rolled backward on the hard ground towards the open. The alleyway was a dead end with no exits. Her prey was trapped inside without even a fire exit to climb. Running footsteps from behind distracted Melody. She spun to face them and recognised the graffiti artists from earlier.

"Sirena," the acidic and familiar voice laughed from the darkness. "You're slow in your old age."

The words meant nothing to Melody, but the voice was right. She knew it.

The garbage can fell beside her with a loud thump. Its lid fell near her foot. Without looking, she jumped forward towards the alley, her dagger held ready for an overhead thrust that never arrived. The alleyway seemed to yawn with boredom. Would she enter the alley and risk attack from the unseen, or would she wait here like a coward until sunrise?

After so many years, she still held many more years in abundance. But the chase had taken so long.

Melody picked up the tin garbage lid and held its handle. It was thin but would serve as a shield of sorts. It would end tonight, she decided.

The darkness swallowed Melody, and her eyes readjusted to the murky gloom. Bold steps carried her forward. Her eyes peered past the bin lid, flicking side to side to survey the shadows. All noise disappeared, save for the traffic sounds from blocks away. Melody's fingers gripped the hilt, practised from years of training, years of experience.

He rushed upon her from an apparently innocent place, expected but not. Ancient steel flashed towards her with a snake's speed, crying as it clashed with her own response. The clamour of steel bashing and sliding away, ringing through the night, drowned the Demon's laughter.

Then he disappeared.

Breathing hard, Melody shifted her gaze left to right. "Where are you, coward?"

Instinct saved Melody, shifting her to the left as the Demon's knife stabbed where her head was half a moment earlier. Her arm swung backward and the garbage tin lid clanged. A harsh grunt. She turned to see him. A shadowy figure with two fiery eyes filled with insane hatred. The head shook itself, clearing its thoughts, before the creature lunged for her.

Melody jumped, parting her legs like scissors as the Demon passed below her. At her leap's apex, she twisted, somersaulting while slicing through the air with her long dagger. It connected with the Demon's shoulder. He roared a mixture of pain, rage and surprise.

Whirling to face her, the Demon lashed with his blade. Melody uttered a cry as she landed on uneven ground. If her stance had been better, the blade would have killed her. But she landed on something loose; it moved, twisting her ankle, so she fell, and the blade whistled harmlessly above her.

Melody's legs struggled to find a steady stance. They wobbled, and she fell. The garbage lid rolled away. Pain lanced through her neck and the base of her skull.

Blackness overcame her.

For how long unconsciousness held her in its sweet state of slumber, Melody did not know. But when she awoke, the alleyway's dank urine-stinking walls were gone. A soft, warm bed replaced the hard, damp alley's ground, and soft sunlight drifted through an open window; tiny specks of dust dancing in the beams like a dandelion's seeds do in the wind.

The bed's mattress was firm, comfortable and relaxing. A gentle moan escaped her lips as she stretched her limbs to their fullest extent. How long had it been since she last slept so well? She closed her eyes in drowsy bliss and wrapped herself back in the man's arms.

Man? Her eyes, which she had closed for only a second, popped open with surprise. With a cry, she jumped back, pushed the sleeping man's arms away from her. The man's face remained placid in sleep undisturbed by her motion. He moaned gently and turned his back to her.

Who was this man? Then she realised she was as naked as the stranger. But who was he? Had they-?

Her long fingers felt down between her legs until they found the sticky residue. A shocked expression crossed her face.

They had. But who was this man?

Spying clothes nearby, she scooped them up and hurried to what looked like the bathroom. The decor resembled a motel room, an expensive one. But she couldn't remember arriving here. And when she looked in the mirror, another stranger's face stared back at her in shock.

Who am I? What's my name?

Although the clothes she held were a woman's garments, she didn't recognise them. They weren't the stranger's clothes, and she doubted he was a drag queen. His sticky seed dribbling down her legs confirmed that. Her breathing came to her in hurried gulps as she slipped into the clothes.

A shriek escaped her mouth upon looking in the mirror again.

The man must have been light on his feet. There he was behind her. He jumped back in surprise at her scream, hands held up with palms towards her as he backed off.

"Hey! It's okay. I didn't mean to scare you." His voice calmed her with words of baritone sweetness.

Instinct told her to leave now. Go. Now.

So, she did, leaving a bemused stranger behind whose name she still didn't know. And it wasn't until she was in the street that she realised something else. What was her name?

Realising she held a wallet in her pocket, she reached in and took it out. Cash, at least one thousand dollars, sat inside it. Recalling the past fifteen minutes, she wondered how she got it. Then she saw something else inside: three or four business cards. Each had her photograph on them so she looked closer. Oh! The photos differed on each card, but they each matched the lady who looked back from her reflection earlier. Although each card offered a different service, the name was the same.

MELODY KOSTAS

So that's who she was.

***

Craig drew Melody from her hypnotic regression. His mind clawed at parts Melody had revealed, but he focused on awakening her so she would be rested, relaxed and ready to resume her day. At last, Melody's eyes flickered open. She looked about her, recognition registered in her eyes at Craig's office, and slowly rose from the couch. Craig offered her a glass of water.

"How do you feel?"

His client sipped the water at first before chugging down the glass. "Thirsty. How long did I sleep?"

Craig nodded at the clock as he poured more water for her. "You were in the trance for forty minutes. How much do you remember now?"

Melody swilled some water in her mouth, which must have been dry from the talking during the session. After swallowing, she spoke. "Some things are patchy, like looking through darkness. But what about this creature?"

Craig shrugged. "I've heard and seen strange things in my life, but I don't know about demons. Not a lot, anyway. What about the name you mentioned before? (Craig checked his notes) Does the name Sirena mean anything to you?"

Sitting up on the couch, her feet on the floor, Melody shook her head. "It rings a bell but still means nothing."

Craig jotted down another note and stood. "I've never dealt with many amnesiacs before, but your case is different. Most of them never readjusted to life. You seem to have managed that, despite the memory loss. You're lucky you traced your address to people who knew you. What do you do for work?"

"I own a couple of night clubs," Melody revealed after a pause. "Delta worked at one. Quite a few girls from the club live in the same block I own."

"That must keep you busy."

Melody nodded. "I think it must have."

Craig took Melody's hand, a smile on his lips as he watched her eyes. "You will find further rest helps your memory return. It may come as small flashes; a snippet here and a snippet there. Maybe a gush of memories. But they will come to you in a short time."

Melody's grip was strong. She pulled Craig towards her, lifting her mouth towards his, but he slipped away. A confused expression crossed her face like a cloud over the moon. "I wanted to -"

"Your recovery will be thanks enough." Craig wiped his cheek where Melody's breath had breezed over it. "Apart from your fee," he added.

Melody nodded, shook Craig's hand again with a firm grip, and thanked him before leaving.

Craig shut the door, faced his desk, and sighed. Damn! He had never met a woman like Melody Kostas before, but he recognised dangerous when he held hands with her. The raw energy within her grip, sexual and sensual, seductive yet sincere. It reminded him of something he'd read years before. But he couldn't remember what.

There was one thing of which he could be certain.

Melody Kostas was complicated. Before and after the hypnosis, when he'd shaken her hand, he had searched her mind through his psychometric abilities. With other people, he could catch parts of their memories. Usually they came like a dripping tap. Only Melody's memories were held in a ship's broken hull, some sealed off by doors that slammed shut upon him before he caught more than a glimpse. He never experienced that often. It was as if part of Melody's consciousness hid those things on purpose. But he was certain Melody never intended it. Her memory loss was genuine.

Melody was a woman of means, but Craig doubted running a night club was her only means of income. She had mentioned four business cards. Craig wondered what they advertised. Melody's sexual energy, the way it cornered and corralled him like a snake coiling around its prey, concerned him.

If Craig hadn't committed himself to Brianna, he may have fallen under Melody's spell. He had come close as it was.

Memories of the morning came to him. Brianna's expression when he mentioned the appointment with Melody punched through his consciousness. Brianna wasn't a jealous person. She understood his work, how women were his greatest market for readings, and never expressed insecurity about it. And, yes, he knew Brianna's feelings were strong for him as his were for hers. But it was more than that. If only he had touched her before she left in a bad mood.

One thing was certain. Although nothing happened, a dirty guilt crept across Craig because of what almost happened. He was glad he never pushed for a second session as much as Melody probably needed it. Next time, he might not-

A knock at the house's front door, not his office door, snapped his mind from his concerns. Craig stood and walked around towards the bookshelf which he slid aside on silent rollers to enter his living room. The knocking persisted as he closed the secret door over again and sauntered towards the front entrance. Looking through the peephole, he saw a dark familiar figure and opened it with a grin.

"K-"

A sword's tip appeared at his throat, pressing without cutting his jugular. Khan's narrowed eyes flickered from his deep-set sockets.

"You have ten seconds to tell me why you're consorting with *Jacqueline* the Ripper."

Chapter 17

Craig stared in disbelief into Khan's eyes. This had to be a joke. But, no, the blade was real and its sharp steel was icier than a mother-in-law's kiss.

"Jacqueline the Ripper?"

"It pains me, my friend, but I saw the she-bitch leave your home." Khan's eyes roamed down Craig's length. "You're still alive, so I know you're consorting with her. I can't allow that."

Craig's mind calculated the odds. He knew of Khan's expert swordsmanship, and the immortal had enjoyed centuries of practice. Khan could dispatch Craig with a simple flick of the wrist if he made a wrong move. But he had to-

"Hold it right there."

Craig and Khan turned their heads to see Brianna, her hands holding her pistol with a steady relaxed grip.

"Back off nice and easy, sir." Her voice reflected a cool tone. "That is, if you want to keep your head."

Khan ducked, tossing his cape towards Brianna to cover her vision. With a quick twist, he lashed at her with his sword, aiming for her hand, but Craig kicked the side of Khan's knee. The immortal dropped to the ground and rolled away from them, stopping short of landing in prickly rose bushes. By this time, Brianna had removed Khan's cape from her head and gun hand and pointed it at Khan.

Her voice remained calm. "Stop there. No more warnings."

Khan pulled a rose thorn from his finger, from which blood flowed in a crimson stream, and held it for her to see. "Watch, madame." His face was as still as stone. "You will see how serious I am, and your folly."

Craig, ready to strike, focused on Khan. Brianna gasped upon seeing Khan's small wound heal.

Khan raised a mock-interested brow. "If I can heal so quickly from a rose thorn, how quickly do you think I will heal from your bullets?"

Surprise remained in Brianna's voice, but she fought to maintain her composure. "Craig, who -?"

Khan struck like a snake, but Craig punched first, harder and faster, and hit Khan's wrist. The sword fell to the ground with a harmless ringing as it clattered on the cement flagstones. Meanwhile, Khan's free hand caught Craig unawares and tossed him to the side like a limp dishrag. Craig rolled and felt the breeze of Khan's boot missing his face.

Before the immortal realised it, Brianna's fists punched three times in succession. The blows struck with such force that Khan shook his head in a daze. Brianna moved closer, prepared to deliver the final blow, but Khan recovered too fast. He moved with a dancer's precision, appearing behind her with a knife pressing on her throat's soft skin. Khan's other hand gripped Brianna with a millennium's worth of experience as he backed away.

"It's two hundred years since I killed a woman. Don't force me to break my record."

Craig stood ready, calculating. Brianna was an expert fighter herself. They both looked towards each other, calculating each other's next move.

Craig broke the silence. "Khan, I don't understand. Why are you threatening me in my home?"

From the side, someone whistled aloud. Khan flicked his head towards it, but it was too late. A dark, murky mist appeared in the air, flew straight for Khan's face, and disappeared up his nose.

Aware of Khan's distraction, Brianna reversed Khan's headlock and disarmed him. But the immortal showed no resistance. His body stiffened and appeared to fight itself. He stiffened as though an epileptic fit overtook him, foam appearing at his mouth. Words burbled from his mouth.

Craig flashed forward. "Hurry!" With one hand, Craig released the belt from his trousers. Brianna helped him fasten Khan's hands together after throwing the knife to the side.

Khan continued struggling with himself the whole time. Fear combined with a cocktail of shocked puzzlement and determination flashed in his eyes like a rainbow of thoughts and emotions. His chest expanded with a greedy suck of air before a roar bellowed from his powerful frame.

"What's happening to him?" Brianna fought to hold Khan's feet down while Craig forced pressure on his upper body.

"Tyrone happened."

A puzzled look cross Brianna's face for a second but melted when Khan's boot bashed her shoulder. She caught him again and held him down long enough to cuff his ankles.

Before long, a calm fell over the immortal's face and body. He relaxed, the tension flowing quitting his limbs. Khan's eyes stayed open, but instead of resistance, they reflected quiet patience.

Brianna studied Khan's plain placidness. "What do you mean Tyrone happened?"

Craig stood and lifted his bound friend and led him inside. "I believe there's a misunderstanding from my friend here, Brianna. He believes I've been harbouring someone he's been chasing for just over a century."

Brianna's jaw dropped. "A century? What the hell are you talking about? He can't be any older than thirty-five, if that."

Craig allowed Khan to seat himself in the lounge. At that moment, Emily bustled into the house from outside. "What's happened to Khan?"

Turner appeared too, his coat bulging with something Craig couldn't pick out, but it clanked. He looked at Khan, his eyes opening wide. "Hey! I know that guy! Met him back in 1888."

Once Craig had finished securing Khan's arms further with some rope, he looked at their captive. "Okay, Tyrone, you can let him go now."

Khan's face contorted, twisting about and a moan of displeasure and disgust issued from his mouth. The misty shape that entered him earlier re-emerged from his nose and mouth and ears before heading out the door. Brianna watched as it floated past her and out towards the front door which remained open.

"What is that?"

Craig only smiled, and Turner muttered something about Craig "owing the boy and apology but he knew he wouldn't". A moment later, Tyrone walked through the front door looking jet-lagged.

"Did you see that, Uncle Craig?" he uttered.

Tyrone's adoptive father glanced towards the teenager and offered a wink. "I'm impressed, Tyrone," he replied. "But you still need to go to school." Before Tyrone could reply, Craig turned towards Khan. "Are you ready to talk first before stabbing me with your sword?"

Khan drew a deep breath and shrugged. "It appears I made a mistake, my friend. But what were you doing with her?"

"Friends don't hold swords to our throats." Brianna's words cut the air. "I could have shot you. Who are you?"

Craig held his hands up. "How about everyone calms down?" He looked around at them all. Brianna stood closer to Craig, postured to protect him if Khan jumped again, while the immortal Khan sat bound in the lounge chair. Meanwhile, Tyrone sat opposite from Khan in another chair, and Turner hovered near Emily who was standing silent and watching. "Khan, by your outburst just now, do you believe my client is the woman you are seeking?"

Khan nodded, his eyes narrowed as they flicked over Craig and studied him. "I smell the same fragrance around you as when I first met her over a century ago."

Brianna opened her mouth to say something, but Craig lifted a hand for patience. "Why did you threaten my life?"

At this point, Khan's gaze dropped, but it was for only a moment. "I thought she had weaved a spell around you the way she has others."

"Spell?" Brianna's curiosity refused to stay contained longer.

The look on Brianna's face reminded Craig of the outburst she made that morning. This would make explaining difficult. "As Brianna asked, Khan, what spell? Are we dealing with a witch?"

Khan laughed. "It would not surprise me. But, no, your client is Jacqueline the Ripper. The Ripper was never a male. Everywhere I saw death, she was there, and I'm certain she bewitches men."

Craig shook his head. "That's impossible." But then he thought of how something tickled his sexual urges in the mysterious lady's presence.

Brianna stepped in. "You know what he's talking

about, don't you? Did she do something to you?" Her eyes flicked towards Emily who raised an eyebrow of curiosity.

Craig's mind filled with the memory of meeting with his client. "Let me show you what I learned. It's on video, so we can watch it here."

***

After her consultation with Craig Ramsey, Melody caught a bus from the next street. Although nothing occurred for her on a conscious level, Melody sensed something happening from within her psyche. Memories or random thoughts spun, churning in her mind like turbines. The whole thing gave her a painful headache, and she couldn't shake it.

Outside the bus, the world sauntered past as the vehicle travelled, halting now and then. Before long, Melody's eyes grew heavy and shut as she observed the streets and their lights in the advancing dusk. Her head leaned upon the window.

Meanwhile, thoughts wandered through her subconscious, some pausing to tap her dormant conscious side. Other figments raced by, spinning like howling dervishes as they stirred more images and memories. But to Melody, as she lay in her lucid slumber, they presented themselves as disjointed fragments. Some pieces of Craig Ramsey moved through her. Words uttered in the psychic's voice echoed and tumbled past her. She recognised some as memories, but there were others that weren't. At one stage, Craig Ramsey's clothes looked different, older, as though from the Victorian years in old London. Even his face sported mutton chops curling out from his face. Did he have them before? It hurt too much to think of the session.

Melody fought back the sick daze from her mind. Ringing the bell for the bus to stop, Melody stood and waited for its door to open before stepping out into the humid air.

Summer was approaching. She could smell it in the air. But something else hung there too.

A presence.

At first, the being hung in her mind; a dark shape clad in a long jacket that hung to its feet. It reminded her of the man with the glowing eyes whose knife blade scraped along the brick walls and created sparks that danced in the air. But another appeared too. This one was sleeker, lithe and flowing, a feminine force with a fighter's heart. It approached her, breathing down her neck. All the while, the masculine shape followed behind. Was that a laugh?

She hurried, unaware of the other people in the street who watched her lurching steps, like those of a drunk. One approached, a man with kind eyes, but she pushed him away. He regarded her with a surprised expression. Did he know her? No. It didn't matter. She had to move. The shapes were following her.

The feminine shape was familiar. But from where? It walked along beside her. Occasionally, it regarded her with a focused stare before returning its attention to the creature following them. Was this her guardian? A guardian angel she sensed through her throbbing headache? Perhaps.

You owe me ten shillings,
Say the bells at St. Helen's.

The words echoed through her mind and grew louder with each line. But not loud enough for her to miss the sound of steel dragging on bricks. And the laughter.

As though her eyes had been closed for so long, Melody realised where she was. Her mind cleared like clouds leaving the sun.

She was in an alleyway, facing a looming blackness in which anything could hide unseen. The hammering in her chest accompanied her kick-started panic as she turned and hurried back towards the sounds of the street. People hurried about their business, laughing and enjoying the late night trading, unaware of the woman who scurried out into the open.

Fear of embarrassment stopped Melody from running faster, and she slowed to a walk despite the feeling that someone or something continued watching her from the darkness she had escaped. Although it stayed hidden, she felt its withering gaze and insatiable appetite for her. The foreboding stayed with her, clinging like a bad smell.

I'm coming for you, Sirena.

Melody flinched. That name. Who is Sirena, and why did this creature call her that?

Something hammered insider her mind. It sounded crazy, but did she hear a door's squeaky hinges followed by a faint bump? Whatever happened at Craig Ramsey's place, it couldn't be right. What had he done to her?

Impulse pushed her forward so she half-ran towards the train station ahead. Melody could feel hot breath, pungent with the stench of death, upon the back of her neck. Tingles ran up and down her spine as adrenaline pumped harder. Images pushed their way from her thoughts to invade her consciousness.

The guard at the train station's gate said something. But his words echoed and warbled. Was she stumbling? Her fingers fumbled with her Pay-pass and almost dropped it. Still she sensed the thing behind her. Couldn't the guard see it?

At last, the gate opened, and Melody lunged through and hurried towards the train which was pulling into the station. Only as she reached the platform did she dare glance behind her. No one there. No dark predator. Just a guard with skinny, hairy arms and a bulbous stomach bulging over his belt and trousers, and staring at her with a befuddled expression. He shook his head, murmuring something she couldn't interpret, before returning to his office.

The carriage doors opened, and Melody stepped inside, feeling comforted by the crowd of late commuters. Before anyone noticed, she dodged her way towards an empty seat, plonked herself down and released a heavy sigh.

Ah! Comfort and relaxation.

Yes, Sirena. Rest. I'm coming for you tonight.

Chapter 18

Thoughts and questions buzzed in everyone's minds when the video finished.

"Do you record every consultation on video?" Brianna cast a curious glance towards the wall of shelves full of VHS tapes. Stacks of DVDs and CDs labelled as consultation sessions accompanied them. "You have a lot there."

Craig nodded. "Yes, always. These days, it is easy for people to claim things happened while under hypnosis. In my early days, I never hypnotised a woman unless she had a female friend with her, and I had one too. I believe that stopped a lot of false lawsuits and accusations. Too many practitioners leave themselves at risk of sexual misconduct claims. And even if they're untrue... I'm sure you catch my drift. These days, video cameras cut out the need for witnesses."

"Blimey! Any uvver in'erestin' ones fer us ter watch? Nuff said, yeah?" Turner piped up, his face filled with cheeky anticipation. He saw Brianna squirm and Emily about to bash him over the head but gave them a charming smile. "Lawd above! I mean yew must 'ave been single once, right?"

Khan interrupted before Craig answered. "Craig, I must apologise again," he faced Brianna, "and to you too, Miss Cogan," he regarded them both together, "because I can see you never betrayed me at all. When I saw this woman leave your home, after everything I told you, I felt you had fallen for her charms." Khan's face reflected his sincerity.

Craig fingered the collar of his shirt. "It wasn't easy." Brianna turned to look at him. "I felt a psychic pull from her. Only my mind training from Emily over the years helped me resist," he looked at Brianna, "and probably my sense of loyalty to Brianna." *And a good thing too*, Emily's words filtered through to Craig's mind. He shook his head for her benefit. "But you never mentioned that before, Khan."

The immortal shrugged. His fingers played with his sword's hilt for a moment. "I felt her spells over me when I tangled with her in London and Yorkshire."

"And it's obviously strong if you are still hunting her now, Mr Jealousy." Craig grinned, joined by Emily and Turner laughing in the background.

Khan hid a sheepish grin. "Perhaps you are right. But we must catch her still."

"Then let's crack on to it." Craig stood and strode across to find his car keys.

"Wait!" Brianna's voice halted him. "Do you know where to find her?"

"I imagine her home is a good place to start." Craig shrugged.

Brianna paused, watching him, her face a cocktail of concern masked by cheekiness. "If you're cracking on to it, like you said, I'd better come along too."

Craig sensed an underlying tone and paused at the door, Khan already close behind him. He turned back towards Brianna. "Of course. You know her address, right?"

Brianna hesitated, caught Emily's wink in her direction, and grinned. "Like you even had a chance without me," she replied.

Craig was about to exit through the door when he realised something and turned around. Tyrone was still sitting on the lounge-room chair. "Are you coming along?"

Tyrone's eyebrows raised in surprise. "You want me there too?" He looked at Brianna who offered a smile in his direction, and a grin brightened his face.

"If you want. You proved useful before."

Tyrone considered it, glancing at the other adults and spirits in the room, before shaking his head. "Not this time, Unc. I have other things to do, and I don't want to be in the way."

Turner nodded towards Craig. "The boy is comin' along well wiv 'is training, but I 'aven't finished wiv 'im yet. By da time, I'm done wiv 'im, you'll be askin' 'is permission ter come along. Sorted, mate." The Cockney winked in Tyrone's direction. "Right, lad?"

A smile slipped across Craig's cruel lips as he regarded his adopted nephew. Turner was right. Tyrone had come through twice for Craig, each time with success. Whatever training Turner gave him was turning him into an adept psychic warrior. Craig caught Emily's motherly gaze on Tyrone. Although the Scottish spirit didn't like Turner's methods, and maybe his past life, the admiration in her face for the boy shone too.

As the adults slipped out the door, Craig made a mental note to talk more with the boy.

***

Dusk transformed into a velvety darkness that kissed the nightscape like a silent lover. From their perspective in Craig's car, the apartment building looked like one from a Hollywood movie. The building's exterior lights illuminated the entrance with a gentle touch. An array of fairy lights set in the garden beds shone upon the shrubs, eliminating any hiding places without harm to the beauty. Even the miniature pine tree in the centre bathed in the light's cone. Put lights on it, and it would look like a Christmas tree from the Otherworld. A tramp breeze carried a train's braking squeal from the station a few blocks away.

Khan peered through the Jaguar's backseat window's tinted glass. "I believe I can take it from here." He pulled on the door's latch, which remained shut, and shot Craig an annoyed look upon realising the child locks were engaged. "What are you doing?"

Craig afforded Khan an apologetic look. He had sensed from Brianna's touch that she didn't want either of the men barrelling through and disturbing Melody yet. "Sorry, Khan. This is still a police matter. Brianna's the official detective on this case, so she leads."

Khan's face loomed forward towards them. "This began centuries before your parents came into the world. I don't require your permission."

Brianna turned around to face Khan. "Settle down, Khan. We're working as a team." Something caught Brianna's eye, and they followed her gaze.

A solitary figure hurried from the nearby train station. By the person's walk, the car's occupants recognised it as a woman.

"Is it her?" Khan strained his eyes to pick out shapes from the shadowy physique.

Craig hid back in the car, allowing Brianna a view of the approaching person. The detective nodded in agreement. "Yes, it's her." Brianna glanced at Khan. "Stay where you are, Khan. If we approach her now, she can run. I want to talk to her inside."

"Inside?" Khan's voice hissed. "Surely, you jest, Detective Cogan. Inside is the lady's lair. She may have many traps inside for enemies."

"She doesn't know us as enemies yet." Cogan looked at the sword in its scabbard laying on Khan's lap. "Unless you wave that cutlass around at her."

Khan's eyes glowed. "It's not a cutlass, madam, it's a —"

"It's an illegal weapon I could arrest you for." Brianna's words brought pause to Khan who opened his mouth to speak more. But Brianna held a finger to her lips with a shush. Khan resisted, his mouth poised to speak, and Brianna repeated. "Quiet."

"When you two have finished, we have a suspect to question."

Khan and Brianna snapped their gazes towards the apartment building. Melody had unlocked the front door and entered, her silhouette visible through the frosted glass door. Both men faced Brianna who nodded. "Let's go."

The trio left the car and crossed the street. Khan strode faster, his legs propelling him ahead of the others who sneaked glances at each other.

"Should he have brought flowers?" Craig's eyes twinkled. Brianna punched his arm. She tried not to laugh but couldn't stop smirking.

A woman's screams exploded the night air. And they were heart-stopping cries filled with terror mingled with loss. Mournful and panicked.

Craig reached the door and banged hard. It rattled against his blows but didn't give. "Someone! Open the door!" Brianna and Khan arrived at his heels. The shrieks continued, but they moved throughout the apartment building. Craig's eyes darted towards the intercom where he pressed each unit's call buttons. But no one answered.

The woman's cries for help continued. Then they emanated from the front door's speakers.

Brianna's voice sliced like a knife to regain control. "Police! Detective Sergeant Cogan. Open the door. Please."

The screaming woman didn't hear. Her screaming had turned to sobs. "Help me! Please! Some-"

Brianna interrupted. "Let us in! Press the button."

Then it was quiet, save for a sniffle. The door buzzed. "Please, hurry. They're dead. All dead." More sobs and a wailing cry.

Craig pushed the door open. Brianna and Khan pushed their way past before he followed them, taking the stairs two-or-three at a time.

A stench of blood, entrails, and ended life wafted through their nostrils. Brianna and Craig gagged. Khan, however, remained unaffected and hurried faster until something stopped him in his tracks with a horrified expression.

Brianna recognised the scene in a heartbeat. Khan blocked part of her view, but his frame didn't hide everything. Blood ran down the walls, congealed in places, like a crimson river. Their feet squelched with sick sounds on the carpet soaked in body fluids. Every murder scene before this failed to prepare Brianna for the bloodbath confronting them.

Craig vomited hard, splashing his own shoes as it bounced from the crimson-drenched walls. His foot slipped on a body organ he didn't recognise. But someone had bitten a chunk from it.

The woman's screams ricocheted off the walls from down the hallway. Brianna, gun drawn and gripped ready, hurried towards a unit's open door. "This is Detective Sergeant Cogan." Brianna's voice sounded alien to the scene. "Is someone else with you?"

The screaming transformed into sobbing. Another voice, frail and faint, spoke. Was it speaking to the woman who screamed or someone else?

Craig, a handkerchief clasped to his mouth and nose, approached from behind her. "The killer left earlier."

"How did-?" Brianna stopped herself. Craig waggled his fingers at her, his eyes twinkling above his cloth mask. "Smart arse."

Craig side-stepped Brianna and strode through the open doorway. The unit was the same as the hallway: blood-drenched, carpets soggy with it, and walls drenched as though it were a fur coat targeted by an animal lover's red paint. A curse escaped his lips. Then he saw her.

Melody Kostas sat in the middle of the red lake, cradling an old woman in her lap, and rocking back and forth. One bloody hand held her arm in a gentle grip, an attempt to comfort despite death's imminent arrival. A wet sheen glimmered on Melody's face. A long gash in the woman's chest leaked, despite Melody's attempt to staunch the flow. Words flowed from Melody's mouth in a litany of chants. "Please live. Please live. Don't die. I love you."

Craig stepped closer, placing one gentle hand on Melody's back and another on the old woman's grey hair. The latter's eyes rolled to meet Craig's, knowing. He looked into hers and nodded. She knew. Too much time and too much blood lost. But wait. Was that recognition in her eyes?

Brianna produced her iPhone from her jeans pocket and dialled for backup. She murmured something about forensics and an ambulance. Meanwhile, Khan approached Melody. One hand rested upon his sword's hilt hidden under his overcoat. Conflicted thoughts played upon his face as he absorbed the scene and the present. Something about the old woman drew him closer. And the way the young woman wept. At last Khan's features melted, moisture appearing at the corner of his eyes as he loomed above the two women.

The older woman's eyes shifted, almost passing Khan but snapping back to lock upon him. They widened, the pupils dilated, and her eyebrows raised. Words, tinged with death's imminent spell, wheezed from her lips. "You! At last, you-" Then her eyes rolled upwards and back, the whites showed for a moment, before the lids shut. This time, forever.

Silence fell over the unit. No one moved except Melody who bowed her head towards the old woman's face and touched her forehead with her own. Somewhere, a dripping sound beat a slow percussive rhythm. It sounded like water on a saucepan in the kitchen. But with the smell of blood wafting about, who could tell without looking? Brianna stepped close, lowered herself to her haunches, careful not to touch anything, and placed a hand on the grieving woman's shoulder. Khan remained still. Only his eyes flickered back and forth to survey the gore splattered across the furniture.

Then Melody screamed. Anguish filled the cry. Heartbreak and a loneliness like that of an orphan holding her dead parents. Brianna reached to pull Melody closer and offer solace, but nothing could stop the wailing. Nor did Brianna try stopping it, for she knew the pain of losing loved ones.

Craig moved too, but not to comfort. He stepped back, slipped on the bloody carpet and landed on his backside with a squelch. "Get back, Bri-"

"What" Brianna's curiosity changed to shock and surprise. Melody's limbs flailed out, struck Brianna to the ground with a thump that echoed from the walls. Brianna fell back, her arms raised to fend off further blows, with a loud exclamation. "What the-?"

Melody's body stiffened, her breaths whooshed in and out from her foaming mouth, and her eyes swung open until they bulged.

Khan and Brianna both uttered perplexed sounds as Melody's body shook.

"Is she having a fit?" Brianna moved closer, ready to roll Melody on her side, but Khan gripped her shoulder and held her back.

"No. This is no mere seizure." Khan pointed at Melody's legs. "Look!"

Melody's shoes fell from her feet which now appeared discoloured. The tanned skin lost its smooth texture, changed, and deformed. Scales appeared as the bones underneath cracked and stretched. Her legs lengthened.

Chapter 19

Craig's feet and hands carried him away from the transforming body, taking Brianna with him. "Do we have a snake catcher in the house?"

The more Melody's body gesticulated, the more her skin's scales developed, transformed, and defined. Her black trousers came away, flicked to the side by a long serpentine tail with a sound like leather scraped on tiles. Not a word escaped Melody's mouth. Her seizures continued throughout the transmutation. But her eyes stayed shut while her face kept its feminine beauty.

Brianna stood with Craig, eyes transfixed upon the creature. "What the hell is that?"

Craig dodged the tail that flicked at his feet. "What do we do when she wakes?" He turned at the sound of steel withdrawing from a leather scabbard and saw Khan advance towards Melody. He jumped to stop Khan's hand, blocking him at the wrist.

"Out of my way, Craig. We found the creature responsible for the killings. It is our duty to kill her." The click of Brianna's pistol hammer stopped him. Without moving his head, Khan rolled his eyes to spy the firearm jutting into his throat. "Why do you wish to stop me, woman? Can't you see?"

Brianna's face was like marble. "I see," she paused,

aware of Melody's legs moulding together to form the reptilian lower body, "a woman going through changes. She -"

Khan's voice remained strong despite the pistol at his throat. "This is more than menses and feminine issues. She has obviously killed the-"

"Murderers don't mourn their victims."

Craig slipped a pair of cuffs from his own jacket pocket. He snapped one of the woman's wrists to the other. "There!" He grinned. "She's not going anywhere."

"Unless her hands disappear too." Khan relaxed a little.

With a sigh, Craig removed his belt and wrapped it around Melody's body. "Strange how the top half doesn't change."

"But it's normal for the lower half to change?" Brianna's pistol stayed pointed at Khan's throat.

The immortal winked at Brianna, a cocky twinkle in his eye, and lifted a careful hand to push it away. "It appears Craig has found a compromise."

The detective's gaze diverted to the fantastic creature before them. "What the hell happened to her? Is she a Medusa?"

Craig shook his head and brought their attention to Melody's messed black hair. "No. Medusa had snakes in her hair. And she hasn't turned us to stone, so she can't be a Gorgon from the Greek tales. Have you seen one before, Khan?"

The immortal shrugged. "I have seen many amazing things in the past millennium. But nothing like this."

"Past millennium?" Brianna raised eyebrows at Khan. "Are you saying you're over one thousand years old?"

Khan regarded Brianna with a serious expression. "I can remember being part of the First Crusade in 1096.

"And he doesn't look a day over five hundred years," Craig quipped. His tone grew serious.

Khan looked over Melody's body which had since ceased its convulsions. "During that time, I heard talk of an ancient legend about a woman. The Greeks said she had been a queen of what is now Libya, and they called her Lamia. She was a child-eating monster with the lower body of a snake and the upper body of a beautiful woman." He pointed at Melody's inert form. "But it's an old legend, probably old when Dio Chrysostom first orated her tale."

Brianna shook her head in disbelief at Khan's words. "Are you saying we're dealing with an immortal monster?"

Khan nodded. "A child-eater. And no record exists of her death. Sometimes you may find other similar tales, such as Psamathe of Argos who Apollo bedded. Apollo called upon a Lamia to ravage the city's children after Psamathe's father had her put to death. A hero killed that Lamia, but these are legends. Stories change over time, and who can say."

Khan stared long and hard at Melody, his eyes fixed

upon the alien creature. "But they all point to a creature such as her killing children. I know she has killed men, and I believe she killed these women too."

"We haven't checked the others in the building yet." Craig looked about the room.

"What are you looking for?" Brianna asked him.

"Something to sit on that's not bloodied up. I want to sit on something while both of you search the apartment building. Someone has to watch Melody."

"Excuse me?" Brianna's tone filled the room. "If you think you are staying here with a woman naked from the waist down while we-"

Khan held up a hand. "I can keep watch while you both-"

"No! I will stay here and you men can search." Brianna's words fell with finality.

Craig opened his mouth, but Brianna shushed him. "I can take care of myself. Go! There may be another survivor who can identify the killer."

Khan paused and scanned the room about him. Then he checked the floor to examine the ground. He tapped Craig's shoulder. "Whoever did this came in and left through to that room there. See?" He pointed towards the entrance. "Those are our footprints. There's a fourth set leading that way."

Craig nodded and led the way. Khan followed right behind him. They reappeared soon after, Craig's phone in his hand. "Looks like he escaped through the bedroom window."

"How did he get in?" Brianna wondered. "This place is secure as Fort Knox. Check Melody's unit. It's down the hallway to the right. Down the end."

***

Like the other dead bodies, the door to Melody's unit lay in splinters across the floor. Remnants of a bloody boot print stood out on some pieces that lay scattered across the entry. Craig tiptoed through the pieces, careful not to fall or slip on anything. Khan remained behind, stepping where Craig did to avoid messing too many things by their movement. Ceramic shards that looked like parts of what was once a large vase littered the living room's tiles. Khan shook his head, dismay in his eyes.

"Terrible waste. They look like pieces from an older time."

A lover of art, Craig nodded in agreement, and picked up a piece. After a moment, he tossed it to the side. "It's fake. But beautiful, just the same."

Khan snorted, irony tinging his voice. "A common affliction in people, too." Something caught his eye. "The person who did this has already left. Look."

Craig looked where Khan pointed. Footprints, bloodied but faded as the blood transferred to the floor with each step, led amongst the debris from the large vase and the mutilated sofas and couches towards the door. "He was looking for someone. Melody, perhaps?"

Craig bent to retrieve a piece of leather, a sliver of

blood on its edge. Puzzlement crossed his face. "I keep hearing words as though they're whispered or sung. Sometimes I hear it whistled." He paused, listening to his inner voices. "Oranges and Lemons. Does that mean anything to you?"

Khan shook his head. "It's an old nursery rhyme. Common enough in the 1880s during the Whitechapel murders."

"The Ripper's time?"

Khan laughed. "You're hearing it because the Ripper lives in this home. It's her, the one you call Melody Kostas. She's Jacqueline the Ripper."

Craig's eyebrows raised. "I don't believe that. If it were true, how do you explain her mourning over the old lady? No one in their right mind would do that."

"We all believed the Ripper was a madman, Craig. But, I tell you, the Ripper is a woman. Jacqui, not Jack. There is no other possibility. And worse, she's an immortal creature."

Craig brushed his fingers across a patch of carpet. "No. She isn't the Ripper. But she has met him." He stood. "He left shortly before she arrived home. Minutes before. I've just seen him walking down the hallway, wiping his blade on a rag. Oh, and he's singing that song."

Khan's eyes burrowed a hard gaze into Craig. "You're under her spell!"

Craig chuckled. "Not the way you are, my friend." Khan opened his mouth to say something but Craig interrupted. "Yes, I felt that tug of seduction, but I don't when Brianna is around."

"You're a lucky man." Khan patted Craig on the shoulder. "Hold on to that magic, Craig. Hold on to it with a strong hand."

A crushing wave of sadness washed from Khan's hand into Craig. "Are you sure you're not under her spell?" Craig was about to say Khan had been alone a long time himself but changed his mind.

The immortal shook his head. "She is a beauty. If she is immortal too, I wonder how lonely she has been through the years. Perhaps she has joined with many men, just as I have with women. Even monsters such as us need love." Khan's voice trailed, his thoughts moving into private voices within himself.

***

Less than ten minutes later, after they confirmed no survivors existed throughout the building, Craig and Khan returned to the old woman's unit.

"You took your time." Brianna afforded them a quick look and glanced towards Melody. The woman had transformed back into her feminine human shape, her legs where her legs should be. All traces of a tail had vanished. "She changed a couple of minutes ago."

Khan blushed upon seeing Melody's nakedness from the waist down. "You could at least cover her nakedness." He removed his overcoat and lay it over her bare legs and privates. But it didn't escape Craig or Brianna's notice that the man hesitated, his eyes peeping, before he finished.

A moan escaped the unconscious woman's mouth. She stirred. Then her eyes opened, the lids blinking away the light.

"Melody Kostas," Brianna said, her voice gentle. "How are you feeling?"

Craig turned his head, eyes searching, and strode towards the nearby kitchenette where he found a clean glass and filled it. He offered it to Melody as she sat up.

"Detective Cogan? Craig Ramsey?" Melody's eyes resembled a wild animal's shocked stare when she spotted the old woman's body next to her. Another sob escaped. Urgency filled her voice. "Where is he? Did you see him?"

"Who?" Brianna asked.

Then Melody saw Khan looming above them. In a flash, she jumped up, bowling over both Craig and Brianna. "You!" Melody pointed at the tall man. "What have you done?"

Brianna picked herself up. "This is Khan, and he was outside with us when you screamed. Don't you remember?"

Melody hesitated, a mixture of expressions crossing her face. Recognition, disgust, curiosity, disbelief. After a glance in Craig's direction, she returned to Brianna. "Yes. I remember this man. I first met him in 1888. He and another man attacked me in the streets. I realised it was in error now." She narrowed her eyes at Khan. "But how is it you still live?"

"Wait!" The urge to speak overcame Craig's self-control. "You really were alive in the 1800s?"

"Of course, Mr Ramsey. You need not act so surprised. Your psychic visions were correct," the woman replied. "And I remember everything now. Thank you for your help. But," Melody cast a sad glance at her elderly neighbour's corpse, "we have an enemy in common. A demon who has walked the earth as long as I have. I still need your help." Melody noticed her half-naked state and responded. "Please allow me to dress and I can tell you my story."

Chapter 20

"As Khan stated, I am a Lamia. But I am not just any Lamia. I am the Lamia," Melody Kostas said, passing her gaze across Khan, Craig and Brianna. "My life began in an age when Gods and Men walked the world together. My father, King Belus, was a grandson of Libya who fell pregnant to Zeus, who seduced her in disguise as a peacock. The nation took Queen Libya's name, and many years later, I inherited it from my father."

"I must state that Belus is not my biological father, for a God seduced my mother, the God known as Poseidon, Lord of the Seas, from Greek legend. My people called Poseidon Enki. By the same token, Zeus' real name is Enlil, and both brothers were rivals of each other. But they were only Gods compared to humans. In reality, we knew them as our Creators; visitors from another far-flung planet spinning on an orbit that crossed with ours every two-to-three thousand years. Thanks to them and their debauchery, I became the centre of a terrible drama, for which I still pay the price as progeny of the Anunnaki."

"What is the Anunnaki?" Brianna asked.

"What, indeed!" A smile crossed Melody's face. "The answer may shock your sensibilities, Detective Cogan. The Anunnaki were a fact of life to people once. They were visitors from another planet. Some claim they created us, and from what I know, that is probable. They are the powerful beings who used genetic engineering to create the modern human race many millennia ago. When you read the Christian's Bible, you read about ONE GOD. But that God is two beings - Enlil and Enki. Enlil fits the harsh God, the one who hated humans so much that he ordered them killed by the Great Deluge. He felt jealous when the so-called 'Serpent' suggested Eve eat from the Tree of Knowledge. But the one who loved us was my father Enki. He is the one who spoke to the Noahs - there were many Noahs, not one - around the world, and he told them to build their Arks."

Craig had been listening from the side. "And you say Enki, also known as Poseidon, is your father?"

Melody nodded. "But the story of the Demon who attacked my apartment building and killed the women in your streets is the real concern. And I will tell you his story."

***

Long ago, millennia before the Roman Empire grew from two foundlings raised by a mother wolf. I had two brothers - Aegyptus and Danaus. Aegyptus ruled Egypt and two other lands. Aegyptus was a wise ruler and kind to his people. Danaus was the opposite and ruled Crete while I ruled Libya. Danaus hated me because I was a woman, a daughter of the Gods, and ruled Libya which he wanted for himself. He hated even more the fact I created equality between the people of my land, something society since forgot - thanks to Enlil's influence - and your Western Society is still trying to

216

achieve.

Danaus tried to take Libya from me. When I had not found a husband after two years of rule, he tried forcing me by law to relinquish to him. But the Fates brought me a husband named Eyvind from the Northern lands of ice. Eyvind and I had thirteen babies, a mix of three boys and ten girls, and each brought us great happiness.

I would love to tell you we lived happily ever after. But we didn't. It's not such a tale.

For one day, my oldest son Dumuzi vanished at the age of ten while playing by the river with friends and three of his younger brothers. A few of my trusted guards were in attendance, but they found it difficult when the youngsters played by hiding and seeking among the bulrushes. My heart hurt when I learned of this. Years later, the bards would write of the day and tell how my tears filled the rivers. Poetic nonsense, but it carries truth. We never found Dumuzi's body. There were jackal tracks in the sand and mud, but we never found the beasts responsible.

Then came the next tragedy. My eldest daughter, my second child, developed a fever. It came over her quicker than a snake while she played in the courtyard. One moment she was sitting by the pool, playing with a puppy. Her dog's plaintive and worried barks drew a guard's attention, and her skin burned his hands with the burning heat from her glowing red skin. I summoned the best physicians and healers in the land, spared no expense, but none could help Persephone. Not even the old crone from the mountains.

So, helpless, I watched my Persephone die a horrible painful death. The image of her flesh wasting until it became thin and appeared to drape on her bones will haunt me forever. But the memory of her eyes pleading with me are worse.

Two deaths in less than six turns of the moon. Eyvind and I were beside ourselves with grief. Some would say we still had eleven other offspring, but they cannot replace each other. Each little life a parent spawns is a separate soul and personality that carves its distinct mark in their life.

But the worst was yet to come.

Time passed. One year became two, and soon the world circled the sun another ten years. Libya grew and flourished. Eyvind and I continued our duties to the nation, and our remaining children grew. Some bore more progeny, making us proud grandparents. Eyvind, despite the years, looked the same as always - proud, handsome, tall and strong - while the ravages of time and stress wore upon me. Small lines in my skin became deeper lines. A poet of my time wrote: that a pretty young girl is a work of Nature, while an elegant older woman is a creation of Art. He wrote of me, and later writers stole the line, transforming it through time.

All happy times end, and my disaster took place on my fiftieth birthday. I recall waking that dawn with the rich sun peeping through the window's lattice shutters and spreading cross-hatched shadows across my bed's cover. Eyvind was away across the Mediterranean for Libya's enterprise. His empty space in the bed felt horrible, as ever, nevertheless I enjoyed the extra room to stretch myself.

But all was quiet. And a smell hung in the air. The stench of death.

I sat up, ready to call my servants to clear the air, when my hand flew to cover my mouth. For there before me were my children on the floor, dead, next to their own dead offspring. Blood covered the floors and the bottom of my bedspread. And a cold, sticky sensation made itself known in the breeze.

The scream caught in my chest. I ached to release it, but it stayed there, unwilling to come. Their blood covered my hands and my chest. But how could I have slept through such carnage? Why had their murderer not killed me? At last, the scream escaped me and echoed through my bedchamber. Imagine my surprise and my anger upon the guards' arrival! I attacked the nearest one, shrieking at him as I wrested the knife from his belt. A hard pain flashed through the back of my skull.

All went black.

***

My subjects thought me insane. They believed me a killer of my own children. How else could they explain the chilling massacre scene and my survival? No one else could enter the bedchamber without being noticed. My children had only entered less than an hour earlier to surprise me for my birthday. Instead, in my people's eyes, they met their deaths. And I had attacked my guard, too, tried to kill him with his own knife. People's mouths work faster than their logical minds; the negative gossip is easier to believe, more convenient.

And they kept me locked up in my bedchamber with guards inside and out to keep watch over me. I was a prisoner in my own palace. But the worst prison was inside my head. Sleep evaded me, and when it teased me with morsels of slumber, it tormented me with images of my mutilated children that caused me to scream with the mental torture. I would have killed myself if the guards let me approach close enough to grab their weapon. But they already held caution from the earlier incident.

Physicians who specialised in the Mind Sciences, equivalent to today's psychiatry, examined me. The fools determined I suffered temporary insanity and had murdered my children in my sleep. But how could I do that without a weapon? Someone had hacked their kidneys out with a blade, bitten from the organs, and spat them out to the floor. Their blood on my face from when I screamed with my hands to my cheeks was circumstantial evidence.

So persuasive were their words, reinforced with unbendable confidence, I almost doubted myself. Could I have done it?

But, no! I couldn't. I knew in my heart.

At last, after another week, Eyvind arrived home from his trading trip. He burst into my bedchamber and rushed to hold me. Eyvind's warmth filled me as he took me in his arms. For a moment, I believed the nightmare was over. Although my eyes had dried days ago from the unending grief, the wells of my tear ducts found more salt water and squeezed it forth. All the time, Eyvind's calm voice soothed me. I had seen his red eyes, felt his own sadness from within. "Lamia." His voice seemed distant.

I pushed him back, looked into his eyes with all the strength I could deliver. "Someone killed our children, husband," I told him. "They believe it was me. Please, believe me. I couldn't do that to them."

Eyvind said nothing, and the moments dragged as he studied my eyes. He looked towards the windows. "I believe you."

Hope! At last!

"You do?"

Eyvind nodded. "Do you remember the roses you found in the mornings when I courted you?" When I confirmed the sweet memory of a long ago time, he offered a quivering smile. "I delivered them to you myself in your sleep with the help of a charm provided by Thoth. It gave my sandals wings to fly through your window."

"What does that prove?"

"My love, it proves the possibility of entering your guarded bedchambers undetected." His positivity lifted my mood and illuminated the darkness I had wallowed in since that terrible day.

"But we require more than proof based upon our early days."

Eyvind remained confident. "And we do." He sat me gently upon the bed, his voice a whisper. "I suspect a conspiracy against you, for, while I was away, a young priestess approached me. She told me you were in danger of Ninlil's wrath."

"Ninlil?" The name escaped in a noisy rush, and my husband hushed me, his finger pointing towards the hallway entrance. I understood what he meant. So with a hushed voice, I asked why the wife of Enlil - the Anunnaki lord and my uncle - would want to harm me or my children.

"Ninlil is a jealous woman, envious of any who threaten her beauty or her marriage."

My eyes narrowed. "Threaten her? Of what does she believe I am guilty?" I stood to dress myself, determined to meet this spiteful being I had met just the once when the Anunnaki presided over my coronation years ago. But Eyvind pulled me back to the bed.

"The priestess told me of your joining with Enlil." His eyes searched mine. "Is it true? Did you have an affair with him?"

Surprise gripped me. My jaw gaped as I regarded my husband in disbelief. "Never! Not even in the fertility rites. You are the only man with whom I have slept or made love."

His response came quick, filled with certainty. "I believe you. But Ninlil believes otherwise." His voice faded and an expression of revelation crossed his visage. "Unless, it is more than that. Do you know how the furniture shifts and floats when you and I join?"

I nodded, not yet understanding Eyvind's line of reasoning.

"Has there been a time you know when this never happened?"

Curious, I allowed myself the chance to reminisce over our wonderful trysts. No. Never. I shook my head, and relief crossed his face with a sigh.

"Good!" A smile broke from his face again, shining through the dark clouds of my worry. "Enlil disguises himself when having his affairs. Sometimes he is a peacock, others a shower of gold, or otherwise. I wondered if he had disguised himself as me." Seeing I didn't understand his meaning, Eyvind continued. "You and I are soulmates. We have met before, and we will meet many times in the lives ahead. This is clear when we make love because things move. They shake, rattle and roll about us until we finish. Candles will float. So will heavier vases. Then they drop when we climax. It would not be so if we lay with another person."

Ah, yes. Now I understood, but I had no way of testing Eyvind's theory. Having made love to no other, I knew no comparison. Our bed, so heavy, which takes eight servants to lift it, had lifted in the air and dropped with a thud upon our love finishing. I noticed it on our wedding night. But because I never knew another man, I never knew the difference.

Eyvind's face darkened once more. "Ninlil would know if you had joined with her erstwhile husband, and she does not attack without reason." His voice trailed away, his mind lost in thought until his countenance reflected sudden realisation. Before I could ask, he told me. "Ninlil is not attacking you. She is attacking me. The bitch learned I am the bastard son of another God."

A lump blocked my throat. A daughter of Enki, had I married incestuously with one of his kin by mistake?

Eyvind nodded. "I am the son of Odin." Odin? Who is he? "You know him as Enlil, Ninlil's husband."

Shocked, I lost my words. How long had Eyvind kept this secret from me? I had refused to marry my step-brother Danaus because he was grandson to Enlil.

"I never told you of my real father," Eyvind explained, "because I never cared for the gods. Odin tried coercing me to join with him in Valhalla, but I always refuse. I always detested how the gods interfere in the lives of Men and Women as though we are their toys. He tried bribing me with gifts, even promising me a ship that could travel anywhere in time or location by my whim. I refused every time. But there is one gift I could not refuse because I inherited it." His voice carried true sincerity. And when I turned to face him, tears streamed down his face. "Why do you cry?"

"I will pass this gift to you, my Queen Lamia." His outstretched fingers touched my face, and a thumb traced a line on my face. "You are the loveliest I will ever know. By passing this gift to you, our time together in this life will be undone."

What? I shook my head. "What are you-?"

His finger touched my lips, silencing me. "Lamia, You must remain young in your search for our children's killer. I could not do it without you, and the chase may take centuries. So I give my eternity to you."

The coward! He was deserting me when we should be pursuing our killer together!

But before I could speak, his fingers glowed like a fire brand, their warmth spread through my lips to my face and across my body. The energy of lost years flowed into me. And I have remained immortal since.

Without his immortality, my husband aged quicker over the next few months.

In that time, we learned Eyvind's theory was correct. Ninlil hated Enlil's children, and fuelled by her jealousy, she had arranged for one of her agents to hunt Eyvind's children down and kill them, along with every other child from her wayward husband's loins. The gods rarely taint their own hands by doing things themselves.

Eyvind died fighting the Demon. His head left his shoulders in battle, leaving me alone in our fight. But the Demon does not kill Eyvind's children alone. On the night Eyvind and I battled the Demon, my own blade had snapped, and unarmed, I wrested one of the Unnamed Demon's knives from him and raked it through his face before he escaped. But to this day, he still carries that scar. And so, he hunts me as much as I hunt him.

I have chased him through the centuries, and we both survived the Great Deluge brought upon the planet by Enlil to destroy all Humankind and the Nefilim. Enki arranged passage for me with one of the Noahs, and I learned later the Unnamed Demon escaped on another Ark. I thought he was long dead and remarried with another identity in another country. But he returned and killed my progeny again.

But only this knife I took from him can kill him. And

one day, soon I shall. If only I can find it again.

***

Melody turned her attention to Khan and studied his features. "You, Mr Khan, intrigue me. When I fought with one of the Demon's puppets in 1888, I thought you were him." She reached a hand towards Khan's chest. "And I plunged my blade into your heart, right here. How did you survive?"

Khan shrugged, his face revealed nothing, and he answered. "My story is long, too, but my immortality came from a genie that resides in a bottle."

Curiosity crossed Melody's face. "You became one yourself?"

Khan laughed and shook his head. "It granted my wish. And it won't undo it. I am doomed to live forever as you do."

A thoughtful expression passed Melody's face like a cloud blocking a bright sun, and a mutter escaped her lips. "Interesting."

Craig cleared his throat, waking Melody from her mind's voice. "Do we call you Lamia or Melody?"

"Melody, please." She allowed a smile. "The other name is long past."

"And Sirena?"

"A past identity in the 1880s that I abandoned in 1912."

With a thoughtful nod, Craig pressed. "You

mentioned the Demon has 'puppets'. What do you mean?"

"He marks men who he wishes to serve him." Melody paused and inspected one of her nails. "You may have noticed a few dead men on the streets too. I killed them." Khan released a satisfied grin as Craig and Brianna gasped with shock. The ancient woman arched an eyebrow. "Of course. It's survival. There is nothing people understand about the Demon's puppets. He possesses them, and I've seen him control them from afar too. They lose their minds, they change, and once marked, they can't be unmarked. He owns them, and they suffer."

"How do you know we can't help them?" Brianna asked, her voice tinged with concern as she looked at Khan and Craig.

Melody shook her head and blew something off her nail before looking straight at the detective. "Detective Cogan, your psychologists may take them, diagnose them with some mental illness that doesn't exist, and drug them to the eyeballs. But when the drugs wear off, they return to the old way. You can keep them drugged up, but it's a living hell for them. It's a merciful end. Trust me."

Khan's voice carried depth and power. "How do you know they are marked?"

"The last victim I found mentioned a singing voice. He said the Demon's blade sung to him and spoke inside his head." Melody paused. "His name was Henry. I gave him the most merciful death because he was Delta's friend." Her voice drifted, shaking her head as though in sympathy with the memory. "Poor, sweet Henry. He was already touched in the mind, but he had a good heart."

Khan leaned forward. "In 1888, I came running to save you from your attacker. Yet you stabbed me. Why?"

Melody thought for a moment, her eyes looking up to the corner of the room. "Yes, I remember now. Our first meeting. A man smelling of the demon attacked me. The scent is another indicator of the demon's possession. I dispatched him, and when you appeared from nowhere, I thought you were another of the Demon's puppets." She presented an apologetic smile. "Collateral damage. I am so sorry for that."

"Yet you attacked me later in my friend's house. Why?"

Melody stopped, ran a tooth over her lower lip, and nodded. "Yes. I remember. You surprised me again. Your friend Darling was a puppet of the Demon. I tracked him to his home, and you surprised me shortly after I dispatched him. How did you track me that night?"

"I didn't," Khan replied, his voice hard as stone. "I hoped Darling could help me die, but you killed him first, murderess."

Melody opened her mouth to rebuke, but Craig interrupted. "Khan, are we talking about the same Mr Darling who you found beheaded in his home?" Khan nodded. Craig turned toward Melody. "When you kill one of the Demon's puppets, what happens to the body? How do you know you killed one possessed by him?"

"When they're beheaded, a viscous grey smoke leaves their body." Melody noted Khan's recognition. "And you saw such a thing leaving Mr Darling's body, didn't you?

Khan cleared his throat. "I saw-"

"You saw part of the Demon's essence leaving him. That is all I need to say." Her eyes gazed deep into Khan as though surveying him. "And the girls the Demon killed back then, the prostitutes, were my wards. He killed them to draw me out for battle, tormenting me at the same time." A tear formed in her eyes. "He always kills those I love."

Khan pressed with another question. "The legends say Zeus removed Lamia's eyes to allow her sleep. Another says she clawed them out from insanity."

"I had lost my children," Melody responded. "Zeus did no such thing. The coward. My father, Enki, appeared to help me instead. It was the second time I had met him. He offered me a potion Hecate brewed to help me sleep through my madness. But there were side effects. Yes, I fell asleep, but not in body, only in mind, and it awakened certain genes in my system that cause me to change shape every full moon. Sometimes it makes me sleep in memory, so I forget the horrific sight of my dead children and those who followed. In that state, I become as I was until tonight - a woman with no memory by day, and the Lamia creature by night. Tonight's incident woke me from the potion's effect again. And I am back."

"The legends say you killed your children," Khan responded. "How do you explain that?"

Melody replied matter-of-factually. "Not all you hear in legends are true. My brother Danaus spread rumours about my killing my children to undermine my rule. And it worked because he took Libya shortly after."

Brianna clicked her fingers and pointed at Melody. "Did you consider that Danaus conspired with Hera to take your throne?" She shook her finger, jaw set as though sorting thought another idea. "Or what if Danaus had tricked Hera into helping him?"

"Danaus?" A cloud appeared to lift from Melody's eyes. "You may be right, Detective Cogan. My treacherous brother knew a lot about the Anunnaki, and he knew how to manipulate. Such a jealous creature."

"You don't believe her, do you, Brianna?" Khan asked. "You saw her attempt to seduce Craig, how she has-"

"I believe 'er."

They spun towards the sound of the Cockney voice. Turner was floating in the room's corner. He moved closer towards Khan and towards Melody. Casting a curious eye over the latter, he allowed himself a nod before he let loose in triumphant recognition. "Lor', luv a duck! Tell me, Miss Melody Kostas," he said. "Do yew recognise me?" The Queen of Ancient Libya regarded Turner's visage, her eyes scrunched to examine his translucent features, and shook her head in apology. Tuner shook his head. "I am da geezer yew killed in da alley da night yew met Mister Khan. Know what I mean?"

Melody's jaw gaped. "Then you were a puppet of the Demon I seek?"

"Gawdon Bennet! Thee bet yaahr blessed silks, I was!" Turner grinned and winked. "Yew 'aven't aged much!" Turner whistled to himself as he ogled Melody's shapely figure until he caught Craig's mixed expression of amusement and impatience. He regarded Craig with a nod. "I'm sorry fer in'errupting, Mr Ramsey, But I overheard da conversashun an' I remember bits and pieces ov da time. I remember losin' me 'head back then, 'earing voices, I did. It used ter sin'ter me. Later I would wake wiv blood on me 'ands." Turner's shape metamorphosed, shifting so he faced Melody without turning to look. "This lady stopped that da night I met Khan. Sorted, mate. I vouch fer 'er, I do. Nuff said, yeah?"

Silence filled the air. Melody sat taller, happy she knew had an ally in Turner who understood the Demon's power. Craig glanced towards Brianna, noted her expressions and body language, then towards Khan. The immortal knight's mood had changed. At last, Craig nodded and slapped both hands upon his knees. "We still have questions buzzing about," he said, "but there's something we need to decide. Are we working together on catching this Demon or not?"

Khan nodded, raising his hand. "Aye. Let's do it." Craig suppressed a smile, upon seeing Khan's eyes move towards Melody, and guessed there was more than catching a demon on his mind.

Brianna raised her hand. "I'm in." Craig noted something else hung in Brianna's voice.

Melody faced Brianna. "You sound hesitant. May I ask why?"

"I'm just processing everything." Brianna shrugged, her eyes gazing at a coaster on the coffee table's glassy surface. "A lot has happened tonight for me to process."

The ancient Queen nodded her understanding. "It has taken me many lifetimes," she conceded.

Brianna paused, eyed Khan for a moment before returning her gaze to the Lamia. Then she glanced at Craig who returned a wink in reply. Craig wished he could tell her his own thoughts and feelings on the subject and hoped the wink would be enough.

It was.

Chapter 21

Craig looked up from the dusty volume he had been reading when his ears pricked at the sound, a key sliding into the front door's lock. Craig was surrounded by books in his living room when he heard the key slide into the front door's look. As Brianna entered and shut the door behind her, he shut the dusty volume he'd been reading, plonked it on top of a pile beside him, and stretched as she approached.

Brianna surveyed the messy scene, baffled by the disorganisation, which wasn't something she expected from the normally tidy Craig Ramsey. "Is there a place to sit here, or are your books the new furniture?"

Craig stifled a yawn and moved the books from the sofa to the floor. "I've been researching our friend Melody Kostas." He noticed Brianna's tired eyes and hazarded a guess. "Hard day?"

Brianna plonked herself beside Craig, and the sofa's leather squelched under her. "Yep." She picked up hardbound book from the coffee table to look at its title. "Haven't you heard of the internet?"

Craig hmphed. "I could scour the internet, but these books carry enough information to support almost everything Melody told us last night."

Brianna looked around. "Where is Melody now?"

"She paid for a room at the Hilton," Craig answered. A grin crossed his face. "Khan's out, too, but I don't think he will be at his own lodgings, wherever they are."

Brianna allowed a chuckle. "You noticed that too, huh?" She paused a moment. "What did you find about Melody's story in these dusty tomes?"

Craig stretched again, the sound of his joints punctuated the air, and he released a sigh. "First, Melody Kostas has been around for some time. Her story matches because of the inconsistencies I found in the books. One legend states Queen Lamia had a long affair with Zeus. He was a randy one, always fornicating with anything with ovaries, and he impregnated Lamia with numerous children. Hera, the goddess of matrimony, always forgave Zeus but she always punished the women too - even when it was plain to see Zeus had tricked them."

Brianna shook her head in disbelief. "I always wondered why I never heard of his castration by Hera."

Craig grinned. "I don't know why either, but there's more. One story says Hera caused Lamia's insanity, making her kill her children. The shock sent her so mad she couldn't sleep because she always saw the carnage. Zeus felt bad enough about it because he removed her eyes so she could sleep."

"But Melody has both her eyes," Brianna responded. "How does this help?"

"I don't mean he literally removed Lamia's eyes, although that's what the texts say." Craig shook his head. "No, more likely he caused her to lose her memory from time-to-time. That can explain her amnesia, and I would say the recent shock of seeing the murder scene last night re-triggered her memories. Have you heard of Hercules?" Craig asked, and Brianna nodded. "He was a son of Zeus, too, and Hera pulled the same trick on him, except she caused Hercules to kill his children. She did nothing to Hercules' mother. Poor Hercules wasn't as lucky as Lamia because he realised what he had done."

"It sounds like Hera was mad as a cut snake," Brianna decided aloud. "No wonder Zeus -"

But Craig interrupted her. "Careful. Chances are she's still alive, and I don't want to tempt her." He winked at Brianna. "Only joking. How did you go at work today?"

Brianna shook her head. "What else did you learn?"

"Only enough to see there are different tales about the Lamia. She even turned into a bogey of sorts, a tale used to scare kids at night. The poet Keats even wrote something about the Lamia which I'd like to know how true it is."

"Such as?"

"Its truth. Keats wrote about a youth named Lycius who met a beautiful woman. Although he didn't know, the beautiful woman was a Lamia - a serpent turned to human form by Hermes in exchange for other information. A friend of Lycius arrived uninvited to their wedding and recognised the woman. He expressed contempt for Lycius' wife and called her a serpent. Lamia vanished, and Lycius died that night."

Brianna paused for a moment. "Do you reckon she

murdered Lycius?"

"Possibly," Craig responded. "Or maybe Apollonius, Lycius' friend, was something else. He was able to 'see through' Lamia and her 'illusions' or 'charms'."

"Lamia was a trickster?" Brianna leaned forward in interest.

"Or Apollonius may have been the Demon." Craig raised an eyebrow at Brianna. "You seem bent on Lamia's guilt."

Brianna rolled her eyes. "You have got to be kidding. I watched her attempt to seduce you on the video you shot. And Khan's putty in her hands now too. Neither of you men will admit it. She has weaved a spell over both of you."

Craig chuckled. "She has no chance against you, Brianna," Craig winked, "I'm not into scales, you see." Then he pointed at the other books that were stacked like a child's building blocks, only made from dead trees and parchment. "Anyway, Lamia has been around a long time, and even ancient Babylonian texts mention her. That matches with her story too."

"And what have you concluded?"

"If I had not seen her change into that creature, which matches Keats' description of the Lamia," Craig removed his reading glasses to rub his eyes, "I would have thought her a fantasy-prone woman, well-versed in literature and ancient history." He looked back to Brianna. "I'm inclined now to believe she's the real deal."

"What of her mentioning the Anunnaki?"

Craig thought a moment as he folded his glasses and shut them in their case which shut away in a drawer of the coffee table. "I've heard things about the Anunnaki for a few years now. None of the sources are mainstream, but I'm cautious enough to be careful what I say about them. From what I can gather, they were ancient astronauts and have visited this planet a few times in ancient days." He paused. "Anyway, what about you? What did you find today?"

A ringing sound cut through the air before Brianna opened her mouth. Craig's eyes searched the room, but the books hindered his floundering hands as they searched. At last, his probing fingers found the phone behind a sofa cushion.

"Yes?"

Brianna caught some words, but others were garbled. Craig nodded then responded in surprise. "What?" He checked his watch. "This early?" Craig shot a concerned glance in Brianna's direction. "How can that be?" A pause. "U huh. Okay." He lifted his wrist and checked his watch. "Give us ten-to-fifteen. We'll be there."

"Who was that?"

Craig was lifting books and hastily shoving them back in the bookshelves. "That was Khan," he replied, grunting as he tidied up. "Can you help with this please?"

Brianna looked in consternation. "You said we'd be there soon. What's going on?"

"He's down at the police station, and he used his one phone call to ring me." He lifted five more books and placed them one at time into the shelf. "A little help, please? We don't have much time."

Brianna remained where she was. "Why? Can't we clean this later."

"No time to explain," Craig puffed, but by the time Brianna picked up the first book, Craig had finished the job. "Never mind." He lifted his jacket from the sofa's arm, slipped into it, and patted his pocket with a jingling of car keys. Craig reached in and removed them. "Let's go."

***

Craig's Jaguar roared like its namesake as it raced through the streets towards the police station. It was just past eight o'clock, and Brianna heard Craig's stomach rumble in reply to his car's moans. Brianna turned her head at the sound. "You sound how I feel."

Craig allowed a smile. "You were going to tell me what you learned today."

"Oh! Yeah! It wasn't much, but it may prove useful." Brianna removed a notepad from her belt. "I had a hunch after Melody's story, so I checked it out. Do you remember how the murders always happen at night or in darkness?"

Craig's eyes turned thoughtful and his voice took a thoughtful tone. "Yes...?"

"I checked the dates of the murders. Most of them happened during the time of a New Moon. Isn't that

238

crazy?"

Craig opened his mouth to respond when another voice interrupted from behind and startled them both. "Not on a full moon, yew mean?"

"Shouldn't you be wearing a bell or something?" Brianna responded with impatience. "Stop popping in and out, can't you?"

"Popping in and out?" Emily responded from next to Turner in the backseat.

Brianna wondered why the spirits were in the backseat, almost said something, but ignored it. "Yes, Turner, I mean there was no moon. Does that mean something to you?"

Turner chuckled. "Awright! I don't know abaaht deese days, but in me time, we stole from 'ouses in complete darkness. Thee see, we 'ad no street lights like yew do today. No one could see us as they can durin' a full moon. Yeah?"

"So he found it easier to operate in secrecy." Craig chewed his lip as he negotiated a corner and dodged a red light. "That makes sense."

Brianna grinned. "Thanks, Turner, because that answers my next question. I looked up Jack the Ripper's victims and found they died on moonless nights too."

Turner chortled. "Glad t' be of service, m' lady, but what'ya willin' t' pay me?"

Brianna narrowed her eyes, turned her head to face Turner, and held out her hand, clicking her fingers.

"Hand it back, or I'll find a way to torture you, even if you are dead."

Turner reflected with an innocent expression. "What are yew talkin' about?"

Brianna clicked her fingers, louder this time, and stared through Turner's eyes. At last, he reached inside his jacket pocket and extracted Brianna's Casio G-Shock Mudmaster watch, which Brianna snatched back.

"Keep your hands off my things," Brianna said before she returned her attention to Craig. "Dr Kroot would be upset to learn that as he considers himself the Ripper expert."

Craig grinned. He knew of Dr Kroot, the police medical examiner whose mind appeared unhinged from spending too much time with the corpses. Brianna had told Craig before of how she caught Kroot serenading a corpse with a Frank Sinatra impersonation. "The moon phases are interesting if he's still attacking then, despite the increased light. Anything else?" Craig glanced at Brianna as he waited for another traffic light change.

"Dr Kroot mentioned something about two of the bodies from Melody Kostas' building." Brianna paused. "They were cut up with a blade similar to a Liston knife. ("The Ripper's weapon," Turner piped.) But it can't be the same one we took from Toomey because that's locked away in the evidence room."

"Could that mean a copycat?" Craig wondered aloud.

"Maybe," Brianna replied, "or it could be the killer is working with someone else."

The queer aroma - a putrid cocktail mix of disinfectant, vomit and something else Craig couldn't name - hung in the air like death's deodorant. It tickled Craig's nostrils enough to make him cringe as he entered the police station's reception area. To the side, a prostitute argued with a uniformed officer about whether her handcuffs were real (an offence by the state's Firearms Act) or a mere novelty. No, she didn't have the key, and no, there was not trick switch on the set to open them. Both she and the arresting officer paused their discussion to view the psychic and the detective who passed by before they resumed their discussion. Nearby slouched a drunk who snored the tune of the dearly unconscious with the occasional DT-induced chatter in his slumber.

Behind the reception desk sat the desk sergeant - an illustration of overindulgence in doughnuts and fatty food combined with a lack of sleep. He looked up from his computer screen and stood to address them. Perhaps he was tired because he didn't recognise Detective Sergeant Brianna Cogan at first until she flashed her badge.

Craig introduced himself and stated he was visiting Khan.

"Khan?" The desk sergeant appeared distracted by the discussion between the other officer and the prostitute, but more interested in snatching glances at her luscious assets.

Craig snapped his fingers to wake the desk sergeant. "Hello! Yes, Khan. One of you arrested him this evening. I'm his representative."

The desk sergeant eyed Craig with derision. "Do you mean the guy we found in the alley with blood over his hands and a body at his feet?"

"What?" Craig glanced at Brianna. Surprise covered his face and reflected Brianna's expression. He turned back towards the desk sergeant. "He didn't tell me that."

The desk sergeant shrugged and looked back at Craig. "He's been trouble ever since he arrived. Charged with resisting arrest, assaulting seven officers - four of them are in hospital now - and he's been trouble in the cell too." He was about to say what else happened when a ruckus erupted from a hallway, echoing along the walls enough to make the other officer and prostitute pause in their argument. "What the hell?"

Craig's eyes gleamed with a cheeky smile. He raised his hand, swept it across the desk sergeant's field of vision. "You will take us to my friend."

The desk sergeant's eyes glazed. "Yeah, well, you can talk to him for yourself." With his eyes staring ahead, the officer stood, turned, and shambled through the swinging door that led to the cells, the direction from which the fighting sounds came.

Craig strode in the sergeant's wake, Brianna following him with quick steps and hissing in his ear. "What the hell did you do?"

"I made him speed up," Craig replied, casting a wink in her direction.

"But you can't do that!"

"Sure I can." Craig turned the corner and strode after the shambling officer. "See? He's doing it."

"But you-"

"Do you normally take people to the cell's area to visit?"

"Sometimes," the officer answered, turning a blank stare towards Craig and Brianna.

"And you have no problem with this?"

The desk sergeant grinned. "Nope." His eyes had lost their glassy stare. "You've always done well by me and the boys, Mr Ramsey."

Brianna's face was a mirror reflecting more surprise when she realised. "You hadn't hypnotised him after all?"

The desk sergeant laughed. "Mr Ramsey? Hypnotise me? Not at all. I had a feeling he'd arrive when this nutcase rang him earlier. I'm used to this."

Craig playfully punched the desk sergeant in the shoulder while Brianna paused with an exasperated look on her face. "How are the wife and kids, Roy?"

"Hayley's still in and out of the hospital," the officer responded, "but the doctors reckon she'll be fine. The boys are fine too. Did you know I'm going to be a granddad?"

The shouting and banging noises had subsided by the time the trio arrived.

Khan's cell was on the corner of intersecting passages. Two of its walls were solid, the others comprised a set of bars with a sliding gate. A single toilet sat against a wall, its steel rim and seat having lost its shine years ago, and a limp man lay across it with his head buried in it. Three other limp bodies, alive but unconscious, sat piled on each other in the corner next to a bed upon which Khan sat next to only one other man: a skinny mouse of a man who remained silent and staring ahead while hugging his legs closer and rocking back and forth. What appeared to be a knife with a two-inch blade, its metal streaked with blood, sat on the floor outside the bars.

Upon hearing their approach, Khan looked up, recognised Craig and Brianna, and allowed a smile to cross his lips. "It's about time you arrived." He indicated the conscious inmate beside him. "Gary, here, was telling me about how he," Khan indicated the unconscious man smelling toilet water, "smuggled a knife in here past the boys in blue before trying to shave my throat with it." Khan fingered his throat which bore a fading scar from a puncture wound. "Wait until the women see this!" He winked at Craig who grinned back and imagined what evidently transpired.

The desk sergeant fetched the knife from the ground, shook his head, and placed it in a plastic bag he extracted from a pouch on his belt. Then, facing Craig, he jerked a thumb towards Khan. "Do you know this guy?"

Craig suppressed a smirk. "Yes, I do. Why is he here?"

"A patrol received a call from an anonymous source and found your friend above a dead girl with a fancy looking knife in his bloody hands." The desk sergeant shuddered. "He was covered in blood spatters when they brought him in. The girl was gutted like a fish, just like those others we found."

"But I didn't do it!" Khan's knuckles turned white from gripping the jail's bars.

Craig faced Khan. While walking to the cell, Craig had patted the desk sergeant on the back which was all he needed to gain psychic impressions of what the officer saw when Khan arrived earlier. What the desk sergeant said was accurate. Khan was a mess when the arresting officers brought him into the station. Bloodstains on his white shirt cuffs had turned a coppery tone now. Some spatter drops were on his shirt's front too. "What were you doing in the alley, Khan?"

"I was heading to the nightclub district on a hunch when I heard a lady screaming and a scuffle." Khan rubbed the back of his head, a chagrined expression on his face. "I should have known." He looked towards the officer talking to Brianna and whispered to Craig. "It was just like 1888. The woman I thought I was saving attacked me. But it wasn't a woman. It was a man. And he sprayed mace in my face. Then someone knocked me out. When I woke later, I saw another woman on the ground. Someone had cut her to ribbons, and I held the knife. At that moment, the police officers arrived, and I couldn't escape in time." Khan held his hand out towards Craig long enough for the psychic to brush it with his own, long enough for another psychic vision. Khan told the truth.

Craig turned towards the desk sergeant. "Roy, who was the dead woman?"

The officer shrugged. "A homeless woman."

"Not the usual victim profile." Brianna raised an eyebrow. "Yet you said just now the weapon looked like the same knife I took from Toomey."

"And she was cut up the same way too," Sergeant Roy added, casting an eye at Khan.

"Khan is innocent," Craig said, raising his hand to pass it in front of the desk sergeant. But Brianna grabbed Craig's hand, pushed it down, and faced the desk sergeant.

"I can vouch for Mr Khan. He is assisting us with the investigation and was with us on another crime scene last night."

Relief flooded over Khan's face as he heard Brianna's vote for his character. His eyes brightened as a smile beamed from his mouth. The desk sergeant appeared confused for a moment, looked at Khan with a sceptical look, but reached into his pocket, found the swipe tag, and opened the cell door for Khan to leave.

"Thank Christ he's going," a voice mumbled, and they looked to see the skinny mouse man on the cell bench sigh. "He's a bloody nut."

They left the watch house cells and headed back to the main desk where the desk sergeant signed Khan out under bail, which Craig paid.

After slipping his wallet back in his jacket, Craig turned to the others. "Right, let's get out of here."

Brianna shook her head. "I'll head to my office."

Craig looked at her, and Brianna responded to his questioning expression. "I have a hunch I need to check out." She grasped Craig's hand and gave it a squeeze. "I'll call you when I need a lift."

***

After signing the release papers and swapping money for Khan's bail, Craig led his friend to the car park. All the while, something niggled his brain, a sense of foreboding. Something didn't seem right, and he couldn't place a finger on it. Even when they sat in his Jaguar's comfortable interior and he started the car, the engine's purr failed to relax him.

Craig turned his head towards Khan. "What seems wrong about this whole thing to you?"

Khan, who was also sitting in silent contemplation, shifted his gaze from the passing streetlights. "Besides men wanting to be women in this day and age?"

Craig realised Khan had been thinking about the drag queen who had duped him earlier that evening and chuckled. "That's not what I meant, but close. Why were you targeted and framed?"

Khan's face remained still as a Zen pool. "Our adversary believes we are close to him."

"Or he's close to us."

"The bastard knows we're looking for him. And by that, I don't mean the police. He knows I am after him."

Craig raised an eyebrow. "And how does he know?"

247

Shock spread from Khan's face like a frilled-necked lizard's frills. "You can't be suggesting me?"

Craig shook his head. "Not you. No." He turned the car's steering wheel, taking a corner faster than usual, and braked to avoid hitting a slow driver ahead of him. "Earlier, I noticed something when I grabbed your hand at the cell."

Khan nodded for Craig to continue, but Craig was waiting for the driver of the car ahead to decide what he was doing. At last, the car manoeuvred into an all-night car parking facility. Craig pressed the accelerator and moved forward.

"I saw the face of the woman, I mean man, you ran to help. I saw him." He paused again for the traffic. "His eyes looked familiar." Craig's voice drifted off as visions came to mind. But instead of recollections of visions, they were memories of something else. Was it a dream? Yes.

Khan clicked his fingers. "Craig. What is it?"

Craig's voice whispered. "Oranges and lemons."

Khan shook his head in impatience. "Would you stop bringing up that old nursery rhyme?"

Craig shook his head. "Sorry, Khan. There's something nagging at me, and it's not just that rhyme. I feel like it's a warning, but it's disguised as an invitation."

"You're talking in riddles, my friend. I don't understand."

The headlights of Craig's Jaguar washed over a familiar figure standing in the driveway of his home. The woman's raven tresses blew about her in the breeze to reveal her beautiful skin and eyes.

"Your girlfriend's here," Craig cracked, throwing a wink in Khan's direction. "Can't you both find a room of your own without visiting my place?" He laughed when Khan punched his shoulder.

As soon as Craig stopped the car, Khan stepped out to meet Melody who approached him. Her nose twitched as she circled him like a she-wolf checking her mate. But this one smelled something else.

"Where have you been?" Her voice shot at him. "The smell covers you like cheap perfume."

"He's been in jail," Craig announced but not so loud that his neighbours would notice. Melody glanced at Craig, measured his words, and shot a suspicious look at Khan. "The man is innocent. I've paid his bail; and Brianna vouched for his innocence."

"I perceive his innocence." Melody traced the long nail of her forefinger across Khan's chin, and his eye twitched as he refused to show pain. "He may stink of the Demon, but he doesn't carry his mark." Then she stood back, flashing another searching glance at him. "And if he did, I would kill him on the spot."

Khan grinned. "And if you did, you would kill me again and again."

"Your curse would be my pleasure." Melody winked. Her hand took his before her mood shifted. "I know of Gretel's passing. The police rang me at the club." Craig glanced at her with curiosity, and she explained. "Gretel came as a runaway. I gave her a waitress job, and I became her next-of-kin. Even if they unrelated, I treat my girls well."

A despondent expression fell over Khan's face. "I am sorry I failed to save her."

Craig paused, regarding Melody and Khan in his house's exterior light that buttered their features in a golden hue. They looked happy, probably because they were both immortals and found comfort in the companionship. But for how long? The same uneasiness that washed over him in the car tickled his skin now. What was going to happen?

"Is all well, Craig? You look as if-"

A ringing from Craig's pocket broke Melody's words of concern. Craig lifted the phone's screen, "It's Brianna," and he answered. "Hi, it's Craig."

"Craig," Brianna's voice sounded whispery through the phone. "I'm still at the station. You won't believe it."

"What?"

"The knife. It's missing from the evidence room."

Craig's eyebrows raised, and he reiterated what he heard for the benefit of Melody and Khan. "But isn't that under lock and key with top security?"

"Yes, it's supposed to be." Brianna's voice whispered through again. "Listen, Craig, can you come pick me up, sugar buns?"

Sugar buns?

Craig hesitated at the nickname. What a peculiar one. He shrugged. "Yeah, sure. Just let me fix a few things here first."

"Better hurry," Brianna's voice rasped like a phone sex operator's siren call. "I'll be waiting for you."

Craig looked at the phone, his quizzical eyebrow raised while the other eye scrunched. "That's Brianna," he said, strolling to the front door which he unlocked for Melody and Khan so they could enter. "Come on inside and make yourself at home. Tyrone can help you with anything you need. I'm off to pick up Brianna."

"Excellent!" Khan declared, shaking Craig's hand. "I could use a good drink after tonight." He turned about, faced the front door and headed towards it.

Melody waited with Craig and gave him a warning look. "Hurry back." She glanced over her shoulder at Khan who was banging on the door and calling for Tyrone. "Craig, the Demon is up to something because non-Lamia are not his usual target."

"The same occurred to me too. But I thought he had killed non-humans before."

"Come on, Melody!" Khan's voice boomed from inside the door. "Let the man fetch his mistress. Craig, you are satisfied with just the one, aren't you?" His laughter filled the air.

Craig caught the expression on Khan's face, a look of conflict and reminiscence entwined. He touched her hand for a brief moment. "He reminds you of someone, doesn't he?"

Melody nodded. "And it's been a long time since I met another immortal, and one as bold and cheeky." She shook her head. "Sorry, I was talking about the Demon. Yes, he has killed non-humans too, but he does that with a different purpose. He is trying to lure me out."

"This time you have friends helping you."

"Be aware, Craig. The Demon loves to target people to whom I am close." Her eyes reflected a yellowish light that seemed to glow for a second before fading.

A passing car's lights cast a faint glow across the scene and revealed a tear building in Melody's eye. For a moment, Craig stood in awe of the mixture of warrior, queen and woman in Melody. For all the strange things he knew about her - the monstrous shape she could become, the timeless immortal, and her roles - Melody was still a human. The car's headlight beams disappeared, plunging darkness over them, and Craig remembered. "I have to go."

He afforded a brief wink before turning and hurrying to the car.

Melody's voice followed him. "Be vigilant, Craig Ramsey."

He nodded and waved over his shoulder before sitting in the Jaguar's comfortable seat and flicking on the ignition with a roar.

***

As Craig negotiated the late night shopping traffic, Melody's words echoed through his mind. Be vigilant. It

252

stirred memories of the previous night's bloody scene, the massacre. And it also reminded him of the time, some months earlier, when Inspector Myles asked for his help with investigating another spate of killings. It seemed hard to believe.

According to Melody, this killer was the same one who mutilated the other women. And the ones before that. He thought he had caught the killer, a social miscreant who Craig, and another officer had trapped on top of a shopping centre car park. They had cornered the killer before he jumped to his death, dying on impact with the ground three storeys below. Although the man had admitted and confessed to the killings, they never found the weapon.

Although it was easy to understand how no one else had caught the killer, it annoyed Craig that he hadn't. How had he missed it with his psychic abilities?

Before the negativity engulfed him, Craig shook his head because he already knew the answer. No one is perfect, not even him with his sensitive ego. Years ago, he had learned stage magic and sleight of hand, and he used to perform as a magician too. If not for meeting Emily and several other spirits, he may have taken the path of a full-blown sceptic. So many things can be duplicated through trickery. Movies and theatrical people have always been able to fake a bloody gunshot, using squibs and remote control devices. Even catching a bullet between the teeth can be faked although it's a dangerous illusion. History tells of twelve magicians who have died performing it, including Chung Ling Soo, an Oriental performer whose real identity as a Caucasian American came to light upon his death when they wiped away his stage makeup.

Yes, Craig knew he was the real thing; however, society places so much pressure upon clairvoyants and those who claim to possess otherworldly abilities, it ground at Craig whenever he stuffed up along the way.

How easy it would be to leave the spotlight, leave entertainment, leave the circles of psychic practitioners and investigators to live a normal life. That would be lovely, to live the way others did.

Craig slowed the car and stopped to give way to a lady crossing the street. He sat and waited, watching as she crossed. The streetlights highlighted the smooth naked skin of her throat, shoulders and the upper part of her chest. She moved with the ease and grace of a practised ballet dancer, flawlessly, a contrast to the bouncy businesslike gait of a catwalk model, although she could have been one or the other. A quick movement captured Craig's attention, drawing his gaze towards a man who rushed behind the lady, heavy feet pounding the concrete in his hurry to cross before the light changed. However, he kept running, turning to the right on the path and running in the opposite direction to the woman and into the shadows; his white shoes bobbing like rabbits tails. Then they disappeared in the shadows.

Yet no sooner had they vanished, another tall figure loomed from the darkness. The man, shrouded in darkness, slipped through the shadows with the grace of a spirit. But Craig knew it wasn't the case. This one lacked that same feel and presence. At first, it stalked the way a predator might approach its prey. But it exuded an evil aura more than hunger. It carried malevolence as it stepped with purpose in the same direction as the woman. Like a homing device, the tall figure's gaze remained glued to the woman, but for a moment, it glanced in Craig's direction as it passed.

Craig shuddered as the shadowy figure regarded him. The rest of its face remained indiscernible, but he recognised the eyes that glowed like hot coals from a furnace.

The Demon from his dreams!

It was there!

A horn behind him beeped, startling Craig from the vision so he jumped. The traffic lights had changed, and he hadn't realised it. Winding down his window, Craig waved the impatient driver around him and received another indignant beep as the car roared past.

But Craig ignored it as he moved the car to the side of the road and parked before jumping from his car.

Apart from the streetlights which only added to the shadows of the trees, shrubs and bushy foliage, Craig saw little. Where was it? Where was the woman? He scrunched his eyes, peered through the darkness and moved about to search for any other sign.

There!

The tall figure bobbed as it closed in on its prey.

Chapter 22

Craig trotted closer. Craig stayed as close to the bushes and cover as possible to blend in and remain hidden. This slowed him, and although he wanted to protect the woman, he wanted to catch her ominous stalker by surprise.

With excited fingers, Craig dug inside his pocket for his mobile phone. It wasn't there.

"Shite!"

He didn't have it with him. Where was it?

Well! No time to worry about that.

Mindful of the trees' massive roots that threatened to trip him, Craig dashed from shadow to shadow and kept a watchful eye on the stalker. He wished he was a ninja, for every tread upon a lurking leaf or chunk of squelchy ground echoed and resonated like a bowling ball down an alley. His quarry would undoubtedly discover him. But the towering shadowy figure revealed no signs of hearing him and strode closer to the woman.

Fifty metres still stretched between Craig and the couple when the man reached the woman. He opened his mouth to cry out, warn the woman, but it was too late. Then Craig stopped.

The woman turned at the last moment to face the man. A chuckle erupted from her as she tickled her follower. "Boo!"

The man who towered over her by at least a foot laughed and bent to lift her by the waist and turned with her. But her playful struggles caused them both to fall to the soft grass by the path. They continued giggling and laughing and stopped to look in Craig's direction. With his heart beating, Craig paused, overcome with curiosity. The couple knew each other. He peered through the shadows and realised the man in the black cloak was wearing white makeup with black around his eyes. A pair of glasses sat upon his face which occasionally blinked a red light.

Craig sucked in a breath and released it in relief. Trick glasses! He chastised himself under his breath. Why hadn't he recognised them? He once owned a pair as a kid.

Happy to learn his suspicions were unfounded this time and relieved at the woman's safety, Craig turned to head back to his car.

He didn't see what happened next as blackness fell over him, and he slipped into unconsciousness.

Chapter 23

The first thing Craig noticed was pitch blackness. He knew he had woken, but for how long he had been knocked out, he didn't know. A blunt pain hung in the back of his head like someone had inserted half a tennis ball through his skull. The pressure made him wince as he tried to move.

Something prevented him lifting his hand to rub the sore spot. It bit his skin and reminded him of something recent.

His voice sounded unfamiliar and distant as it escaped his parched throat. "Colonel Blaze?"

A tortured scream erupted from his mouth before he realised something had sliced his skin. It felt like a fiery needle had scraped him.

But no other sounds came to him. No raspy breathing from a silent observer. Not even the scuff of shoe tread in the darkness.

However, a horrible pungency reached his nostrils. A stench of death. Then his fingers touched cold steel. Chains. Visions filled his mind. He saw a large man, covered in stinky sweat that glistened around his throat, huffing as he carried part of a large carcass into the room. The vision grew brighter as fluorescent lights flickered to life and cast a sickly glow across the room. A cow's carcass, skinned and bare, flopped onto the table upon which he lay chained and shackled. The corpse passed through his body, blood trickling from its already drained veins to the table, and Craig repressed the urge to vomit. A large saw whirred to life and sang a deathly chorus as it descended from the ceiling above towards him and the carcass. Its spinning teeth ripped into the meat, slicing it. And Craig wanted to scream, but he knew it wasn't happening. This was the past he saw, a ghost of times long gone.

Then the vision faded, leaving Craig alone with his heart beating like the drums from a Tarzan movie.

Pain flashed through his joint like lightning as it tore through his arm. The scream blasted from Craig's mouth like a searing ball of hellfire. His head burned and throbbed. And when his screams stopped, his chest rose and fell with each greedy suck of breath he could take. The vision faded to blackness, and he was alone in the dark again.

***

"But the devil didn't have me yet!" Khan's eyes were wide with the excitement of his tale. Melody listened from the side, her face a picture of deep thought, and dodged as Khan brandished an empty Jack Daniels bottle like a sword. "I weaved, ducked, and parried. The blighter was good, but I possessed three hundred years of experience then."

Tyrone was impressed. "Do you forget things as an immortal?"

"Only humility," Melody interrupted with a grin.

Khan swung about, staggering a fraction from the

heavy drinking, and lifted a finger in rebuke. But the sound of a phone ringing interrupted them.

"That's Craig's phone!" Emily's eyebrows raised. "I never heard him return."

Everyone looked around, their gazes falling upon a sheepish-looking Turner whose white ghost complexion turned a pink rosy colour. Emily clicked her fingers and tapped her foot, her hand outstretched.

"Hand it over, Mr Turner!"

The thieving ghost reached into his jacket pocket, rummaged about, and found the phone which he held out to Emily to took it away. She gazed at the screen. "It's Brianna!"

Tyrone took the phone from Emily and answered. "Hey, Bree, how are you doing?" A frown crossed his face as he listened. "Uncle Craig's at the station now to pick you up." He paused. "Yeah, he left about two hours ago when you rang him." Melody and Khan raised their faces in deep interest. Tyrone raised a hand to quiet their words. "You never called him? Then who-? Yeah, okay. We'll be here."

Tyrone switched off the phone call and looked at Turner, anger in his eyes. "Why do you have Uncle Craig's phone?"

An embarrassed expression was his only reply as the Cockney ghost shrugged.

"The ruffian can't help himself!" Being the only one who could do so, Emily punched Turner in the chops, with a blow her fellow Scots would have appreciated as the English ghost dropped to the ground. "Pray the lad is unhurt, or I will-" Emily stopped herself. "Did you say Craig has been away two hours, and no one wondered?"

Turner stood with shaky legs and rubbed the spot on his mouth where Emily's blow had hit him. "Gawdon Bennet! Thee didn't seem an' all worried abaaaht 'im, y' know wh't ah mean?"

Emily landed another blow that caused everyone who heard it to wince. Turner spun and fell to the ground, upsetting the bottles on the coffee table. "I didn't know you had stolen his phone." With a flick of her crimson hair, Emily turned and headed out the door. "I can't understand how you came to be Tyrone's guardian spirit."

"Where are you going?" Khan called after her.

"Brianna will be here soon herself to pick us up to search," Tyrone told her.

Emily offered a smile to Tyrone, her hand cupping his face. "You're a good lad," she offered him. "And I'm proud of how you're growing up. I'll find your Uncle Craig myself, and then I'll be back to let you know he's all right."

And with a wink, she vanished out the door.

***

Another slash. This time it traced from his solar plexus to his navel, where it stuck for a moment, before jetting towards his pubic bone.

Craig howled in pain. The wounds felt deep enough to expose organs and burned as though touched by pokers. To push the pain from his mind, Craig hissed. It soothed, but his body still wanted to curl up.

"Do you want to die, Mr Ramsey?" The voice sounded cold, harsh and hateful, and possessed evil intelligence. It was an intellect so vile, it made the James Bond movie version of Blofeld sound like a boy scout.

Craig forced the words through the fiery pain. "And. Miss The. Fun?"

A deep chuckle rocked and echoed across the room. "I have waited to meet you for some time... Craig Ramsey."

Craig shivered as a cool breeze wafted across his sweaty skin. He hissed in pain again. "Should. Have. Tried. Yellow Pages."

"I once watched you some years ago," the voice replied, taking a memory lane voice.

"That explains the fogged up windows." Craig couldn't resist commenting.

"You use humour to distract yourself from pain." This time the voice whispered next to his ear. With it grew the stink of death, and it drifted across Craig's nose and into his nostrils where it pervaded his throat until he choked and dry heaved. "But will it keep you from mental pain?"

Craig's eyebrow lifted in the blackness. "What does that-" Something round touched his finger. An instant later, a psychic vision engulfed Craig.

***

The darkness swirled like the water curling down the drain, tinged with grey blood, from the movie Psycho. Only it lacked the staccato slashes of the stringed instruments. As it washed over him, the current drew Craig into the plug-hole's abyss and into a recognisable scene he had not set eyes upon in years. He rubbed his wrists, now released while in the vision, and memories absorbed him like liquid in a paper towel.

It was Craig's old home, a small house he once rented years ago when life was new with youthful optimism. The quiet suburban street he stood upon once played host to the neighbourhood children playing street cricket. Today, all was quiet and bare, except for a red Ford Fiesta parked two houses down the street towards where he knew a single mother lived with her three or four daughters. And he couldn't remove his eyes from the house before him. It had once been home to him and Celina. Above him, the sun shone hard, yet it cast no shadow upon the bitumen. This wasn't merely a psychic vision. It was a reconstruction of an event for him.

With caution, Craig stepped onto the lush green lawn of the footpath and towards the front pathway lined with shrubbery on either side. Reconstruction of a memory or not, the brick paving stones had the same bump in the middle with the weed pushing its way between the cracks. He had tried so many ways to kill the weed, but no matter how many times he sprayed or pulled it out by the roots, it returned with a vengeance and waved its yellow flowers in defiance. It was the plant version of Eensy Weensy Spider, for it always came back up the cracks.

The front door, brown and wooden, beckoned him as the security door squeaked open for him.

Craig's heart hammered hard as he stepped towards the closed door. The sounds of singing drifted from behind it, voices he had not heard in years. The door opened as though by an unseen hand, and he paused at the step as he beheld the sight within.

A tsunami of pain, mental, not physical, but just as terrible, passed through Craig as he watched Julia, not dead, but alive for now, toddling across the living room's carpeted floor towards the large television. She held the remote control in her hand and was flipping channels. Loud music blared from the speaker. The nursery rhyme, Oranges and Lemons, and a ghastly animation played from it. What rubbish did they play for toddlers and young children? Yet Craig as watched her, he couldn't help grinning through the pain and wished he could touch his little girl. But it was an illusion, a projection of psychic vision, and one can't hold a shadow any more than they can catch the wind with bare fingers. Craig opened his mouth and mimed his daughter's name.

Her little fingers paused on the television remote. She turned to face him, looked into his eyes. "Daddy!"

What?

Julia ran with stumbling steps towards Craig, her pigtails flying about. His heart wanted to stop. She was so pretty, and the finger of sunlight shining through the window danced from her light brown hair. He had forgotten how he ached to feel her arms around his neck, to hold her close and -

She passed through him.

Craig had felt ghosts pass through him before. It's like walking through a light gossamer sheet, but it permeates you instead and feels like fine feathers. But this was worse. He felt his heart wrench from want.

Julia walked backwards through him again until she faced him. "Daddy?" Her voice was soft, but he heard it still against the heavy background music. "Why can't I touch you?"

"Julia!" A young woman walked into the room, wiping her hands on a tea towel. The suds from dishwater were heavy on her fingers. "Daddy's not here. Who are you talking to?"

A perplexed look crossed the little girl's face, furrowing her otherwise smooth brow as she looked at Craig. Then she glanced back to her mother. "Just playing, Mummy."

"Go, change into your other clothes to visit Grandma and Granddad, will you?" Celina's voice cracked, and Craig stood to regard his first love.

She was as beautiful as he recalled. Celina's hair normally hung shoulder-length in a blonde waterfall that cascaded and bounced. But now it was wet from a shower and was brushed back from her face to reveal her fine features better. It emphasised her crystal-clear eyes and delicate chin. He ached to touch her, to hold her again one last time.

Craig's jaw dropped in surprise as he realised. This was the day Celina and Julia left to visit her Celina's parents. Later that day, they would die on the roads of Mount Lucrapana!

What if he could stop them?

Craig watched as Julia hurried away on her little legs to her room. Then he stood and looked into Julia's brown eyes. Old memories popped into the present like bubbles in champagne. He still loved her, but it didn't feel the same as back then. Pain from the loss remained, but this time...

***

He was in the dark. Again.

Oranges and Lemons. The song continued playing. Its volume cranked higher until the sounds rattled through his bones and into his being. The vibrations sickened him, made him want to vomit and explode. And tiny spots of red danced before Craig's eyes which still swam in salty water from the vision. Then the music stopped, and relief flooded his screaming body's flesh and bones. Every nerve sighed, thankful for the reprieve.

"Tears!" The harsh voice whispered in the darkness beside his ear.

The spots rushed in, alighting upon Craig's face, and he smelled searing flesh before the pain seized him and ushered a scream from his emotion's bowels. And as he cried, he realised how much sadness he released. Sadness for Celina, sadness for Julia, and sadness for their loss to him.

"It hurts to lose someone, doesn't it, Mr Ramsey?" The voice mocked him in the darkness. "Did you see them before they died?" Craig refused to answer, gulping back the sobs as other memories rose to the surface along with his self-hate and loathing. Why couldn't he have lent Celina his car instead? Why didn't he take away her car keys, hide them, so she couldn't find them and had no choice but to use his instead?

The voice rose in volume. "You petulant baby! Which part did you see?"

Craig stopped his crying, not because of the voice, but because something else occurred to him. "Why did you show me?"

"It hurts, doesn't it?" The unseen captor paused. Was that a smirk behind the silence? "It wasn't a quick death, you know."

Craig's brow furrowed. He held it a moment before realising the bait. His lips hardened in resolute silence.

"No, Craig, it wasn't a quick death at all. What did the authorities tell you? They swerved? Hit a tree?"

But Craig stayed quiet. Only the sound of his watch's sweep hand ticking reached his ears. He tried concentrating on the sound, allow the distraction to clear his head of the pain.

The demonic creature had other ideas. From his other ear, Craig heard the intake of breath, the grin behind it, and then it spoke. "Do you know she yearned for another?"

Craig fought back more tears. He recalled someone

tried moving in on Celina and him once. But Celina remained faithful to him. He knew for a fact. His psychometric visions would have picked up anything else.

"She wanted him so bad."

Doubt stole into his mind like a thief through the night. There was a way Celina could have cheated on him without him knowing. Tyrone and his late sister Debbie, his adoptive niece and nephew, had done it. Could Celina have too? No! He couldn't believe it.

"You're full of shit."

Yet the voice persisted. "Yes, Craig, she wanted him. Every time you boned her, every time you joined her, and every time her legs wrapped around you as you thrust, she imagined it was him. And she didn't call your name when she died. It was his."

Every word permeated Craig's mind and created a new vision. Each image featured Celina having sex with another man. In one vision, Julia stood outside the open bedroom door as Celina writhed in ecstasy with a faceless man. Tears flowed from Craig's eyes. He couldn't stop them. Tears of anger, frustration, hurt. He knew they weren't so true, yet the visions persisted, smashing the precious memories he held of the woman he loved the most in younger days and his little girl.

"And do you know who she was, Craig?" The voice paused, smacking its lips.

Craig's lips trembled. "She?"

"Yes. She." Footsteps. A slight scraping sound from

his feet. "She who you loved and who betrayed you."

Craig's voice came like a zephyr. "Celina."

"WRONG!" The voice boomed hard, echoing against unseen walls in the darkness. "She was related to the snake you befriended. She was the Lamia's daughter!"

Craig's jaw dropped in the darkness. What? Silence replied, waiting, listening to Craig's breath rasp from his dry throat.

"That, Craig, is why I had to kill her. Do you understand?"

The music from Oranges and Lemons cranked again, blasting the air, echoing from the walls about him, and vibrating into his core. It wasn't the words, nor was it the music. It was the volume. It permeated his mind, rocketed through his spine, and jangled his nerves.

Oranges and lemons,
Say the bells of St. Clement's.
You owe me five farthings,
Say the bells of St. Martin's.
When will you pay me?
Say the bells at Old Bailey.
When I grow rich,
Say the bells at Shoreditch.

Shock filled Craig's chest, constricted his throat, and trapped the words inside him. All he could do was move his lips in silent rage. Through the darkness, he mimed the words. "I will kill you."

Suddenly light blazed through the room with blinding

intensity. Craig groaned and shut his eyes hard against it, squeezing his lids against the assault. Rough fingers pried at his eyelids. Craig tried shaking his head to stop them, but one powerful hand gripped his skull like a vice and held him still while fingers compelled his eyes to open. A dark shape moved across the light like a moon across the sun and blocked the painful rays. But by doing so, Craig's eyes focused upon something worse. Much worse.

When will that be?
Say the bells of Stepney.
I do not know,
Says the great bell at Bow.

The first thing Craig noticed were its eyes, the same blazing red coals he had seen in nightmares. To see them in dreams was terrible; but in life, they curled his stomach. However, where the eyes burned, the face looked like a victim to the red orbs. At first, Craig thought bandages covered it, wrapping it like an Egyptian mummy he had once seen in the London Museum. But a second look revealed no shape under the bandages, and the wrappings were more like a wilted pumpkin's skin, cracked with age and dehydration. Yet, it wasn't a skin he had seen before. Moreover, the stench! Craig wished he could free his hands to hold his nose. The best he managed was screwing his nostrils up, but that only opened them more, and breathing through the mouth made it worse. The creature, because that was all Craig could call it, poked a grisly piece of flesh from its mouth, which was a hinged slit, similar to that of a sock puppet. With a slurpy flick of its tongue, it grinned, the slitted mouth stretching until it seemed it might crack and break.

Words, none of them complimentary, and all of them born from surprise, spilled from Craig's lips. He couldn't help it. His mind, tortured from the visions and now the incessant super-loud music blaring through his ears, snapped.

The pumpkin creature bobbed its head closer to Craig's eyes, its mounded nose pressed against his, and it roared. "You want to kill me? You think you can, mortal?" It stood back, rocked its head in laughter loud enough to accompany the blaring music. And from its grotesque non-lips screamed the rest of its song. "Here comes a candle to light you to bed, And here comes a chopper to chop off your head! Chip chop chip chop the last one is DEAD!" It screamed the last word hard into Craig's face, its putrid breath forcing through his nostrils until he gagged.

Craig almost missed what happened next. The creature moved too fast for his eyes catch more than a fleeting glimpse, like looking through a strobe light in the darkness. A flash. A blade.

Pain ripped through his shoulder as a blade sliced through his pectoral muscle and bounced off bone.

Darkness fell, covered by a crimson curtain. The last thing he heard were voices, somewhere in the distance.

But it was too late...

Chapter 24

Cold water embraced Craig's face, followed by the comfortable pressure of a wet handkerchief. A buzzing sound filled his head as he opened his eyes against the light of the torch in his face.

"Craig!"

A familiar voice. But cotton wool in his mind slowed his recall. He blinked and groaned. An ache behind his eyes, similar to sinus pain, throbbed while the glands in his throat threatened to pop.

"He's waking up." That voice again. A woman's voice. "Craig, are you okay? Can you talk?"

Pain flared in his left shoulder, hurt like hell, and he stifled a moan. His words remained trapped in his sore throat. His mouth tasted like fine sandpaper, and his tongue refused to cooperate.

The woman's voice spoke again. "Craig! It's Brianna. Don't move, Tyrone is coming with the car."

Tyrone? Yes, he knew that name. And Brianna. Yes!

At last, he found the strength to open his eyes against the brightness. His other hand lifted to push it aside. "Am I alive?" His voice croaked. Craig shook his head. "Water, please."

Plastic pressed against his parched lips. Water flowed against the opening and touched his tongue, which reacted in surprise to the flow. He choked on the sweetness as it passed to his throat.

"Easy." Brianna's hand cradled his head as she took the bottle from his mouth. "You need to sip it. Don't gulp."

"Where am I?"

A pause. He sensed other people about but they remained in shadow.

"We're at the meatworks near Narrawa," Brianna replied. "It took a while to find you. Was it the Ripper?"

"That shoulder wound looks like his mark," another woman's voice reached his ears.

"Sex on legs," he muttered, uncertain why. An uncomfortable silence reached his ears. It lasted only a moment. Something told him he shouldn't have said that. But it hurt to think and know why. "What happened?"

Other sounds reached his ears from the left. He turned to face whatever it was, and a large shape loomed from the darkness, cape flowing around a towering presence. He uttered a scream and struggled to stand. Brianna's voice shushed him, hands held him close to her soft breast. That felt like home to him.

"It's only Khan and Melody." Brianna's voice flowed through him, comforting. "What the hell did that killer do to you?"

"The Demon is that. A monster. He loves to induce fear before he kills." The dark shape spoke with a baritone voice. "I know he was here, but I couldn't find him. The creature moves like the shadows."

Ah! That's Khan. Of course. Craig's recall finally started to work.

The sex-on-legs woman's voice responded. "Yes, he was here. But he's fled. To where, I don't know."

"You disturbed him." Craig forced the words, and they shuddered as his voice shivered. "He was here." Sobs wracked his body, making him shudder. It hurt his shoulder, but he couldn't stop. "The bastard killed Celina and Julia." He sniffled warm snot and water up his nose, almost choked on it, and the words flowed. "I have to kill him or die trying."

Meanwhile, the woman, who Craig recognised now as Melody, examined his wound. Her warm breath on his skin tantalised him, causing him to blush when he remembered calling her sex-on-legs in front of Brianna, and she stood back. "The Demon infects men with his knife. I can smell the knife and the Demon's presence on Craig, but he is not infected. Something protected him from that."

"That would be his past exposure to ectoplasm." Emily's Scottish accent was an added welcome relief to him. "It creates a healing effect that never stops, besides other things."

Craig's eyes fought to focus in the light from the torches and rested upon Melody's face. He could see Brianna, but why couldn't he see Emily? "I can't see you, Ems."

"You're uninfected by the Demon," Melody explained, her voice soft and hypnotic, "which is lucky because I would have killed you, otherwise, out of mercy. My guess is the Demon tortured you and affected your mind. It's a psychological attack, but you can recover from it."

"That would explain why you can't see me," Emily's voice floated to him. "But you can hear me, my boy."

Khan, who had been watching from outside the room, re-entered. "The young lad is here with Craig's car. Can he walk?"

Brianna moved, taking Craig's right arm around her neck, and stood, standing him beside her. Craig's legs shook, weak as a kitten's, but he found his footing.

"The car is just outside," Khan said, moving in to help on Craig's left side. Then he saw Craig's injury, rethought his strategy, and looked at Brianna.

Brianna shook her head. "I have him. Can you drive? I don't want Tyrone driving unlicensed. If another officer catches him, it'll create unwanted problems."

Khan laughed. "Can I drive? You must be joking. Of course, I -"

"No, he can't," Melody responded. "But I can drive Craig's car, if that's what you mean." She poked her tongue, a human one, at Khan. "Some of us immortals choose to live in the present rather than the past."

Before long, they strapped Craig in the backseat of

his Jaguar, Tyrone beside him with a concerned look on his face, and Khan sat on the other side. Craig lay with his head back on the seat and closed his eyes as Melody started the car. Brianna gazed at Craig for a moment through the side window before approaching Melody's window.

"Melody, I'll follow in the police car. We're going to Craig's place."

"Shouldn't we take him to the hospital with that wound?"

Emily had been watching Craig with a worried motherly gaze. "He doesn't need a hospital. The physical wound is healing now as we speak, thanks to the ectoplasm."

Melody examined the wounded man in the back. "I'm impressed." Facing Brianna again, she added with a whisper, "Okay, his place it is then. He will need rest, and I'm concerned by whatever mental tortures Craig suffered."

"Me too," Brianna nodded, casting another look through the window at Craig.

"We can help him better at home than any hospital." Emily clapped her hands at Melody. "Now, go, will you? Time is ticking. Take us home."

***

Melody drove the car away, her headlights shining the dirt path towards the main highway, and Brianna hurried to the police car she had commandeered from the station earlier. When she reached it, she noticed

Emily waiting in the front passenger's seat.

"I thought you'd be with Craig."

"Dear, I could do that, but that rotten haggis Turner is with Tyrone. He's in their front passenger seat. I can't stand the sight of him and don't trust myself near him." She turned and flashed a grin with a wink. "Besides, I don't trust him enough not to steal from the police car. He'd as likely hot wire it and steal it later."

***

Craig awoke from a dreamless slumber with a start. Lights, red and blue, flashing in his eyes had woken him with a start. A cockney voice reached his ear and exclaimed about "the cozzers". Disoriented, he snapped glances to the left and right. "Where are we?"

Tyrone placed a comforting hand on his uncle's arm. "It's all good, unc. We're home, but the cops are here too."

Craig's head swam and his neck joints hurt from a stiffness. He stretched. "What? Why? Did someone call them about my being missing?"

Khan and Tyrone shook their heads. "No one called them," Tyrone explained. "Even Brianna kept it to herself."

Craig allowed a smile to cross his face as he saw a back-lit uniformed officer approach their car. The officer leaned towards the driver's window, which Melody opened for him.

"Good evening, ma'am," the young uniform greeted

Melody. "Do you live here?"

Melody shook her head. "No, but its owner is in the back."

The officer moved towards the back door. Craig stirred, ready to move forward, and hissed as his wounded shoulder and chest protested. He moved more gingerly and stopped upon realising blood stained his shirt. He tapped Khan who reacted in surprise at the blood and understood Craig's concern. If the police saw the wound, suspicions would rise. The quick-thinking immortal covered him with his own cloak and gave him his own top hat.

Khan opened the door opposite to the officer, and Craig stumbled out, stiff-legged and hobbling like an old man as he fumbled to cover his bloody stains. He feebly attempted a winning smile for the policeman.

"Is everything okay, officer?"

He saw Craig and came around towards him. But Craig was already covered by the cloak. The policeman paused upon seeing Craig's otherwise dishevelled appearance.

"A hard night, sir?"

"It was an office party." Craig flashed another smile, hoping he wasn't too bruised.

"Costume?" The officer eyed the strange cloak and hat.

"Yeah, I dressed as a magician who had done one too many kids parties." Craig paused. "They can be murder for some."

The policeman raised a quizzical eyebrow before shrugging. "Are you Mr Craig Ramsey?"

Craig nodded. "How can I help?"

"We received a call from your neighbours." The officer pointed to flashing lights from Craig's house. The front door was open, and a couple of other police officers were checking the broken door. "Neighbours reported hearing shouts and sounds of fighting." He eyed Craig's face, maybe seeing the fragments of bruises there. "How long were you at the party?"

"Since 6pm." Craig's voice belied a slight slur, due in part to his earlier torture.

"It's 4am now, sir."

Melody stepped in. "It's been a long party, and Craig is feeling unwell." The officer wavered as Melody spoke for Craig, and Melody's experience as Libyan Queen and night club owner came to play. "Have you caught the people responsible for the noise, or are you intending to charge my friend for something?"

The officer hesitated, his eyes wavered across Melody's attire - a mix of nightclub wear and vixen garb - and he swallowed. "I'm sorry, ma'am," the officer looked towards Craig, "and I'm sorry to you too, sir." He looked over his shoulder. "We caught one fellow on your front lawn. He was unconscious and looks beaten up. We're taking him for questioning."

At that moment, another police vehicle arrived on the scene and parked behind Craig's Jaguar in the driveway.

Craig's head lolled as he faced it, but a smile crept across his face. It was Brianna. She stepped out of the vehicle, a picture of confidence and poise as she approached them. "What is it, constable?"

The officer turned towards Brianna who flashed her badger for him, and he told her the story of the break-in. Snippets of the conversation reached the other three's ears. Something about sounds of fighting, smashed window. Craig stepped towards the front lawn and spotted glass scattered about the grass like sharp glittering confetti at a sadomasochistic wedding.

"They broke in another way," Khan commented, guiding Craig in case he fell. "They smashed this window from inside, otherwise it would be on your carpet."

Brianna's voice floated towards them. "Yes, I live here too." A pause. Craig looked towards Brianna and realised their story about being at a party could fall apart. Then he spotted a faint apparition next to her whispering in her ear. Turner? Brianna paused. "I was at the station earlier, working on a case, and I'm home now." She looked towards Craig, gave him a short nod and another towards the police car with the flashing lights. "Is that the kid there? It may relate to a case that Craig and I are working on. Yes, we live together, not that it's your business, constable, and you can stop the attitude, thank you. I will interview the boy at the station soon."

Brianna left the constable to scratch himself, and continue his job, and approached Craig. Bags hung under her eyes, filled with unclaimed sleep, and managed a smile. "They caught one kid on the lawn, and apparently there's another one inside in the kitchen. They're both beaten up pretty badly."

As Brianna finished her words, a policewoman carried another youth out the front door and along the path towards the waiting police car. Craig spotted the lad and shambled over towards him with his hand outstretched. The policewoman saw this, didn't realise Craig's intentions, and manoeuvred herself in the way. Meanwhile, Khan hovered nearby in case Craig, who was still unsteady on his feet, needed help.

Brianna spoke for the uniformed officer's benefit. "It's okay. He only wants to touch the lad." Realising that sounded wrong, she added, "I mean he's Craig Ramsey. He wants to check for vibrations."

A sceptical yet puzzled look crossed the officer's face. But upon seeing Brianna's badge on her belt, the officer nodded. Craig leaned forward, took the lad's hand.

The lad, about fifteen-or-sixteen years of age, reacted in surprise and adopted a curious look when Craig took his hand. "What the?" Then he shook Craig's hand a moment before the psychic broke contact. "I broke into your home. Why are you shaking my hand?"

Craig eyed him with derision. "I didn't. I held it. You shook it." With a shake of his head, he waved the officer towards the car. "Take him away. I have all I need." Yet his mind painted a confused expression across his face still.

"What is it?" Brianna asked.

Craig allowed a smile. "They took nothing. Looks like my security systems caught them in the act and forced at least one out before the police arrived."

"Security system?" Brianna lifted a confused eyebrow. "What do you mean?" Then the penny dropped. "Do you mean Sifu Yong?"

Craig winked with a tired nod.

Brianna held Craig's hand briefly, allowing the touch to send him her feelings. "I want to stay home, but I ought to interrogate those kids. Is it related to our case?"

Craig nodded. "I don't know if you will learn much more. But if you think it will help, I'll keep the bed warm for you."

Chapter 25

The first uniformed cops drove away with the two youths locked safely in the back, with Brianna following. Meanwhile, the third and fourth officers stayed behind to clear up other things.

Craig wished they hadn't. There was something he neglected to mention from his visions. A third youth had invaded his home, and Craig guessed this would-be thief was hiding inside somewhere. He wanted to question the kid, and he didn't want the officers in his way.

Craig cast an eye at the two officers. "Thank you for coming. I feel safe knowing you guys were quick on duty."

One officer, a young woman who appeared more makeup than anything else, acknowledged him with a nod. "We don't know how many broke in. And they smashed some things, too. Do you mind if we come in so you can tell us if anything is missing?"

Ah! That's why they hung around.

Craig shrugged. "Sure. But I am pretty beat right now from the party. It can wait until later, right?" He passed a hand before her eyes as he delivered his words with the hint of a commanding tone.

For a moment, the officer wavered and hesitated. But the second policewoman, who looked like she had broken up bar fights on her own and kick-started her electric toothbrush, approached and broke the spell. "It's all a formality, sir."

At any other time, Craig would have persisted, but his head hurt too much. He figured it best to continue; he could still send them away after a cursory glance. "Sure. I can see what obvious things are missing, I guess, but I think you have everyone of them."

Craig approached the front door, walked in, and looked around. What a mess! Most of it was near the rear entrance, the lounge room, and the kitchen. His visiting room for clients remained unscathed, but books lay strewn on the floor, including the volumes he read the previous afternoon. Some pages were bent, but none torn. Several slashes spewed stuffing from the sofa. Craig reminded himself to talk to Sifu Yong about that but he doubted the Oriental spirit would recompense him, anyway. Apart from that mess and the broken crockery in the kitchen and dining room, Craig found nothing missing.

"It looks like everything's here," he stated, matter-of-factually. "Just small stuff that's damaged." However, he noted upon touching his coffee table that the boys had been searching for something.

At that moment, Sifu Yong, looking resplendent in a fine changshan (a traditional Chinese dress), appeared near the doorway to the back garden. Craig spotted him, lifted a finger to his mouth to hush the Chinese spirit as though scratching his nose, and coughed. Yong nodded his head and regarded Craig's friends with a serene gaze. Craig allowed himself a smile, glad that Sifu Yong was visible to him, even if he was faint. That meant his spirit vision was returning. Thank the Universe.

"Nope." Craig smiled at the officers. "Nothing missing. I'd say we were lucky."

Officer Make-Up nodded, looked towards Officer Big Bertha, and they both excused themselves. Calm as a Zen master, Craig shut the door behind them. Then he waited a moment, checked they police car was leaving, before striding towards the Sifu Yong.

The Chinese spirit who haunted Craig's backyard Kwoon and taught him martial arts regarded Craig with studious eyes. "You need rest. Where have you been?"

Craig shook his head. Other matters needed attention. With a sweeping hand, he introduced Khan and Melody. "Sifu Yong, you know Khan -" The spirit bowed in recognition. "And this is Melody Kostas, also known as Lamia, Queen of Ancient Libya." Yong's eyes registered surprise at Melody's plain youth, but regained his composure, and bowed to her. Craig continued, "What the hell happened here tonight, Sifu?"

Yong ignored Craig's tone and turned to exit the door. "You received uninvited guests. Please, follow." He passed through the door as though it never existed.

The three flesh-and-blood people followed Sifu Yong into the Chinese-style garden, past an artificial stream and a pond filled with golden koi, towards a shed Craig had converted into a Kwoon. The door was already open and Craig flicked a light switch as they entered, bathing the room in bright light to reveal a martial arts studio that would have made any Hong Kong movie producer salivate with envy.

There, in the centre of the room and tied by his thumbs with his hands behind his back, sat a dark-skinned youth. His eyes bulged at the sight of the three new arrivals.

"Let me out of here," he called, struggling at the thumb ties, but Sifu Yong, invisible to the lad, clipped him over the ear. The boy yelped in surprised pain and swore. "Who did that?"

Craig crouched in front of the lad and examined him. "Why did you and your friends break into my home?"

The lad quietened and clammed his mouth shut. Craig slapped the boy hard across the mouth. Spittle flew across the floorboards. But the boy remained silent.

Craig remained calm. "The police were here. I sent them away with two of your friends."

The boy's silence answered, but his eyes spoke volumes of how hard his brain was working.

"It's a matter of time before the kid with the mohawk talks." Craig looked towards Khan and Melody. The latter nodded while Melody itched to say something.

"Let me talk to the boy. Maybe he'll talk to a chick." Melody said the last word with derision. Perhaps she didn't like the boy or the word, but she spoke in his language.

The boy lifted his head as Melody approached him

with a sultry look in her eyes and licking her lips. Her supple body enticed his eyes, attracted his attention.

Then Melody's eyes changed, swirled like a kaleidoscope, colours shifted into each other and back again, and the teenager stiffened with his jaw slack. A second later, Melody's body shifted, her pants falling to the ground, and she transformed into the Lamia creature of old, half-snake and half-human. Craig marvelled at the opalescent scales of Melody's belly and the pearlescent lustre of their surface as the lama slithered towards the boy.

But the lad didn't run, nor did he flinch from the horror before him. Slack-jawed, he fixed his eyes fixed upon hers. Craig recognised the fixated expression; he was a master hypnotist, but Melody's power was greater in that regard. For that matter, Craig was glad Melody was on his side. The psychic stole a glance which revealed Khan's awestruck expression too. No doubt existed in Craig's mind; Khan's feelings towards Melody had changed in the last twenty-four hours.

Even in her serpentine form, Melody kept an alluring air of sophistication crossed with sexuality. With the slightest of sounds as her weight brushed against the matted floor, Melody brought herself within two inches of the boy's face and flicked her tongue. Its tip touched the captive's nose enough to make him twitch.

"Hello, young man." Her voice sounded like smoke and hot wax and sticky honey and aroused Craig as much as the boy must have experienced. "How are you feeling?"

A muffled sound issued from the lad's inert lips. His

eyes were round as golf balls.

Melody nuzzled his throat as her serpent's body twisted and embraced the lad's body. "Do you often break into other people's homes?"

To this, the boy managed a slight nod.

"I bet you do. And you're so brave and gutsy about it, too." Melody brought a hand down towards the boy's hip. "Why did your friends come here?"

The captive's lips shuddered and sweat beaded on his forehead as his breaths came in excited bursts. "A stranger paid us."

"Paid you?" Melody's voice remained as seductive as a phone sex operator, alluring yet mocking. "How much?"

"Five hundred for each of us."

"Five hundred?" Melody's face showed no surprise, but a slight sneer appeared at the corner of her mouth before disappearing again. "Five hundred, eh? What would you do with five hundred dollars?" The boy's eyes moved to his top right. But before he could answer, Melody prodded with another question. "Who sent you?"

The lad shrugged. "I never met him. Greggo did the talking. But I saw him from across the street. He was tall, wore a hat like the one he wears." He nodded towards Craig who was still wearing Khan's hat.

Melody's eyes glanced at Craig, then at Khan, and narrowed. It was as if she suspected him. Craig removed the hat and handed it back to Khan in case Melody would turn on him.

Melody's voice remained honey-sweet like Shania Twain in You're Still The One. "Did he look like either of my friends?"

The boy shook his head. "He looked like a rotten vegetable at first. But his face had bandages around it and looked like they leaked. Someone was with him too."

"Someone else?"

Craig and Khan glanced at each other with puzzlement.

The lad nodded. "Yeah."

Melody glanced at Craig with a raised eyebrow. "What did he look like?"

The lad shrugged. "Baldish. I remember the shine off his head. He looked spaced and reminded me of a dirty old man."

Melody caressed the boy's cheek and elicited a pleasurable murmur. "Not as handsome as you, my Adonis, eh?"

A dopey grin crossed his face. "I wouldn't know."

"Yes, you do." Melody moved in closer. "You're just turning me on with your coy act, aren't you? What did you come to steal?"

"We were told to steal some dagger."

Craig's face exuded puzzlement. "A dagger?" Khan

shushed him as Melody paid them a scornful look.

The lamia faced the would-be burglar again. "A dagger. What kind of dagger?"

The lad gulped. "I never saw it. But we were told we'd know it when we saw it. The thing was meant to have pictures of Greek gods on it or something."

Melody afforded another glance towards Craig and Khan who reflected their interest too. Craig wanted to ask questions himself, but Melody only nodded at him with a wink before returning to her prisoner. "What else can you tell me?"

The lad shrugged. "That was all. He was going to pay us more upon delivery."

"Where?"

"Across from the Pleasured Snake. But we couldn't find it. That's why I came in here. I spotted the dojo inside here, while we were breaking in at the back, and I spotted the spears. I figured if I found it, I would get a big bonus for it."

"I see," Melody mused to herself. She passed a hand over the burglar's eyes, lulling him to sleep before returning to her human shape. Melody bent, picked up her underwear and long black pants, and slid into them. All the while, she appeared nonchalant about her nakedness from the waist down. Meanwhile, Craig averted his eyes out of modesty and respect, and Khan refused to take his eyes away from her shapeliness. Melody grinned as she approached them and Craig in the eye. "This sword the boy mentioned sounds familiar. What do you know of it?"

Craig, his eyes heavy with drowsiness and his head throbbing from fatigue, shook his head and stifled a noisy yawn. "I apologise. I can't stop yawning. I don't know about any such sword except for Khan's story of how he met you in 1888."

Melody nodded, firelight still shone in her eyes, and she passed her hand in front of him.

Chapter 26

Craig awoke from a dream about glowing eyes. The sounds of night drifted through the partly open window. Otherwise, the curtains blocked most of the outside light, but his bedside digital clock's luminous screen displayed as seven o'clock. Something warm moved against him, and he turned his head to see Brianna's slumbering form next to him. One of her naked arms lay draped across his chest. A few images flashed across his mind as he reached to touch her skin, and he smiled at the psychometric vision of her stealthy entry into bed to avoid waking him. Even under sleep's spell, he had responded to her presence although he remembered nothing of it now.

He tried sitting up and winced at the pain in his shoulder. What had the Demon used to cut him? Not his blade? That would mean the Demon had infected him, wouldn't it? Then the memory of the abattoir returned with full force to his consciousness; he scrunched his eyes against the painful images. Then he remembered: the house, the break-in, the youth's interrogation, and blackness. Why was everyone taking pleasure at knocking him unconscious these days?

Brianna murmured in her dreams as Craig slid out from the covers. He found no need to wake her. She needed sleep too, unlike his immortal friends. Craig wondered where they were now.

As if on cue, the sound of cutlery scraping china reached his ears, and the delicious aroma of hot food enticed his mouth's saliva glands to action. Food! Craig rubbed his empty belly, stood, and stretched. He was naked! Who undressed him? What else happened here while he slept?

A few moments later, he had dressed himself and headed downstairs. By the sounds from the living-room, Khan and Melody were discussing stories from their pasts with Turner and Tyrone.

"You lot sound fresh for people I doubt have slept in over a day." Craig stepped into the kitchen to see Melody had been cooking. She waved away his curious look in anticipation of his next words.

"It's something I grabbed from a local Indian restaurant. I hope you like curries. Are you hungry?"

"Absolutely." Craig's mouth closed his eyes to appreciate the mouth-watering smells. "I'm famished." He noticed Khan playing pool with Tyrone. The immortal eyed up and sank two balls with a satisfied look adorning his face. Craig turned towards Melody. "How long have I slept?"

Melody counted the plates against the number of wakeful souls. "The whole day. We cleaned up for you." She nodded to the sofas. "Some furniture we covered with some sheets from the closet. Tyrone and your Scottish spirit Emily helped." Craig thanked her, ignoring the sound of Tyrone's moans at losing to Khan, and Melody offered a smile. "Is Sergeant Brianna still sleeping?"

Craig nodded. "How did you go with the third burglar?" Melody eyed him with a blank look. "The kid in the kwoon, I mean," Craig added, jerking his head towards the outside gym.

Khan wandered over to Craig, grasped his sleeve, and took him away with a whisper. "We disposed of the lad."

"What?"! The surprise leapt from Craig like a shocked rabbit, but Khan shushed him and jerked his head. "Over here."

Once away from the crowd, Khan explained. "Melody sniffed the lad. He was infected, Craig. You know what that means."

"The Demon had cut him and possessed him."

"Yes. It also means the Demon knew what you learned from the lad. It's like one of your electronic bugs planted on someone."

"A wire?"

Khan nodded. "Only this one is a psychic kind. There was only one way to deal with it." His voice was low and matter-of-fact.

Craig's mouth opened in shock. "You killed him?" He looked around in surprise and horror. "You killed someone in my house?"

Khan remained calm and quietened Craig with a look only an immortal with many years of experience could manage. "I'm not telling you how we handled the problem. But it's done, and the police have no reason to come after you. That's all you need to know."

Craig was uncertain. "But Brianna -"

Khan placed a calming hand upon Craig's shoulder. "Brianna is having a nice sleep. Being a soldier, she would understand."

"How can you be sure?"

"Because this is war, my friend, and the authorities have no jurisdiction on the supernatural. Nor do they know how to handle it."

Craig placed a hand upon Khan's and saw what happened. The immortal was right. Melody had resumed her Lamia form and killed the lad who died of a heart attack, in much the same way her other victims had died, the same way a rabbit dies when killed by a python. The blood stopped in the veins and forced the heart beat to halt. Yet no bones broke either. No fingerprints, no other marks. Just a dead lad who would be found on the riverbank later tonight.

A knowing look crossed Khan's eyes. "You saw, didn't you? We had one of Melody's faithful take the boy away. No one will know a thing."

"Hello, there, Sergeant Cogan!"

Khan and Craig whirled to see Brianna entering the bright room, blinking in the glare. She offered returned greetings to the house-guests and smelled the curry with a starving look.

At that moment, Emily bustled into the room and clapping her hands. "Come on! Dinner's ready, everyone. Be seated, be seated." She turned to face Turner and glowered at him. The Cockney breezed past her with a sheepish look upon his mug. "I would deny you supper, but you can't eat, anyway. You haven't lifted the silver again, have you?"

Turner shook his head and continued by in silence, his eyes shifting as he passed.

The dinner conversation started light as they tucked into the naan bread, rice and assorted curries. Then it changed to the cleanup of the room. All the time, Craig feared what would happen. What would he do if the intruder turned up in conversation?

As it happened, Khan had thought of it already.

"Sergeant Brianna," he said, his baritone catching everyone's attention. "Pray tell, what did you find in the interrogation?"

Brianna's expression changed, clouds appearing from an otherwise blue sky. "Now, that's a story of its own. But in short, one lad sang like a bird. Something scared him, but I don't know what.. Apparently they had a leader by the name of Brian. He was here too."

Khan remained calmer than a placid lake on a sunny day. "Is that so?" He looked towards Craig and then at Melody. "I saw no one else."

Melody and Craig remained quiet. Melody showed no signs of discomfort. However, Craig's stomach rumbled hard. Although he kept plenty of trade secrets, he hated keeping secrets and lying, especially by omission, about what he knew.

"The kid said Brian had spoken to a large man about breaking into your home." Brianna chewed a piece of naan bread and swallowed. "They were looking for a sword."

"What kind of sword?" Craig asked, fighting back beads of sweat. He was certain Brianna would recognise his guilt when she eyed him, her eyes full of calm, but she said nothing.

"He said it had pictures of Greek gods on it and an inscription." Brianna chomped on some butter chicken. "Do you know what he means?"

Craig wiped sweat from his brow. "Maybe. But I think it was a dagger. Isn't that like the one you mentioned, Khan?"

Brianna watched Craig's eyes, the flicker of a grin appeared at the corner of her mouth, and she glanced at Khan who nodded.

"Yes, it's the one I grabbed from Melody." He turned to the ancient queen who was polishing off her plate and smacking her lips. "Do you remember our first meeting, lover?"

"Like it was a century ago," she replied. "What happened to that dagger?"

Khan thought for a moment. "I handed it to a collector friend of mine, someone related to Craig as it happens."

"Why are you sweating?" Brianna asked Craig when all eyes settled on him. "Are you having trouble with the curry?" Craig shrugged, chewing on a piece of chicken hot enough to melt his throat to slag. Brianna grinned in response. "Or is there something else you want to tell me about the kid who was hiding in your kwoon?"

Craig's eyes opened wide, surprise etched in his forehead's lines. "What?"

Everyone else remained quiet enough that the sound of a nearby grandfather clock's ticks echoed through the room.

Brianna grinned, unable to hold back the chuckles. "Melody already explained what happened with the kid." She winked and everyone else joined in with the laughter.

"Gotcha!" Tyrone laughed, his high-pitched giggles eliciting more laughter from the others. "We fooled you!"

Craig surveyed everyone around him, a smile slowly spreading from his mouth. "How?"

Brianna leaned towards him, pulling him closer, and gave him a kiss on the lips. "Relax. I understand what's happened. I think we'll be fine. This is a war with the Ripper, after all, and no one else would understand."

When everyone stopped laughing, Brianna added, "But I want to know about the sword or dagger or whatever it is. This Ripper Demon wants it for something and believes it's here. Otherwise he wouldn't send people to break in when he knew you would be elsewhere."

Craig shrugged again. This time, Turner spoke.

"I know ov da weapon," he responded, surprising everyone because he lost his Cockney accent for a moment. "Lor' luv a duck! Besides lookin' after young master Tyrone 'ere, I 'ad ter make sure i' arrived ter yew safely from London. Did yew get it?"

"What weapon?" Craig wanted to know.

"Lawd above! Yew must'a received da package by now , innit.," Turner responded. "It should 'ave arrived in da last fortnight. Sorted mate."

Craig shook his head and wondered what Turner meant.

"I know the parcel!" Emily replied, and everyone turned towards her. She gazed at Craig and spoke excitedly. "It arrived on the morning you were heading out to Brianna's place, before she moved in here. You were late to leave and in a rush."

A memory came to Craig, the "aha" kind that left pennies trickling over the floor. "Yes! There was a parcel. What happened to it?"

"It's in the hallway behind the table where you left it!"

Chapter 27

Craig hurried from the dinner table towards the front hallway. Near the front door stood a wooden table upon which stood two photos. And there he saw it. The large package, wrapped in brown paper and looking pleased with itself for playing hide-and-seek.

Craig stretched forth his fingers, grabbed it from the ground, and stood with it under the glare of the light. For a moment, he allowed himself to look at it and chastised himself with his inner voice at having missed it.

Brianna called from the dining room. "Are you bringing it back here or are you keeping it for yourself?"

Craig realised he was alone and strode back with the package in hand. It was a good weight, so whatever it contained was heavy enough to be a substantial dagger. He ran his fingers across the handwriting but received no psychometric information. Curious! How could they hide it? Maybe changing hands so often in the postal service weakened the vibrations, but that wasn't always the case. Whoever wrote it possessed old-fashioned sense. Years ago, Craig's next-door neighbour, an octogenarian to Craig's early teens, had a similar handwriting style. But this one appeared more ancient by at least fifty years again. The writer must have had an artistic flare.

The high expectation of his waiting friends filled the room. But Craig didn't notice as he turned it over, examined the string tied fast around it with tiny, tight knots, and read the sender's address: an enigmatic "London, United Kingdom".

"That's the one I saw!" Emily's voice woke Craig from his mental musing. "Well, go on! Open it, will you?"

Craig sliced the string with a steak knife from the kitchen drawer and tore into the wrapping. Brown paper flew about him until he discovered a cardboard box. Now, a vision hit him. He looked around, saw a darkened room with dim lights and closed curtains that reached ten feet high. An odour like an ancient tomb or a museum filled his nostrils, and beside him stood a long table. The vision faded quickly.

Brown string held the lidded cardboard box shut fast, and inside the twine, a yellowing envelope caught his attention. The string was easy to untie; it only required the pull of the end to undo the rough bow knot. The envelope slid away, and Craig slid a finger under the flap to tear it open. Inside, another piece of yellowing paper waited.

Craig removed the letter, flipped it open, and moved his lips as he read the first line or two. Its script was as old as that on the package's address label. A strong-minded individual had written it, but the mind was old and had seen much. It reminded him of Khan who sat across the table from him.

Craig bit his lower lip in thought. "This letter is dated

four months ago, yet the person who wrote it is much older."

He read it aloud for everyone to hear.

"Dear Craig,

It is about time you opened this parcel. I sent it along with my faithful spirit friend, Turner, such that he could tell you the rest. I foresaw you missing the parcel the first time, so I took the added precaution.

You will require this dagger. I came across it in 1888, thanks to a mutual friend, Khan Gaston. As you will have gathered by now, he met with a young mystery woman, but I believe you will find otherwise. She is as ancient and mysterious as the lost continent. Appearances can deceive, but she holds honour. You can trust her and Khan.

Although I never knew the name of the lady in question, I believe you will know her as Lyrica or something as musical. I never met her, but her vision when I touch her dagger is enchanting. I can discern a small part of the dagger's history. The Lamia lady knows more.

But she does not know this.

I see two visions of your future. In one, you die, and so do all you love - including the Lamia, your policewoman companion, Tyrone, and your friend, Khan. So will many more from this world. Heed my advice of the Dagger, and you will all live longer.

Khan left the dagger in the care of my family and organisation, along with many other treasures from the ages. But it has gathered enough dust. Its duty and destiny draw closer.

The dagger has a companion, and the man known as Ripper carries it. Not only does he use it in killing women. The knife you hold in your hand now is one of the two instruments required to kill him. Thrust it into his heart from the front. Thrust the second through his heart from behind. Marry the two blades so they touch. And the ancient Evil will perish. Never separate them once they come together, or the Demon shall rise again. When He perishes, so will his curse upon his male victims.

I know you will try to find me. So I can only warn you. Do not try.

Your great-great-grandfather,

Reginald Ramsey II"

"He has your name!" Brianna's words echoed Craig's sentiments as he looked at the paper in disbelief.

Craig turned the paper over, brushed his fingers across the surface, and his perplexed expression grew. "The date at the top states he wrote this in 1892, yet it's post-marked two months ago in London!" He mouthed the next word. How?

Khan and Melody both reached forward for the paper, but Khan reached it first. After a cursory glance, he nodded, handing it to Melody. "It is Reginald's handwriting, sure enough. He is your great-great-grandfather." He saw Craig was opening the box.

"Khan, remind me to ask you more about my

ancestors."

All eyes set upon Craig as he gently shook the box's lid to remove it. The bottom part dropped into his other waiting hand. Then reaching inside, Craig grasped and held up the blade for everyone to see.

The same wonder swept through Craig as voiced by Tyrone and Brianna when they saw the wondrous weapon. Polished beyond perfection, the blade glinted as it caught the light. The reflection tracked its way from the handle, past fine holes and grooves in the blade, to the tip. Exhilaration filled Craig's chest as he allowed himself to express his appreciation. Careful not to touch the blade's edge, in case he cut and infected himself, Craig admired the engravings in its handle. For a moment, as he watched the pictures, he fancied they moved. A Herculean figure strangled a lion while other dead lions surrounded him, a serpentine creature with bat-like wings flapped them, and an indescribable creature screamed as though in pain. But the figures were not Greek, Roman or Egyptian.

Craig glanced up at Melody, holding the weapon toward her for inspection. "Melody, is this the same knife you lost?"

Recognition mixed with a sense of relief appeared on Melody's face. She nodded while holding the knife in the light. She flipped it through the air, caught it neatly in her hand by the blade, and delight sparkled from her eyes. "Ah! Yes! It is the same."

"You first held not long after your husband died." Craig's words filled the air, flowing from his mouth in a dreamy stream. "The figures are not Greek. They're older than Babylon."

"Older than Atlantis," Melody confirmed. "The man with the lion is Gilgamesh. The winged creature is an Akhekhu, maybe the same I met as a young queen so long ago, and the other creature is the Unnameable Beast."

Craig nodded. "But the weapon was not yours in the beginning."

Melody stopped, her eyes narrowed as she lifted her gaze towards him, and everyone remained quiet. "No. It was not mine. I wrested it from the Demon soon after he beheaded my husband, Eyvind." A tear formed in her eye. "He was the last of my original family. If only..." Her voice drifted away.

Brianna shook her head at Craig with unspoken words that carried volumes of meaning. She felt Craig had said too much and upset Melody.

Khan diverted the subject. "The only thing is we now need the other dagger. Where is it?"

Craig's eyes lit with excitement. "Melody, did you say I'm uninfected?" She nodded. "I believe I know why I'm uninfected. I wasn't cut with the real blade. The real blade is at the police station in custody."

Brianna shook her head. "No, it's not. Do you remember I returned to the station last night before we went hunting for you? Well, I went to check a hunch about the knife."

"And?"

"It's not in the evidence room. Someone has stolen it."

Brianna's took a breath; her lips tightened for a moment as she did. Then with a sigh, she replied. "I have a hunch we'll know for sure in the morning when I can see the security footage."

Chapter 28

Craig and Khan faced each other, swords ready, as they practised in the kwoon.

Rivers of sweat flooded from Craig's skin. The perspiration from his forehead flowed past his eyebrows and stung his eyes. But he ignored it and slashed his Katana at Khan's equally drenched body. Lithe as a snake and quick as a mongoose, Khan side-stepped, parried Craig's sword, and delivered a kick towards his head. Craig bobbed his head backward and the boot missed his face. But it was a feint. Without losing balance, Khan re-diverted his kick and connected with Craig's wounded shoulder.

A shock of pain flared through Craig's shoulder and distracted him. That was all Khan needed to pass Craig's otherwise good defences. He slid inward, slashed towards Craig's throat with his own blade, and stopped short of touching his skin by a mere bee's penis width.

"Perhaps you should rest that shoulder more."

"I'm fine." Craig shrugged and gave the shoulder a gentle massage. "The wound has closed over already." He pulled back the t-shirt's collar to reveal the smooth skin below. Only the slightest scar remained: a faint white line. "But it hurts like hell when kicked by your heels."

Khan marvelled at the speed of Craig's healing. "I have never seen a mortal recover as fast as you. Are you sure you haven't met a genie like my Azriel?"

Turner chortled from the sides where he and Tyrone were watching the melee. "Emily told me yew 'ad contact wiv ectoplasm some years back. Is that right?"

Craig replaced his t-shirt. "A long time ago, yes. Besides enhancing the psychic abilities I already had, it enhanced my body's healing speed." Still puffing from the workout, Craig grabbed two bottles of water and tossed one to Khan.

"I wonder. Can it bring you back from the dead?"

Craig swished a mouthful of water and swallowed. "I hope that revelation comes late."

"Old age is fine," Khan philosophised, "but immortality is more a curse than a gift. With no one to share the long life, it's a lonely time."

"But you never know when you can meet someone worth the wait." Craig winked. "You and Melody bonded fast."

The immortal chuckled.

"Gawdon Bennet! You've given 'er da sausage, 'aven't you?" Turner's voice rang from the side.

Khan's face remained as still as a statue's. "A gentleman says nothing." But he leaned closer to Craig and winked. "But the furniture floated an inch or two and dropped when we finished."

***

Brianna stretched back in her desk-chair and yawned. The past forty-eight hours ached through her joints and her neck. Then she saw the woman standing inside her office.

She stopped her surprised scream and sighed as her heart slowed again. "Emily! You should ring a bell or something if you keep popping in like that."

Emily smiled. "I'm sorry, dear. How well can you see me now?"

"Like you're flesh and blood." Brianna motioned to a nearby chair. "But you're not completely solid, either. If I look hard, I can see through you like peering through coloured glass."

"Your psychic abilities are growing well. Have you noticed anything else?"

Brianna pursed her lips and bit the skin inside her mouth and nodded. "Something, but I'm not sure. Do you mind if I ask you something?"

"You may."

Brianna checked the door, and seeing it closed, spoke in a quiet tone. "Do you remember Melody mentioned what happened when she made love to her husband?"

Emily allowed an amused smile. "She gave ample detail, more than a lady of my time would. Was there anything in particular besides how he used his -"

Brianna grinned. "I mean the thing about the heavy vases moving?"

Emily's eyes widened, and a smile shone. "Do you

mean the floating?" She laughed when Brianna nodded. "Oh, yes! Yes!"

Brianna raised an eyebrow. "Are you having an orgasm from the thought, or is something else happening?"

Emily laughed with a tear rolling down her face. "No! It's not that, dear. What it means is you have found The One. It never happens with others, only with your true soulmate."

"But I've knocked furniture over before."

"Not like that, girl!" Emily had trouble speaking for her laughter. When she settled enough to talk, she continued. "Has that happened with you and Craig?"

"Six inches," was all Brianna said, but it brought a laugh from the Scottish spirit.

"Oh, bless you, lassie!" Emily surprised Brianna with a hard hug. At last, she let her go. "Things are going well. I'm happy for you. My husband and I -" She stopped, as though lost in memory, and changed the subject. "You mentioned checking on security cameras from the evidence room. Did you find anything?"

Brianna was still thinking about Emily's behaviour. She had expected Emily's congratulations, but she hadn't foreseen that level of happiness. But taking the subject change, Brianna went with the flow. "Yes, but I'll tell you more when I arrive home."

***

Craig was a new man by the time Brianna arrived

home. A day of alternating meditation and workouts in the kwoon with Khan and Sifu Yong allowed him to clear his mind and body. The previous night, although he had slept since his kidnapping by the Demon, and his subsequent rescue, a pale man with hollow eyes had stared at him from the mirror. But late this afternoon, his eyes shone with their familiar strength and light, and his complexion glowed; it was better than the greyish skin.

Craig looked up from reading the junk mail when Brianna dropped her keys on the table near the front door. Where he looked better, Brianna appeared tired but happy.

"How was your day?"

Brianna smiled and tipped her head back as she stretched upward to kiss his lips. Soft and loving. He liked that. "It's been a long day, but you'll love hearing about it."

"Oh?"

"Mmm hmm." Brianna looked around. "Where is everyone?"

Craig chuckled. "Melody is at her club. She attended a funeral this afternoon for the girls who died at her home." Brianna opened her mouth, a concerned look on her face. "It's okay." Craig anticipated her concern. "Melody knew you were working and wanted to be alone, anyway. Khan attended with her, and I imagine he's with her now, too. Tyrone's out somewhere on training with Turner. I don't know where Brianna is, but she likes her space sometimes too."

"Good." Brianna took Craig's hand. "You're looking better."

"Much better. Meditation and exercise helped."

Brianna hummed. "That leaves the sexual healing to be done then."

"Hold on." Craig laughed as Brianna tried to lead him to the bedroom.

"To what?" Brianna's eye twinkled with a cheeky light. Her hand connected with him and slid lower.

"There's time for that later," Craig allowed a grin to cross his face. "Tell me about what happened today."

Brianna pretended to pout before winking. "Yeah, plenty of time. In a nutshell, I scoured the video footage from the evidence room. It took a lot of time on my own because I trust no one. But I did it."

"What did you find?"

"It was Tony Gifford who took the knife from the evidence room. I don't know how but he passed the locked door and the evidence room's guard."

"You guard the evidence room?"

Brianna nodded. "We can hold all sorts of evidence there. Sometimes it's drugs or guns. If anything goes missing, the guard is accountable. Inspector Myles is questioning the guard still, but from what we saw on the video, Gifford passed without him noticing. But, and you'll love this, the video image fuzzed out not long after Gifford reached the door. The next image shows him leaving with his leather jacket appearing heavier on one side."

"Didn't he go on leave?"

"That's right. He's supposed to be on leave, but I remembered hearing he visited not long after his release from hospital. I assumed it was a check-in with the bosses, but obviously not."

"So what now?"

Brianna shifted from one foot to the other. "I took a warrant out through Inspector Myles, and he placed an APB on Gifford. When we arrived to search Gifford's place, he wasn't home. It doesn't look like he's been there for some time. The Inspector also ordered a check on Tony's bank accounts by subpoena. Can you guess?"

"His accounts are cleaned out, yet there's no paper trail to show where he went?"

Brianna shook her head. "No. One account is empty. He emptied it the day he left the hospital. The other accounts with the same bank still hold cash. His credit card's untouched."

"And what's happening with that?"

"Inspector Myles has suspended Tony Gifford without pay, and the Inspector has had the bank freeze his accounts. We're checking other banks, too, in case he holds funds elsewhere. But we'll flush him out."

Craig bit his lower lip. "So we know Gifford took the weapon. The confessor guy cut Gifford with it the day you caught him. It's a fair assumption to say the Demon infected him. He's the new killer."

Brianna nodded. "We'll get him. It's only a matter of time."

"There's something else, too," Craig added.

"What?"

"It's later."

Craig picked Brianna up in his arms and carried her through the bedroom door.

Chapter 29

Coloured lights swished across the nun as she emerged with Bible in hand from the darkness. A sea of faces murmured at her presence. The drums beat a slow tempo as stepped in rhythm across the floor towards them, and although she knew none of the audience, they all watched with dry-mouthed expectation. Her robes, black and heavy dragged along the wooden floorboards, and she almost stumbled. The rhythmic drums provided the sensuous back-beat to melodious Gregorian chants. Enigma's Principles of Lust provided the perfect introduction as she reached the pole, lifted the edges of her robes and lifted a high-heeled shoe towards it to perform a perfect stretch: luxurious, sultry, and seductive. The bible dropped to the floorboards at her feet.

Down in the audience, Turner watched with wide-eyed wonder and pupils the size of saucers. Next to him, a punter let loose a loud wolf whistle, joined soon by others. A five-dollar note hit the stage floor. His hawk-like eyes caught the movement, and he slid a hand towards the currency, but the dancer's robe fell onto the note first. He looked up at the dancer, a sheepish grin on his face. Although invisible to everyone else, Turner reacted when he saw the dancer rebuke him with a shake of her head.

Turner sat back, looked at the punter next to him.

"Awright geeezzaa! The lady detective moves like a dream. But do 'er legs match?"

Khan and Craig pretended not to hear Turner. If two men responded to an "invisible friend", it mightn't look good, even in a strip club.

However, Khan allowed a glance in Craig's direction as the stripper, dressed in a nun's habit, removed her wimple and tossed it to the side. Golden hair reflected the spotlights as it tumbled past her shoulders like a waterfall. "I can't believe you talked Brianna into this."

Craig allowed a smile as he admired Brianna's form. "I offered, but I can't walk in heels the same way."

Craig and Brianna had hatched the plan of masquerading as a stripper in Melody's club, with the lamia's permission, to draw out either Gifford or the Demon. So far, they hadn't caught sight or wind of either, but they had made good money from tips thrown by the punters.

Brianna twisted through a specially choreographed routine on a wooden chair, removing first one stocking to reveal a long tanned and luscious leg before rolling her head on her shoulders to whip her hair in the air. The male audience, and a few women, roared their approval.

Khan surveyed Brianna's supporters among the sexually charged audience. "Craig, it's been two weeks now since we followed this plan of yours. I don't think Gifford or the Demon are taking the bait."

"They will. We need to keep our eyes peeled."

"Perhaps he senses the trap."

Craig shook his head and tried to ignore another punter who called at Brianna to come to him. But the dancer ignored him, rolling her hips under her robe, which she lifted to reveal both bare legs as she approached the pole. Then turning to face the audience, she leaned against the pole and used it to support her back as she slid to the ground. Then she tantalised them, lifting the edge of her gown up, a smidgen with each drum beat. The view she afforded was to see but a smidgen beyond the area between her knees, yet the audience whistled their approval. More notes and coins hit the stage where, unseen by the majority, Turner picked up coins the best he could without attracting undue attention. Luckily for him, all eyes were on Brianna who stood with a cheeky expression and opened her habit to reveal sensuous curves. Her tanned skin showed no flaws, and a black, sequined bikini left something to the imagination.

"I will bet a lifetime of the hardest liquor you can stand," Craig responded.

"I'm immortal."

"An average lifetime then."

"I can consume a lot in that time." Khan raised a suspicious eyebrow. Then he noticed Craig's gaze focused across the room.

"Don't look. He hasn't noticed us." Craig turned his own eyes back towards the welcoming sight of Brianna swinging on the pole. "It was lucky I caught the light bouncing off his balding head. Turner, let Brianna know Gifford is here."

"Right yew are, guv."

Unseen except by any who lacked the psychic ability to witness spirits, Turner shambled beside Brianna and whispered to her. In response, she winked her understanding to the Cockney spirit. Yet, another punter took it as a sign that the exotic dancer was flirting with him. He held out a fifty-dollar note towards her, and Brianna picked up a prop donation basket and held it towards him. The punter shook his head, leaning over the edge of the stage towards Brianna. She lifted a high-heeled shoe to keep him at bay.

Seeing the punter's persistence at climbing on stage, Craig moved to stop him. Khan stopped Craig with a warning look.

Craig grinned at Khan. "Thanks. I didn't think."

"The quarry is so close. We need not telegraph our whereabouts to him." Khan pointed towards the scene, and Craig soon realised he needn't have worried.

Brianna's stiletto heel pressed into the man's chest and pushed him backward. To a casual observer, it appeared as part of the act. But it wasn't. A burly bouncer with a chest like an Olympic pool appeared and warned the patron while Brianna continued her dance routine.

The final strains of Principles of Lust filled the air with the tempo slowing. Brianna gripped the pole so her spin slowed. She descended in a gentle drop to the floorboards where she picked up the bible. Facing the crowd, she opened the book and a plume of blue flames licked from its pages, and the stage lights faded to black. Only her face and shoulders remained lit in the darkness. The flame's light reflected from her sweat, adding enticement to the punter's imaginations.

Three beats later, she shut the book.

Lightning flashed and thunder clapped and rolled from the stage.

She was gone.

A moment later, the lights blazed to light to reveal an empty stage. The punters clapped and whistled, and others moaned their disappointment. The sexually frenzied wanted more of the bikinied nun with the smooth tanned skin.

Yet, they soon forgot when the next dancer emerged with a fresh routine to tease their eyeballs and entice money from their wallets.

Meanwhile, backstage, Brianna hurried past the next exotic dancers who congratulated her on the performance. Brianna nodded to each, a pleasant smile plastered on her face until she reached the dressing area. Brianna wished she had her own dressing room, but Melody stated the dancers didn't have them. Besides, the girls were too busy preparing themselves to perve or anything else. They were there to perform shows and keep money flowing from the customers' wallets.

If her friends were right, Gifford was in the audience, so the Demon would also be close.

Brianna swallowed, licking dry lips, and hoped their

plan worked. If she could entice the demon to follow her, they would trap it and capture it tonight. Her friends would stay close behind her but inconspicuous to avoid alerting their quarry. She had no idea what would happen with Gifford if the Demon refused to release its grip on him. But that would come later.

Brianna hurried to dress herself in denim jeans, flexible enough to allow movement in a fight, and a tank top that boasted her feminine assets. She checked in the mirror's reflection and removed any stray glitter that strippers love like fairy dust. Once certain everything looked right, Brianna picked up her handbag containing Craig's prop bible and strode to the side door. With a nod and bye to the security guy, she emerged from the bustling backstage into the quiet dark alley.

Her senses sprang to life. Ears pricked for the slightest sounds from behind, Brianna's eyes looked for the tiniest sight of danger. But there was nothing in the alley. Why would someone wait so close? Silly question. The Demon possessed an arrogance that precluded worrying about capture by authorities. Why would he worry when he possessed men? And according to Melody Kostas, the Demon possessed considerable fighting abilities and could move like a ninja. Furthermore, he could appear as a bookish priest with a weak chin, a homeless vagrant or even a college student. She held strong suspicions Gifford suffered the same fate: possession by the Demon. But where else was he?

Brianna's steps carried her without incident or sign of anything suspicious until she at last reached the bus station. Still, her eyes and ears remained alert. She saw neither Demon nor bald-headed rogue cop. Craig and Khan were following from a distance, but they remained out of sight two bus stops down the line.

A tramp breeze scuttled loose papers about. They looked like they were chasing a rogue plastic cup that rolled ahead along the footpath.

From somewhere in the station, drunken slurred voices reached her ears. It sounded like two drunks fighting over something: one male, one female.

Smack! A fist exploded against either a jaw or other body part. The male scream that echoed, accompanied by sobbing, told her the guy had lost that argument. A vision came of a man rolling on the ground, his hands cupping his injured groin and pride.

Brianna missed her chance to see. The headlights of the approaching bus appeared. She checked her watch, smiled to herself, and tapped a hasty text message to the others.

"BUS APPROACHING NOW."

The bus pulled up with a squeak of brakes at the stop, and its doors opened with a pneumatic hiss and clatter. Brianna stepped up, swiped her transport pass, and sat three seats behind the driver. The bus was otherwise empty. The driver waited a few minutes, checked his watch, pressed the switch to shut the doors, and the bus moved forward.

Brianna tapped another text.

"ON THE BUS NOW. NO SIGN YET."

It appeared tonight was another failure. No sign of the Demon. Not a trace of Gifford. She was sure either of them would have attacked by now. And they weren't picking victims from elsewhere either. For although the Demon hunted primarily those descended from the Lamia, pure humans also fell prey to the Demon or his hosts. The hosts usually showed less discrimination and picked a particular class. Those infected by Demon in the 1880s - the time of Jack the Ripper - targeted prostitutes. Lamia owned no brothels then, and three of the canonical five victims shared her gene pool. But the other two weren't. They were killed by association either through personal connections, friendship, or because they also traded sex for money or drugs or both. And many others fell victim to the Ripper's demon blade without the attention of the newspapers.

Besides her masquerade as a stripper, Brianna had laced herself as bait further by close contact with Melody to capture her scent. They hoped that would entice Demon more.

If tonight, the seventh failed attempt in a row, was anything to go by, either the Demon had disappeared and moved on for another few decades or he knew of their trap.

The bus emerged from the bus tunnel, which is one of many like a rabbit's warren under the city, and entered the open city streets. Brianna watched the people and cars the bus passed and searched for any clues, anything to show they missed their quarry by a little. But nothing caught her notice.

No one waited at the first stop. It sat there, a lonely shelter adorned with the poster for an upcoming movie called La La Land. Brianna realised it had been years since she last visited the cinema. Work had always consumed her. Perhaps it was time to change that although she would probably enjoy something like Deadpool more than a Woody Allen musical.

The bus approached the next stop, her stop. Brianna reached for the bell and pressed. The bell dinged, punctuating the hum of the bus' engine. She looked through the window ahead and saw Khan and Craig waiting. Brianna looked forward to arriving home, having a hot shower, and relaxing in bed.

A few seconds later, Brianna realised something was amiss. The bus' didn't slow. She pressed the button again, a few times. Couldn't the driver hear it? The bus continued at the same steady cruising pace.

"Oi!" Brianna called loud enough to wake the dead. "That's my stop!"

The driver glanced towards her and back to the road ahead without slowing. His shoulders remained hunched, a little tighter now.

"Stop the bus now!"

The driver replied with rolling laughter, and she spotted the glow of eyes reflected from the windscreen in front of the driver.

Chapter 30

Was it instinct or premonition?

Khan lifted his hand to hail the bus driver and swore when it failed to slow.

The route sign above the bus' front window flicked to "Not In Service" seconds before it passed them. The breeze of its wake blew the leaves and debris from the street into the air.

Craig and Khan exchanged looks and ran after the bus, waving their arms and shouting. But it didn't stop.

"Time for the backup plan." Craig retrieved his phone from his pocket and speed-dialled a number. "Melody! Come and pick us up. The game is on."

Chapter 31

The bus driver's laughter outmatched the din of the bus' engine. The bus surged forward faster than the speed limit, but not fast enough to tip as it turned corners. And its driver continued to laugh as other car drivers sounded their horns in protest and indignation.

Meanwhile, Brianna stepped from her seat and moved towards the middle of the bus, closer to the back door. Her eyes searched, and she considered the strength of the windows. Would she be able to kick through them fast enough? How fast could she pull the back door open against the pneumatic motor? A million other thoughts raced.

Without a doubt, the Demon was here in the bus. The brilliance from the driver's eyes was enough to prove that. But where was Gifford?

As if to answer the query, the driver's body trembled, spasmed and shuddered. His head tilted back, the cap falling off to display a hairless head. Gifford? From her seated position, one hand gripping a pole for support, Brianna watched in incredulity as Gifford's mouth gaped wide. Clawed fingers sprouted from Gifford's mouth and expanded like a stout plant. Something clicked, the sound filled the air with the same grossness as a breaking neck. But it wasn't a broken spine, for Gifford's jaw unhinged, the chin dropping to his knees.

Then the rest of the unearthly creature crawled from the orifice.

At first, it was thin and wearing a black suit that resembled clothing from two centuries ago. White ruffles peeked from the end of the black suit jacket's sleeves. Feet clad in leather shoes with silver buckles stepped to the floor to reveal the full body of the parasitic Demon. In the meantime, Gifford's jaw returned to its normal shape with a slosh then a slap. The rogue police detective shook his head while nursing his jaw with one hand. The bus lurched as he regained control of the wheel.

Brianna held tight to the pole to stop herself falling from the seat. Her eyes wouldn't leave the ghastly sight of the Demon which now filled out, appearing more humanoid now than like a half-inflated balloon.

And its eyes! They burned brighter than coals from Hell's furnace as it strode closer.

Through the side windows, Brianna noticed they were in the side streets where things were quieter. Fewer houses stood here, and her mind raced to recall in what area this was. Then she saw the river bank and recognised the area. They were still in the metropolitan area, but this was near Queens Park. Of the few houses in the area, their lights were out, leaving the area in darkness save for the lights in the bus. An old area with elderly residents who retire to bed within minutes of sundown.

The vehicle's engine chugged down into lower gears as it ascended a hill and away from the river. But Brianna didn't have time to watch those details and waste worry on that.

The Demon, its face still looking like a rotten pumpkin wrapped in a dirty muslin sheet, approached. Its mouth resembled the sliced lips of a Halloween jack-o'-lantern, but the eyes that staring back at her resembled a human's eyes. If the eyes were deeper set, Brianna would have thought the creature wore a mask. But as it approached within two feet of her, she realised it was disfigured skin as though burned. Did all demons look like this?

"Good evening." The lips moved the way a human mouth would speak. But the voice was cold and harsh as Craig said. Its eyes regarded Brianna, surveying her form. For a moment, Brianna felt uneasy as the Demon's eyes assessed her physical assets. "You dance well," its lips formed a stiff sneer, "for a police officer." Its dark-skinned hand with rough fingers pointed to a seat. "Won't you sit?"

Brianna refused to move or take her eyes from the sinister spectacle before her.

The creature chuckled. "Did you believe I would not recognise you?"

Brianna shifted her weight for a stealthy backward step.

The Demon turned his head a little towards Gifford who was behind the bus' wheel. "You know about Detective Gifford, don't you, Detective Cogan? I believe he works with you."

Brianna shook her head. "I don't work with him unless my fists are busting his face." She allowed herself the hint of a smile as Gifford's shoulders tightened behind the driver's wheel. Her words must have reminded him of the bloody nose she gave him.

The Demon's eyebrows, a thin line or wrinkle on its brow, rose in question. "I don't understand. He spoke well of you as though you had once been lovers."

Brianna hesitated. What? But she recovered. "Unlikely and untrue. The mummy's boy is a dreamer."

Its mouth twisted in a sneer as it chuckled; a deep fruity sound. The bus lurched. Gifford must have touched the brakes in anger. The Demon swung around. "Settle down there. I'm talking to the woman. You will have your turn soon enough." He turned back to her. "He is such a jealous man. Imagine my surprise upon learning women had joined the police force. I thought it a joke. But then I saw you two months ago." He nodded at Brianna's questioning expression. "Yes, before I acquainted myself with Tony Gifford. I have watched you for some time. And now," it licked its lips, "I find you and Gifford were never lovers..." For a moment, the Demon appeared thoughtful, but about what?

Brianna didn't see it coming. The Demon's fist connected with her jaw, Brianna's vision transformed to a black canvas dotted with sharp stars, and her shoulder glanced off the arm of a seat as she tripped on the step in the middle of the bus. Instinct told Brianna to crawl backward towards the back of the bus. Logic told Brianna it was a dead end. Reality agreed.

But the Demon didn't follow her. He had turned towards Gifford, flicked his head towards Brianna, and laughed. "She's all yours, Gifford, as I promised. Have your way with the bitch."

Through blurry vision, the detective watched as Gifford, who had parked the bus by now, pass the Demon. He licked his lips with delight as he approached. But it was a different Gifford. The old Gifford, although a sleazebag, possessed some form of sanity; now, humanity no longer lived there.

Gifford half-danced and clicked his fingers to a tune only he could hear. An unnatural lust, the hunger of a crazed man, illuminated his eyes from within. His fingers fumbled with his belt, its buckle jingled as it released, and he popped the zip of his black pants before letting them drop to the ground. He licked his lips with a wink, and the unheard tune in his head transformed into a hum - You Can Leave Your Hat On. Joe Cocker and Etta James would roll in their graves to have heard it. They made the tune sexy, but now Gifford's hummed rendition would scar the prostrated detective for life.

Brianna tried to move, but the grogginess from the Demon's blow still hampered her. She tried to kick, but Gifford caught her foot and gripped it hard. With his other hand, he waggled the finger of his spare hand in the way he would admonish a naughty child, and tut-tutted. Then he fell upon her. His breath - hotter than a Sahara summer, stronger than a corpse's body odour, and harsher than an income tax reminder - assaulted her nostrils and neck. He tried kissing her while his fingers fumbled with her jeans.

Chapter 32

Gifford stopped, a surprised look on his face as he felt a bulge, the kind you never find on a woman down there...

"What the-?" His eyes flicked towards his prostrate victim's face.

But Brianna's face didn't welcome his eyes. Gifford's eyes opened wide enough they could have popped from his eye sockets. "What-?"

Craig's steely eyes sparkled at him; his mouth grinned ear to ear in amusement. But before the detective could respond, a harsh pain filled his face as his nose exploded from Craig's vicious headbutt. A second blow made the detective roll away, crying in pain and holding his nose. Blood spurted and Sergeant Tony Gifford sat up and cradled his bloody face.

"Sorry, Giff, old chap. You're not my kind." Craig lifted a foot and pushed hard against the surprised man's chest. The detective seemed to fly backward before landing on his back in a disgraced heap, crying and moaning in pain. Craig sprang to his feet, regarded the blubbering mess.

The Demon who had been standing with his back to them, but watching through a reflection in the glass windows, whipped around. If surprise registered on his face, the pumpkin-skin bandages hid it. But his features froze for a moment. A moment later, the Demon recovered and strode forward to attack the new arrival.

The Demon's voice registered surprise. "You were an illusion?"

Still dressed in Brianna's clothing, Craig winked and pursed his lips like a kiss. "The best."

Do you want me to take him? Tyrone's voice spoke from inside Craig's head. Earlier that evening, Craig allowed the boy to channel into his body, and using a trick Turner had taught Tyrone, they transmogrified Craig to resemble Brianna. He had been the one who performed the exotic dance routine onstage; not Brianna.

No, thanks, Tyrone. I've got this. Go, get the others.

Meanwhile, Tony Gifford scrambled away on hands and knees to pass the angered Demon. He reached the driver's seat, hit a button, and rushed out the bus door as soon as possible.

Craig stepped forward, his gazed focused on the Demon, and delivered a triple punch to its face. Its skin looked squelchy like a vegetable's, but its jaw felt human. The Demon staggered back in surprise. Craig advanced again, but the Demon blocked his next punches. Whatever the Demon was, man or supernatural creature, it knew how to fight. It also knew how to hit.

Craig aimed another combination of blows, but the Demon blocked them before lunging forward to deal a blow to his chest. The wind whooshed from Craig's lungs as he staggered backward. The Demon dealt another punch. Craig blocked in time with his left forearm, but painful pins and needles paralysed the limb. Less than a moment later, a hand reached out, grabbed Craig's other fist and twisted hard like a corkscrew. Craig's pained scream cut short when a foot kicked into his chest and sent him flying against the back seat of the bus.

The Demon chuckled. "Tony told me you were a master fighter."

Craig strained to speak. "Melody said you talk like an old woman."

The Demon strode forward, grabbed Craig by the collar with one hand and punched him in the face with the other. Craig dropped like a ton of bricks.

But Craig shook his head to clear his brain. "Not yet. Too soon."

Not realising the meaning behind Craig's words, the Demon laughed. "It's never too soon to die." He lifted Craig, wrapped an arm around his neck, and applied a headlock. A fist crashed into Craig's face with the power of a sledgehammer. Craig squirmed, burying his face in the Demon's side, his left hand reaching for one foot while his other hand grabbed for what little hair grew on top the Demon's head. His fingers tangled, gripped, and pulled. His hands and body moved like a circle. While the right hand pulled down on the Demon's hair, pulling his head backward, Craig lifted with his left hand. The Demon fell off-balance and to the floor hard enough to shake the bus.

Then Craig caught sight of something the Demon couldn't. A grin crossed his face. Emily! But before Craig realised it, the Demon picked him and tossed him like a rag-doll towards the front of the bus. Emily's face registered surprise as Craig hurtled towards her, and he seemed to pass through her. But it wasn't so. Once they made contact, Emily passed into Craig, possessing his body. He felt her presence wash inside him, peaceful, determined, and a hint of her Scottish anger. Emily gained enough control to delay Craig's passage through the air, which allowed him to twist enough to land on his feet without overbalancing.

The Demon rushed him. But Craig stood his ground, faced the Demon, and placed his hands together as though in prayer. His mouth moved, but not of his volition, as another had possessed him.

If the Demon noticed this, he showed no interest. His intent was simple. Kill Craig Ramsey.

Strange words filled the air; words the Demon failed to recognise; phrases unfamiliar to Craig although they left his lips.

Something exploded from Craig with the crack of thunder and the force of a lightning bolt. And it struck the Demon like a steam locomotive through a paper wall. It carried flames that enveloped the Demon, wrapped around him, and filled the air with the acrid stench of burning meat. Demon flesh. Green-blue flames licked at the Demon who flew backwards towards the back seat where he landed. The impact shook the bus.

Craig grabbed a pole and avoided falling to the

ground. "What the hell was that, Emily?"

The Scottish spirit emerged from Craig's body, fainter than usual, and appearing tired. She appeared pale. "It's a heat charm I generated." She puffed, seating herself. "But it took more from me than I expected."

Astonishment controlled Craig. "How?"

Emily managed a weak smile. "Something I learned in my past life."

Movement from the back of the bus caught their attention. Craig looked in time to witness the Demon rise on shaky feet with equal astonishment tattooed on his face. But the Demon soon regained his composure, sighted Craig and ran hard at him with arms pumping like pistons. Craig remained firm, his own eyes spotting what the Demon's arrogance missed. As the Demon prepared to lunge and tackle him, Craig dropped to a horse stance, twisted, and punched the Demon square in the face. The Demon's feet flew forward while its face halted, stopped by Craig's fist, before it crashed to the ground like a sack of pumpkins. Craig dropped on top of the Demon, driving his elbow into its chest. But it was short-lived. The Demon forced a strong hand upward and pushed Craig away, standing with a fury-filled face.

The sounds of shouting and heavy footsteps at the bus door distracted the Demon. With a glance past Craig's shoulder, his narrowed eyes took in the number of extra people. He whirled and charged along the aisle to the back window and dived fists-first through its safety glass and into the night.

Craig puffed hard and turned to face the new arrivals. "About time," he puffed hard, "you turned up."

Brianna pushed her way past Khan to check on Craig's well-being. A gentle hand brushed across his brow. "Looks like he packed a hammer through your face. Sit down for a moment."

Khan assessed the damage in the bus and on Craig. "Your plan worked, but the next time you switch places with Brianna, and disguise yourselves as each other, please let me know first."

It hurt Craig to chuckle, but he managed. Brianna finished checking his injuries which were almost re-healed due to past exposure with ectoplasm. "Khan enjoyed watching your pole routine tonight." She winked. "You turned me on too."

Craig reached for a backpack Brianna (the real Brianna) had with her. He ripped it open and withdrew the ancient sword from it. "Let's rip the Ripper before he gets away."

Chapter 33

"Ripper's getting away."

Khan pointed towards a figure darting into the murky distance. "Unlikely. Melody picked up his scent and is after him now. Turner's along with her." He looked back at Craig. "Are you right to follow too?"

With his sword strapped to his back, Craig nodded and brushed past Khan. "We've got to catch up before he escapes. He's likely to hibernate for another fifty years to rest up for the next generation."

Now recovered, Emily rose and followed alongside Craig. "Dear, I can see the sparks leaping from your eyes. I haven't seen you this angry in a long time. What is it?"

Craig shook his head. "Not now." He turned back to Khan and Brianna who were just leaving the bus. "Hurry up, you two."

Khan exchanged looks with Brianna, but they said nothing. Meanwhile, Craig picked up a jogging pace. His limbs hurt, but he didn't care; it spurred him on harder.

They followed Melody's trail uphill along the winding road that led to the south-side's cemetery. Brianna opened her mouth to say something as she floated alongside Craig but chose to say nothing. Craig already knew which cemetery this was and what it meant. To him, it was a fitting place to capture the Demon.

But he had to survive it.

Emily's shape regained its normal luminous opacity, and she allowed Craig to power on ahead with determination lighting his eyes. Brianna and Khan caught up to her.

Khan voiced his wonder. "What's got into him? Has someone starched his underwear?"

Brianna's responded with a gentle whisper. "It's Celina. His first wife. She and his daughter Julia are buried up there."

An empathetic look crossed Khan's face. "Oh. I see."

Brianna filled in the rest of Khan's questions. "And earlier the Demon told Craig he had killed them both."

With an understanding nod, Khan quickened his gait to stay pace.

Chapter 34

Hilltop Cemetery installed its first long-term guest Leonard Statton who had died of consumption in 1872. Being one of the town's founders and a man of wealth had its benefits. A handsome stone crypt, guarded by a marble bust of his countenance, marked his final resting place. Its location at the top of the main hill allowed his spirit to watch and view what was once a beautiful little town. Once a resting place for wealthier families, the cemetery changed over time until it became a hotch-potch of expensive crypts, medium-priced but larger burial plots, and solitary graves for the rest. To some, it resembled a poorly planned town of death.

Yet it didn't matter. Death, the ever-progressive entity it is, always treats everyone the same. No matter how old, how young, or how wealthy or not, it treats everyone the same. Everyone except Melody Kostas.

Mixed feelings filled her as she stalked the Demon's scent towards the cemetery. Shadows loomed and reached from the trees. Their skeletal fingers lurked at the dirt pathway and distracted her from the bumps and potholes that threatened to trip unwary feet.

But Melody's preternatural eyes pierced through the gloom and picked up the different grades with ease. An October breeze cooled the air and teased her hair. Her fingers held fast to the dagger, ready to strike. A quiet whistle caught her attention. She turned, glancing through the blackness, to see Turner waving his arm for her.

Turner was standing at the edge where the trees met the outer gravestones. He pointed for Melody to see. Ah! There was the Demon's host Gifford!

"'E is hidin' 'round that tomb there."

Quieter than the shadows, Melody nodded and glided through the darkness. Turner floated along behind her. Although a spirit, he still recalled the time the Demon infected him in his living years. He had forgiven Melody for ending his physical existence, but he recoiled at the idea of meeting the Demon again - even if he was impervious to physical harm from him.

Melody was already at the crypt and held herself close to the masonry as she stole towards the corner.

Cold steel sliced through the air and rang upon hitting the stonework with a clang that rang through the air. If it had been two inches closer, the knife would have removed her nose. Gifford stepped from around the corner with a cold laugh and stabbed again. This time, Melody ducked and rolled to the side and away from the tomb, closely followed by the killer. She sprang to her feet, ready, knife gripped in a defensive posture, in time to see his knife's point striking for her throat. Melody's other hand struck the blade to the side, her knife hand slashed across his chest, and Gifford grunted as he retreated backwards. They paused a moment. A look of horror crossed Gifford's face. He lifted a hand to his chest, held it there for a second or two and moaned in shock. Then with a wink, he grinned, and removed his hand to reveal that no blood gushed from his torso. Only his shirt had suffered.

"You're still fast."

"You're still destined to die."

Movement from the side caught Melody's attention. She glanced and realised the error too late. Fire coursed through her shoulder as the Demon's blade tasted her flesh and sipped her blood. Already a numbness coursed through her left limb.

Gifford chuckled, but it was the Demon's voice speaking from within. He retreated backward before Melody counterattacked. "You will die sooner." He narrowed his eyes, watching like a cat with a mouse, and a finger of moonlight reached from behind a cloud to touch his blade. No sooner did the blade reflect than Gifford lunged forward towards Melody.

The blade clanged against something solid that stopped its snake-like strike. Gifford's jaw dropped in surprised disappointment as turned his head to see. Khan stood next to them, his sword held in one hand which had blocked Gifford's blade. The other hand tipped his top hat to Gifford. "Good evening. Mind if I cut in?"

Gifford jumped backward, supernatural strength and agility somersaulting him so he stood upon a nearby crypt. The crypt's occupant, a little old lady with a netted hat, emerged through its walls from inside and looked upward at the intruder. But Gifford and the Demon inside him either didn't hear or ignored her protests as she tried to shoo them away with an umbrella.

At last, Craig and Brianna arrived, breathing heavy but ready for a fight. Craig's visage was a mixture of thunder and lightning upon seeing Gifford laughing from his perch. Unaware of their presence, the rogue cop threw taunts in the Demon's voice at Melody and Khan.

It was the advantage Craig wanted. His eyes darted one way and the other until they spied a shorter gravestone.

Thankfully, no spirits hung around it. They were too busy watching the spectacle. Apart from the occasional odd couple fornicating beside their graves, they rarely saw such a thing.

Craig took a run, jumped and kicked from the smaller gravestone. He landed behind Tony Gifford with enough noise to awaken the already-listless dead. The ghostly residents cheered from the ground as Craig snaked an arm around Gifford's throat and delivered a massive punch to his kidney. Gifford swung the Demon's knife up and backwards towards Craig, but the psychic was quicker and pushed hard. The possessed man teetered on the edge but saved himself by springing over Khan's head to another tomb. He rolled on the marble top and jumped again as though his boots had springs before landing.

Their possessed foe turned and afforded a smile from his tortured mouth before shuddering. His jaw dropped open the way Craig had witnessed earlier and his eyes sagged. But this time, the Demon melted away from Gifford's body in full view. Both Gifford and the

Demon staggered upon separation; the mortal from the disorientation of regaining conscious control, and the other from similar.

Khan's voice hissed as he whispered to Craig. "Nice work, my friend. Now we have two bastards to kill."

"Et vincere nemo dividat." Craig only winked back with a knowing look in his eyes.

"Divide and conquer." Melody's eyes lit up upon hearing Craig's Latin.

Gifford's eyes darted back and forth between Khan, Melody, Craig and Brianna. Upon sighting the latter and her determined features, he stepped back before turning to flee. However, the Demon stayed and squared off in a defensive posture against Melody and Craig who both advanced with determination. A smile cracked from his bandaged features.

"The snake and her Son-in-Law." The ancient antagonist let loose with another putrid chuckle.

Melody appeared confused. "Son-in-Law?" Craig didn't answer. But Melody recognised the look upon Craig's face as he slid the knife from the scabbard on his belt. Two and two came together for her. "We share common goals."

Psychic and Lamia advanced towards the Ripper Demon.

The Ripper's eyes opened wide with recognition of Craig's knife. "Where did you find that?" The creature glanced towards Melody who responded with a shrug as she circled around him. The Demon looked at his own blade which had similar designs to those on Craig's knife, and a grin blossomed across his face. "Not that it matters."

With a snap, the Ripper's knife extended to sword-size. Swollen scars, where eyebrows once sat, bobbed up and down on his face. Craig raised an eyebrow, pressed a switch on his knife, and reacted with excited surprise when his own knife transformed into a sword too.

As though their thoughts were one, Melody and Craig rushed at the Demon. Their swords blurred in the moonlight like pinwheels in a cyclone. Steel clashed with steel and slid like a noisy metallic hailstorm. At first, the Demon held them off with ease but their crushing advance slowly pushed him back.

In desperation, he dodged around the gravestones, oblivious to the spirits disturbed by the fracas. Only Melody and Craig, who could see the spirits, experienced that distraction. Craig sent them a telepathic message, "Please stand back," as he dodged a slice that barely missed his skull. But some stayed close.

The fight turned as the Demon lined his two opponents up so he could fight one at a time rather than both at once. His sword strokes and parries focused hard upon Craig, who felt the pressure as he stepped back to avoid a downward stroke.

But that opened Craig for an unexpected kick to his midsection that sent him flying. Melody dodge in time, but Craig crashed into the wall of a crypt. His head cracked on the stone, and he dropped to the ground in a dazed heap.

The world spun about Craig who was barely aware of Melody taking over for him in the melee. Affected by his spinning brain, his feet refused to work as he struggled to stand.

A moment later, the world exploded as two thunderclaps filled the air with two bright flashes. They echoed in his head, and through the ringing sound in his ears, he heard Brianna's pained cry rip through the air.

Chapter 35

A few minutes earlier, upon his separation from Ripper, Gifford realised he no longer had the Demon's power within him.

He stood for a moment, disoriented, his eyes moving as he weighed the odds. They appeared too great for him. He had no sword skills and no sword, and he had seen how his four adversaries fought. The fact hit him hard. Ripper was powerful and capable of doing terrible things to him, but the others would do worse if Ripper failed too. He couldn't match that. So he did what any other coward does when things look bad.

He turned and ran.

But Brianna caught his movement. Before Gifford could take more than a dozen steps, she tackled him to the ground. He squirmed on the ground, rolled to his back and scored a lucky hit to her head. By luck, Brianna had turned her shoulder, so most of the blow's power glanced. But it was strong enough to push her back.

Too late, Brianna saw the pistol, its barrel pointed at her chest. Time slowed for her as adrenaline coursed. She knew Gifford stood too far away for her to stop him. Her limbs tensed to dodge.

Too late. Cordite ignited. It exploded. The gunshot's

thunderous boom filled her ears.

She knew her time had come. She couldn't dodge in time.

But Khan moved faster. Blood showered Brianna as Khan's throat exploded. The bullet continued its passage, tore through the sleeve of Brianna's leather jacket as it passed her, and thudded into a crypt's wall. Pieces of stone exploded, stinging her face as they scattered and fell.

Khan's body thumped to the ground at her feet.

Brianna barely noticed Gifford's footsteps thump away in flight as she screamed Khan's name and dropped to hold his bleeding body. His eyes displayed a curious mix of pain, recognition, and calmness, which Brianna couldn't understand. Memories flooded back, including when she watched Craig take a bullet to the face. Craig had caught that bullet between his teeth. But Khan's teeth had caught nothing. And Brianna saw another man from her past, a lover long dead. For a moment, the shock grabbed her. Khan's lips trembled as he struggled to speak. But no sound came. Khan's eyes closed in death.

Brianna sat and cradled Khan's head close for a moment. A movement to the side caught her attention. It was Emily standing beside her.

The Scottish spirit allowed a smile as she placed her hand upon Brianna's shoulder. "Relax, lass. Khan needs no comfort, and you don't want to give him the wrong impression when he wakes."

Brianna's jaw dropped. "Wakes?"

Emily chuckled. "He has lived long, and died many times... and lived again."

Brianna moved from underneath Khan and gently lowered his head to the ground. Part of her wanted to kick him, but she realised she had tricked herself. "Is that true?" She looked at Melody who fought beside Craig against the Demon still. Melody flung herself into the battle with vigour. Had she noticed Khan's fate or...?

"I'd forgotten!" Brianna stood, checked her own pistol was in its shoulder holster. "I'd better get Tony then."

Chapter 36

Craig froze. A gunshot!

However, Melody continued regardless and rushed at the Demon with an onslaught of sword strokes. It was just as well too. Melody's barrage of swings distracted the Demon who diverted his attention from Craig to parry them aside. She pushed with each attack, and he deflected each of them with ease. And each time he side-stepped or parried, he laughed.

"You're good still," Ripper chortled. He ducked and rolled, holding up his blade to block a downward strike. "But one question." He pushed across with the blade and sparks flew from between the swords. "Why didn't you train your progeny to fight?" He giggled while dodging another stroke, jumping easily above the blade. "Was it because you wanted to kill me yourself?" Melody grunted as she swung again. Steel clashed on steel. The Demon rolled to the side. "Or do you secretly enjoy watching them die while you live?"

Melody roared with thousands of years worth of anger and frustration. She renewed her strokes, changed her strategy, and slashed harder. But the Demon laughed and dodged each stroke with the same untiring ease.

To the side, Craig had recovered his senses enough to stand. A quick glance across the cemetery showed

Brianna was still alive, Gifford was dashing towards a knot of trees, and Khan lay motionless on the ground. Brianna seemed indecisive, though, and cradled Khan's inert body. Didn't she realise Khan's immortality? He would be back soon. Then Emily appeared beside Brianna.

The fighting moved closer to Craig again, and it turned out the Demon didn't realise Craig stood behind him, sword in hand. Craig grinned upon the realisation: Melody had deliberately manoeuvred the Ripper Demon towards him. But her strength was fading and he had to move fast.

It was now or never.

Silent as a cat, though still shaky on his feet, Craig lunged forward towards the Demon with his own sword. Moonlight glinted from the tip's blade. But the Demon dodged to the side, a gloved hand pushing it to the side. Yet Craig's body momentum continued forward, and his full weight crashed into the Demon. They tumbled together to the ground, a thudding mess of tangled limbs and bodies.

Melody side-stepped to avoid being pulled down with them. She raised her blade, waiting for the opportunity to plunge her sword deep into the Demon. But the Demon and Craig's wrestling made it difficult as they each fought for an advantage. Craig was on top of the Ripper, one hand upon the creature's sword wrist, his weight pressing his opponent to the ground. But he couldn't hold him long. Melody circled, her eyes scanning for an opening. Anything. The Demon fought back hard, kicking repeated blows hard into Craig who held on like a leech.

Then Melody saw it. It was the opening she needed. Craig had moved to the side. By accident or design, it didn't matter. She raised her sword, and -

She winced and cried in pain. Her stomach! Crippling pain! Her eyes dropped, one hand went to her stomach, and touched warm blood that gushed across a steel blade, the demon's blade. It twisted inside her as the Demon threw Craig to the side like a rag doll. The Demon stood, a putrid leer crossing his face, the swathed bandages stinking enough to make her vomit from the stench and pain. A gloved fist struck her across the face.

Melody fell, moaning as pain lanced through her guts. She tried standing, but the Demon back-fisted her again, and kicked the sword from her hand. It clattered to the side. His face moved closer to hers, death on his breath, and she looked into his eyes.

"Don't you recognise me?" His voice hissed at Melody, and in pain, she shook her head. "Sister."

Melody's eyes snapped wide open. The words forced through the pain that crippled her. "Danaus?"

The Demon opened his mouth to laugh, but a fist filled it. Then another.

Melody dropped to the ground again, crying in pain. Craig knelt beside her to check the wound. It didn't look good. Melody's inner organs were visible through the long gash in her stomach. Would Lamia survive this? He didn't know.

The Demon, however, was still moving and raised himself to his feet again. Craig stood to his full height, ancient sword in hand, and dashed towards their opponent. If only Craig were quicker, he could have done it. But the Ripper moved quicker than Craig could see. He side-stepped Craig's lunge, grabbed the wrist that held the sword, and punched Craig hard in the face with the other hand. Craig was already groggy when he attacked the Demon. This new blow created new stars in his vision. The sword left Craig's grip. He blindly grabbed for it, but a knee blasted into his face, and Craig fell. Before Craig could blink, a bright flaring pain filled his consciousness, centred in his left shoulder, as the Demon stabbed him with the blade. Craig cried aloud in pain as it seared through him like fire through his veins. Tears welled like springs, and blood spurted and stained the soil beneath him.

Craig screamed again as the blade withdrew. He opened his eyes, looked up towards the grinning Demon who was preparing for the final decapitating stroke, and stared straight into his opponent's eyes, eyes of death.

Chapter 37

With his blade poised to strike, the Demon faltered. It was the slightest hesitation and puzzlement filled his eyes. Perhaps Craig was the first to do so, even while laying on a burial plot.

But it didn't matter.

They made eye contact. That's all Tyrone needed.

For although Craig maintained full control of his body and limbs, the teenager's consciousness remained inside Craig's body. Watching and waiting.

At the moment Craig established eye contact with the Ripper, Tyrone's consciousness leapt from his uncle's mind and into the Demon's mind. It took less than a second. This was the time for which Turner had provided spirit training and taught him how to possess people's bodies. It worked on humans, even some animals, but this was the test Tyrone craved.

The Demon's body shuddered. It stiffened, gesticulated, held its hands at its throat and gurgled, and its eyes opened wider in panic. "What did you do?" Its voice boomed and echoed across the cemetery, but the dead were already awake.

The spirits gathered around to watch. Although they had never seen the Ripper before, they knew his evil.

They lusted to watch the Ripper's demise like schoolchildren gathering around a schoolyard fight. And they laughed. Why hadn't they thought of it?

Craig ignored the disembodied spectators and did his best to stand. Turner appeared beside him, shouting at the Ripper. "Get 'im, laddie! Y' got 'im. Do it!"

The Demon's eyes moved in their sockets, reflecting its inner horror, as one of his hands moved. He resembled a stringless marionette, horrified at the possibility of surviving without strings, yet fascinated at the same time. Then he screamed as he realised the purpose.

"I have him!" Tyrone's voice echoed from the Demon's mouth, despite the lips not moving.

The hand, which still held the Demon's weapon of death and possession, turned the blade towards itself. Discoloured juice oozed from its face and peculiar pumpkin skin, the fluid of nervous sweat. Craig nodded with excitement and urged his nephew on. "You have him! Come on, Tyrone!"

The Demon uttered an angry growl, convulsed hard. "Get out of me! You have no right!"

Then the blade's tip touched the Ripper's solar plexus. The Ripper's eyes bulged from within his Halloween mask of swathed bandage flesh. He shook his head side to side in denial and struggled to push the knife away.

Although something inside the Demon's own mind had not given up, the Demon screamed in anticipation of its end.

Chapter 38

Meanwhile, in another section of the cemetery overlooking Statton's river, two shadowy figures raced and darted between the gravestones. In the lead, Gifford cast desperate glances over his shoulder. His breath huffed as he kept running, the fear of being caught pushing him forward. Behind him, Brianna followed with the grim determination of a wounded animal.

It had been years since she lost a teammate to Death. The images of Tom's lifeless body in her arms while serving in the Army invaded her mind, but instead of hindering, they spurred her onward. They had never caught Tom's killer, she could catch the rogue cop. She ran between the tombstones, but being taller than Gifford, she found it hard when he swerved and changed directions. Brianna pushed her hands outward to avoid falling over a tombstone that stood at an angle from the uneven ground. Her breath exploded from her lungs. Why was she tiring? She rarely felt fatigue so soon when running. Perhaps it was the uneven ground. This wasn't a normal obstacle course. But this felt different.

She looked up and cursed. Gifford had vanished. She swung her eyes side to side but found no sign of him.

Something clicked by her ear. The unmistakable

sound of a gun's hammer pulled back. The pistol's barrel poked the side of her head.

"Do you really want to take me in?" Gifford's voice said from behind her.

Brianna closed her eyes and thought of Craig. "You killed a lot of women that night."

Gifford sniffed. It sounded loose and snotty. "That was Danaus. He made me do it."

Brianna spun, stepping back so that the gun kept contact with her. Her right arm trapped Gifford's gun hand while she gripped him for control. Before Gifford could respond, her palm smashed his nose. Cartilage crunched into his face, and Brianna forced him to the ground. The gun dropped from his hand, clattered along the top of a grave's cement top, and dropped to the grass. Gifford grunted, his free hand flailed and gripped Brianna's hair. Brianna kicked a leg over Gifford, but he twisted, pushed her off, so she tumbled to the ground.

In a flash, Gifford stood and kicked at her head. Brianna caught his foot, twisted, and Gifford screamed in agony as he dropped to the ground.

But he didn't hit straight away. It took half a second longer. Brianna watched him disappear into blackness, heard his body thud. Something cracked loud. Brianna gasped. Was that what she thought?

She stood on tired legs and gulped upon seeing the gaping blackness. Where was Gifford?

Instinct saved her, stopped Brianna from stepping

forward, and she sighed with relief. She hadn't seen the open grave. To the side lay the safety tape usually placed as a warning. Someone had torn it down, possibly vandals or kids. Her ears strained to listen as her eyes adjusted to the six-foot-deep hole's gloom.

Gifford's twisted body lay motionless at the bottom, barely visible in the murky depth, his head cocked at an impossible angle.

"Broken neck is perfect for you," she spat.

Something distracted her. Movement to the side.

Brianna glanced, almost jumped in startlement, but she relaxed when she realised it was a little girl nearby.

"What are you doing out so late, little one?"

The girl couldn't have been over three years old. She didn't answer Brianna but stood there, silent, with a stuffed toy dog in her arms that stared back at Brianna with a goofy grin. The child craned her neck, stepped closer to the open grave, and looked with impassive eyes at Gifford's dead body.

Brianna followed the girl's gaze at the corpse. Something moved down there. Shadows. They swirled around Gifford's body. His voice screamed from the hole, chilling Brianna's marrow, as she noticed his spirit form emerging from the body. But the shadowy fingers grabbed him and dragged the spirit's body deep into the ground.

Shocked at the sight, Brianna stepped towards the little girl to shield her from the horror but stopped. The little girl was a spirit too!

Cherubic eyes gazed upward at Brianna; the hint of a smile appeared. Brianna couldn't resist smiling back, but the child turned, her hair shining in the moonlight, and pointed across the cemetery.

She looked where the little girl's finger pointed... and followed.

Chapter 39

Despite its howling, the Demon had not given up on its life. Fingers like steel gripped Craig's hands and clawed, trying to loosen his grip. The Demon's eyes reflected its own fear. Maybe a prolonged life led the creature to believe it would never die. Its arrogance and ego took a greater beating as Craig pressed the blade of its own sword into its chest. Blood spurted, yet its fingers still tried to pry and push the blade away.

Then something unexpected happened. The Demon's true personality returned. Tyrone's voice screamed from inside it alongside the Demon's laughter. A powerful hand punched Craig backward so his grip on the sword loosened.

"Did you think you could control me forever?" The Demon laughed harder. An internal struggle boiled inside the Demon's eyes which swapped and changed in colours as the personalities of Tyrone and the Demon fought for control of its body.

Although tired from the struggle, Craig backed up a few steps and screamed hard. As his battle-cry escaped his dry lips, he lunged forward, lifted one leg, and delivered a powerful sidekick at the Ripper Demon. The supernatural villain never had the time to register full surprise. Craig's foot connected with the sword's handle and shot the blade through the Demon with a squelch-

and-liquid sound.

The Demon's body stiffened, its head rolled backward on its shoulders, and a tortured mix voices left its throat and rolled across the cemetery to echo from the tombstones.

Another voice cried from behind the Demon. "Step back, Craig!"

Craig dodged to the side in time before another sword emerged through the Demon's chest. It gasped, uttered a single word of disbelief as it looked at the two blades piercing its evil heart.

Then Craig spied Melody, her serpentine body's tail still flicking in pain, pure determination upon her face, and her hand gripped hard on the second ancient sword's handle. Khan, since recovered, had arrived in time to hold on to his wounded lover so she could deliver the second thrust.

But the Demon still struggled, not as much as before; it still lived. The words from his ancestor's letter came to Craig's mind.

"The blades must touch," he realised aloud.

"No!" The Demon croaked and tried to avoid Craig to no avail.

Craig allowed a grim smile to appear as he gripped his own sword's handle. "This is for Celina," he twisted the blade, "and my little girl Julia." His teeth ground as he sliced upward.

Meanwhile Melody still gripped her blade and sliced

towards Craig's. "And this is for all my children and their children."

The Ripper Demon's mouth opened in silent protest. A black mess of fluid ran down its once pristine Victorian garb and pooled on the ground. The moonlight reflecting from the puddle revealed no colour. Its mouth bubbled, and a final gasp escaped the formless lips. The Demon collapsed in a heavy heap on its side, but he turned his head.

His features melted away like fog to reveal a human visage. Still conscious, Melody gasped with recognition.

"Danaus?" Her half-brother.

The bald-headed man who lay there looked to be no older than forty. He nodded, managed a slight smile as blood trickled from his mouth. His lips moved and his voice came with effort. A whispery voice. "If only you had married me, Lamia, like I said."

"Incestuous murderer," Melody spat, struggling to breathe. "You murdered your family, my children, because I despised the idea of marrying you." Her eyes were dim, but flames burned in them. "Go to hell. Tell that bitch, Hera, she failed."

What remained of the Ripper Demon smiled, chuckled blood, and lay still, staring up into the moon.

Emily and Turner appeared beside its body and examined it. They looked at each other and nodded in confirmation before Turner lifted his face.

"'E's dead."

Craig was aware of Melody's mortal wound from the Special Blade. He knew Khan cradled her in his arms, rocking back and forth. But he knew Tyrone was inside the Demon's corpse too.

Trepidation filled his heart, crushing his chest, as he knelt beside the Demon. It seemed wrong to look with humanity upon the creature's body, but he searched for a sign of Tyrone's survival. A finger twitched on the Demon's otherwise limp hand.

Tense seconds dripped like water caught in a clogged drain, slower than eternity.

"Come on," Craig urged. "Come on, Tyrone."

Turner shook his head. "I couldn't train 'im fer dis part. I don't know 'ow ter escape someone else's corpse. If 'e doesn't come aaaht soon, 'e could die."

Emily shushed Turner and cast a concerned look towards Craig. She whispered. "Not in front of Craig, Turner."

If Craig heard them, he showed no sign. His intent focused upon Demon.

At once, the Demon convulsed, startling them all. Even the dying Melody reacted, but Khan held her back gently. A voluminous gas escaped the Demon's face, gathered above it and to the side, before it solidified into a familiar form. The Demon's body crumbled to dust which dissolved further into the ground, gone forever.

Tyrone collapsed to the ground, coughed once, and lay still. Craig hurried forward.

"Tyrone?"

Chapter 40

To the side, Khan cradled Melody's head. Her body had since transformed back to full human form, and she lay still in his arms. The wound in her stomach was a mess of fluid and damaged internal organs. No signs of healing.

Khan choked back a tear as her eyes struggled to stay open. She offered him a weak smile. Her lips trembled as she opened them, but he couldn't hear her words. Khan leaned closer, his ear to hers. And his body shuddered and struggled against the tears. "I love you too, blossom." His lips trembled with the words as his eyes gushed with tears.

She whispered something else.

"What?"

And he choked back sobs as he listened to her parting words.

***

The teenager remained motionless. A pulse in his throat throbbed three... weak... beats... and stopped. Craig placed a hand upon the boy's forehead.

"Tyrone?" Craig listened, watched the boy's eyelids, hoping for a tiny flutter.

But there was nothing. No words. No movement. And no psychic message through Craig's fingertips.

Now two men sobbed, crying over their loved ones' still bodies.

Chapter 41

Craig was sobbing hard, his face buried in Tyrone's lifeless chest, when Brianna arrived. Although he heard her quiet steps upon the grass and leaves, he showed no acknowledgement. Thought and images of the past couple of months mingled with regret, poisoning his mind with pain. Colonel Ryan's words played in his head. Never ignore the living for the sake of the dead. That's what the phantom told Craig when he hunted down his niece's killer. The same words played through his mind afterwards when he realised Tyrone was missing. When Tyrone returned, having changed his mind about suicide, thanks to Turner, he should have taken more notice. Instead of berating his adopted nephew for running away and avoiding school, he should have expressed gratitude for the boy's life. Craig wanted to fly off, to scream at the skies, but all he could do was hold his nephew's body and mourn.

Something gently touched his shoulder. Brianna's hand. He recognised her fingers. He should feel grateful for her life too.

So much loss, so much death. It followed him.

Brianna's words floated to his ears, gentle and kind. "I'm sorry, Craig." Her own fingers ran through the boy's hair. "Has he departed yet?"

Craig sniffed and looked up at her. "What?"

Brianna paused, balancing her moods and words. "His spirit. Has it left?"

He shook his head.

"Then why are you crying?" Brianna pushed Craig back and placed her hands over Tyrone's chest. "You breathe in his mouth; I'll compress. We still have a chance." Craig hesitated for a moment. She urged him again. "Come on! We have time."

She pressed hard three times and counted each one. "One one-thousand, two one-thousand, three one-thousand."

Craig didn't know if it would work, but he decided not to give up yet. He pushed two long life-giving breaths into his nephew's open mouth, pinching his nose. Turner and Emily stood by, watching with hopeful expressions. And the police detective and the psychic detective continued their CPR. It seemed endless. When Craig ran out of breath, Brianna swapped places with him. And they continued for what seemed an hour.

But it was only three minutes. At last, they achieved a pulse in Tyrone's carotid artery, and before long, he coughed, heaving on oxygen.

Craig and Brianna paused her resuscitation attempts to give Tyrone room to breathe. For a tense moment, he stayed still. Only a slight movement of the chest showed he breathed.

When his eyelids fluttered, they sighed a relief. He turned his head and faced Craig to speak with a tired voice.

"Did we get him?"

Craig nodded and gripped his nephew's hand hard. He didn't want to let go.

Chapter 42

What a mess it had been! Although they had caught and stopped the Ripper Demon from killing, Brianna had a mess of paperwork to handle. How could she close off the case, one that the papers had lapped up like vultures for the ghoulish public lapped up with enthusiasm?

Brianna was still adjusting to the supernatural world. How could she add that to the report? What would her superiors think when they read about demons, women who were half-snakes born from ancient gods thought to be mythological, and ghosts?

She felt lucky her immediate supervisor Inspector Myles understood the whole thing when he debriefed her in his office. Mere months ago, Myles had pushed Craig and Brianna together on a case because he believed in Craig's abilities. Back then, Brianna was a sceptic. Now her head spun at everything that happened.

The Inspector's solution was simple. "Take out the supernatural. If it had been God, people still wouldn't believe it."

So Brianna removed all mention of the Demon.

Poor Melody became a victim of the cop-turned-murderer Anthony Gifford. He had a fascination with ancient weapons. The police had found multiple books and magazines about them in his home when they searched his home. That part was true. And he held a reputation for hanging out at strip joints. His co-workers had noticed he talked about prostitutes and strippers like meat, but they hadn't linked this to something deeper. For a short time, the police thought a homeless man named Toomey had committed the heinous acts of murder and cannibalism. But it turned out the weapons belonged to Gifford. Toomey had found one of them where presumably Gifford had hidden it to avoid investigators linking it to him. As it happened, Toomey had personal connections with one victim, which is why Gifford tracked him - to kill him and recover the weapon under the guise of an arrest that went horribly wrong. But Gifford still required a suspect to take the heat off him. He tried to implicate another private investigator, Khan Gaston, who has since proven his innocence. The investigators set up a sting operation to catch Gifford who had stolen one knife from the police evidence room to complete the twin set. In the process, somehow, night club operator Melody died by Gifford's hand at the cemetery. It was beyond their control. Gifford had died while pursued by Detective-Sergeant Cogan, breaking his neck when he fell into an open grave.

The old saying was right. The truth often is stranger than fiction.

Brianna felt tired by the end of the day. She should have taken it off to recover. But the sooner she finished writing the report, the sooner she could put it all behind her. Inspector Myles read it, his lips pursed as though he whistled a silent tune. When he finished it, he looked at Brianna, commented how she looked like shit and needed rest. "Take leave," he told her. She had eight weeks accumulated, anyway.

***

Tired, but happy and accomplished, Brianna arrived home. There was something good about the way the keys to Craig's Jaguar jangled as they hit the table by the front doorway. Was it relief? No, something else. It was home. Soft music played from the stereo in the living room. Brianna's mood lifted, her eyes scanning for signs of life in the tidy house. The murmur of voices in conversation reached her ears. Emily's maternal Scottish brogue and Craig's deep, calm tone.

"Did you talk with Tyrone?"

"Yes." Craig's voice was happy, relieved but tired. "He will continue with school, but he's taking a break again."

"How do you feel about that now?"

Craig paused. "I'm happy with Tyrone. I told him how impressed I am with his study with Turner. But I don't like him hanging out with him either. I'd rather he stayed in school, but we reached the compromise."

"Tyrone's a good lad, Craig," Emily's voice replied. "He loves you almost as much as his Dad. And he wants to prove himself to you, which nearly killed him last night. But he's growing, a young man, and you need to let him grow. Don't suffocate the lad by holding him close and safe. He will push you back. Do you remember how you met me?"

Craig's chuckle was good, even from where Brianna

370

listened. She continued listening, standing back to remain unseen with a smile crossing her face.

"Yes, I remember when I first met you, Emily. Were you sent to meet me as someone sent Turner for Tyrone?"

Emily laughed. "Yes, of course. But I have been with you longer than that. You were younger, just a bairn. I have been with you since your parents died, you poor boy. And as a teenager, you were like Tyrone. Stubborn."

"Like a Scotsman?" Craig replied in a humorous tone.

"Nay! Moreso!"

The sound of a playful punch reached Brianna's ears. She cleared her throat to warn them of her approach, Brianna walked outside into the Japanese-themed garden to find Craig laying on a deckchair in the sun. He looked tired and like shit too. They made such a great pair. Beside him, Emily lay on another deckchair, but she wasn't tanning in the rays.

Craig looked up, made eye contact with her, and gave a warm smile. "Hello, beautiful!" He motioned toward a third deckchair beside him. "Get changed and catch some sun. It's good to recharge."

The November sun was hot. The drinks looked cool and inviting; ice cubes floated and chinked in the glasses that sweated condensation.

Brianna winked. "I'll be right back."

Brimming with happiness and something else that

wanted to escape, Brianna hurried inside and returned to the sun dressed in a black bikini. The sun warmed her with its kissing rays, and Craig's eyes boggled with rapture. But Brianna pretended to ignore Craig's wanting gaze as she lay in the deckchair beside him. She looked at Craig, regarded him for a moment, and said, "Do you see something you like?" Her eyes flickered towards his lower regions.

Emily chuckled to herself and stood. "Do you want a Corona, dear?"

Brianna opened her mouth to reply yes, but changed her mind. "I think a juice, please." Emily's eyebrow lifted. "I mean it's too early for me. Plus Khan's taxed Craig's alcohol supplies enough for now."

Craig laughed at that before his mood sobered. "Poor Khan."

Brianna lazed back, enjoying the sun's embrace as she stretched her arms above her head. "Have you spoken to him since last night?"

"No. He wanted to be alone, and I can't reach him." Craig appeared lost in thought a moment. "I understand how he feels."

Brianna didn't have to ask what Craig meant. He meant Celina. Brianna chose her words. "Something else happened last night when I chased after Gifford. I wanted to tell you but it didn't seem right then." She let the last words hang, gauging Craig's response.

"What's that?"

Brianna accepted her juice from Emily with a thank

you and waited until they were alone again. "Last night, after Gifford fell and died, I saw a little girl's spirit but she appeared solid."

Craig's eyes flickered for a moment. She could tell he fought it back.

Brianna pressed forward. "It was Julia."

Craig smiled, and it was genuine. "Did you?"

Encouraged, Brianna nodded. "She pointed out the gravestone next to hers - Celina's - and told me her Daddy-bear needed me."

Craig wiped a tear. "It's okay. I knew you knew. You see, I saw Celina last night too, and she told me the same. To be happy with you. We've said our final goodbyes."

Brianna smiled, obvious relief showing as her forehead's worried lines almost vanished. "And there's more news too." She was fit to burst, but the words wouldn't come. Then she said, "I'm taking some time off from police work."

"Oh?" Craig's eyebrows rose with concern, then the hint of a smile shone from his face. "How much time?"

Brianna answered with a smile. She took Craig's hand in hers, placed it with her other hand upon her lower belly, and grinned at him.

"As long as we need."

Craig paused as he felt the spark of life from within Brianna's womb. Then he laughed, and all other matters left his mind for that moment.

Epilogue

Melody's voice still spoke in his memories. It hurt to think about her, to remember the loss. She had been so brave as she died. He wondered if he would be the same when, or if, his time came.

Many a time, he had tried to die. Sometimes he even ran full-speed towards Death, but the Grim Reaper would only waggle a bony finger at him. The Three Fates - Clotho, Lachesis, and Atropos - kept spinning his thread. They had probably hung themselves on it by now.

The Jack Daniels bottle clunked on the table with a heavy thud. Then he realised where he was, picked up the bottle and tossed it in a nearby bin. Melody would not approve of him making a mess.

For although Fate had blessed him with immortality, with help from Azriel, it was a curse. At least, he thought so until the other night.

He closed his eyes and remembered.

She said those words before she passed. "I know you, Khan. I knew you before. And I will meet you again sooner than you know. For you are-"

A cracking sound reached his ears. He looked up

towards the blazing fireplace before which sat a large egg the size of a large dog. Cracks appeared in its white shell as it trembled and rocked back and forth. Something inside wanted to emerge, and it knocked hard. Each blow fell heavier than the one before.

And a fist emerged through its side with a yolky splatter.

A woman's hand.

Afterword

Thank you for reading Demon Blade. I hope you enjoyed it.

I wish to thank Kris Verity, author of Bad Nana Unleashed, for her ability to check through the manuscript. She found and reported a lot of things for fixing – mistakes that cropped up from typing in the early hours of the morning, the only quiet time I could find.

The book's inspiration came while writing Dead Cell. The moment I introduced Inspector Myles, a man constantly mentioned but never experienced by the reader, I knew a Ripper character skulked in the background. He had to be there. And so did someone else.

Melody Kostas, the Lamia, came not long after I thought of the Jack the Ripper knife premise.

Originally Melody's character was meant to have a psychic connection to the killer. I just couldn't see how. Then one night, my muse whispered in my dreams, and I realised she was a lamia. But not any lamia. She is THE LAMIA. The original. But she wasn't evil. That would be too easy. How did she fit the tale?

So I rewrote her tale. It took some research into the Greek Gods and other tales from Babylonian and Sumerian times. And what's more the Lamia appears in so much classical literature and also in modern popular fiction.

Having said this, so many stories abound about Jack the Ripper. too. And many authors claim to know who he (or she) really was. I found at least eight different authors (including Patricia Cornwell and Australia's Amanda Howard) who claimed they had solved the killer's identity.

Who is right? I don't know. But I'm certain of one thing.

Only the true Ripper knew.

ABOUT THE AUTHOR

Chris Johnson lives in Brisbane with his family. Besides being a writer, Chris is a magician and a psychic entertainer. He also enjoys reading, watching movies, running, and Kung Fu.

ALSO BY THE AUTHOR

Twelve Strokes of Midnight

Dead Cell (Craig Ramsey 1)

Demon Blade (Craig Ramsey 2)

Bootstrap's Journey

Chris Johnson's books are available in e-book and paperback at most good stores. If you can't find them, be sure to ask for them to be ordered for you – or visit www.facebook.com/ChrisJohnsonAuthor